J.R. MCGINNITY

THE
TALENTED

THE
TALENTED

CHAPTER ONE

Adrienne wound her way through the back streets and alleys of Kyrog, taking a shortcut to the captain's office. Her leather boots kicked up the dust that even hundreds of feet could not pack down as the drought scorching the plains stretched late into the season. Some of the alleys smelled of refuse that had yet to be cleared, but they were quicker and less crowded than the main streets. Adrienne was more worried about running late for her meeting with Captain Garrett than unpleasant smells.

She turned right, in the direction that would take her back to the main street and the captain's quarters, and was surprised to find Lieutenant Nissen coming toward her.

"Lieutenant," Adrienne said, snapping to attention with her left hand resting on the hilt of her sword.

"Adrienne." The smooth voice would have been pleasant had it not been accompanied by those cold green eyes. His gaze ran over Adrienne's leather-clad body, lingering on her breasts and the flare of her hips. "What are you doing, sneaking around the back of the officers' hall?"

"I'm on my way to meet with the captain," she said.

Nissen smirked. His combination of light skin and green eyes was rare this far south of the Almetian border. The man should have been attractive, but whenever Adrienne saw him she got a creeping feeling along her skin and wanted nothing more than to get away.

"I need to go, Lieutenant. I'm running late." She tried to duck around him, but Nissen moved to block her.

"Surely you can spare a few minutes," he said. "I want to talk to you."

"Perhaps later." Adrienne tried once again to get around Nissen, and was once again blocked.

"Join me for dinner," he said, moving closer to her, crowding her against the back wall of one of the buildings. "We can talk then." His hand traveled to her waist, resting on the flare of her hip. "Or we can do…other things."

Adrienne reached reflexively for her sword, but his body was blocking the move, and it stopped her just long enough for her to come to her senses and remind herself that he was a superior officer.

"No," Adrienne said, slipping to the right. "I can't."

Nissen's other hand came up to block her escape, and he moved closer so that his body was pressed against her. He bent and put his mouth next to her ear. "I think you can."

Adrienne froze. Over the years, other soldiers had made occasional passes at her, but never had an officer done so. With another soldier, Adrienne would have blown him off or forcibly ended the encounter. Once, when she had been in her early teens, a soldier had followed her to the river where she was bathing. She had left him gasping on the banks, clawing at the windpipe she had very nearly ruined. Despite being the only female soldier currently serving in the camp of over two thousand, she had never worried that she would start a fight she couldn't finish.

But she wouldn't fight Lieutenant Nissen and risk being expelled from Kyrog.

"Lieutenant Nissen, please," Adrienne said, careful to make her voice sound respectful rather than pleading, "I'm supposed to meet with Captain Garrett."

"You'll have more fun with me," Nissen promised, nuzzling her neck. When she tried to break free, his hand on her waist tightened painfully and he gripped the arm that tried to push him away. "Now, now, Adrienne, don't fight me." His mouth moved to hers, and she brought her knee up reflexively.

Experience had Nissen twisting so that her knee connected with his muscular thigh instead of the more vulnerable area she had been aiming for. He made a tutting sound against her lips. "Bad girl," he said. "I'll have to teach you some respect." He grabbed her other arm when she began to struggle in earnest, pinning it above her head, but pulled back abruptly at the sound of feet hitting the dusty ground behind him.

"What in the flaming Abyss is going on here?"

Adrienne looked to her left and saw Ricco standing there. He was built like a *pago* tree, not much taller than Adrienne but with a thick body and limbs. He could move deceptively fast despite his apparent bulk, and the rage on his dark face made him look every bit as lethal as she knew him to be.

Adrienne was very glad that the savage expression that flashed across Ricco's dark face was not directed at her.

"Rydaeg and I were having a discussion. A private discussion." Nissen's smile was tight, and he moved slowly away from Adrienne. "We'll continue this later," he told Adrienne before leaving the alley.

"Are you all right?" Ricco asked. She could see the effort it took for him not to yell or go after Nissen.

"I'm fine," she snapped, but her voice wavered, and she realized that her hands were shaking.

"Ade—"

Adrienne crossed her arms in a move meant to hide her traitorous hands. Ricco's anger came back as he caught what she was doing. "What did he do?"

"Nothing," she said, but the look in his eyes, so unexpectedly gentle and concerned, was too much for her to resist. She couldn't help the words that spilled from her as she told Ricco about everything Lieutenant Nissen had said and done.

She had barely reached the end of her story when Ricco started heading in the direction the lieutenant had gone. "I'll kill him," Ricco growled.

Adrienne quickly stepped in front of her friend, blocking his way. "Ricco, no."

"I can make you move," Ricco said, reaching out to grab her by the arms.

"Try it," Adrienne said, but her voice lacked heat, and it wasn't the customary bad temper that he saw in her eyes.

She was more than merely shaken by the encounter with Nissen, and Ricco's hands moved up to rest on her shoulders. The weight was comforting, not threatening as Nissen's touch had been. "If I can't kill him, at least report this to Captain Garrett. He would never stand for what Nissen did."

Adrienne knew that was true, just as she knew that she could never go to the captain. She had worked hard to build up a reputation that she could take care of herself, and she couldn't have a man—even the captain—solving her problems. "You know I can't do that."

Ricco looked pained. "Ade, you can't expect me to just let this go."

"I can handle it," Adrienne said, lifting a reassuring hand to his forearm. The nickname Ricco had given her soon after he had come to the camp reminded her of everything they had shared in their years of friendship, and some of the tension left her.

Finally he nodded and let his hands fall back to his sides. "I came looking for you because Captain Garrett was wondering where you were."

Adrienne had almost forgotten about her meeting with the captain. "I have to go see him," Adrienne said.

Ricco forced a smile. "Go."

Adrienne turned to leave, then looked back over her shoulder at her closest friend, the only real friend she could remember having. "Thank you."

Adrienne took a breath before entering the building that housed the captain's office. She announced herself to the page, who turned and knocked sharply on the captain's door. "Adrienne Rydaeg has arrived, sir."

"Send her in."

The captain was sitting behind his desk when Adrienne entered. His stern face, weathered and marred by a thick scar just under his right eye, was not smiling. "You're late."

"I'm sorry," Adrienne said.

Captain Garrett glanced down at the pile of paperwork on his desk, then back up at Adrienne. "Now that you're here, I have an assignment for you."

Adrienne stood straight and alert, her hands folded behind her back, and Captain Garrett studied her carefully with his gray eyes, as if considering her uncharacteristic lack of curiosity about the assignment.

"Is everything okay?" he asked.

Adrienne nodded again. "Everything is fine," she assured him. "What was it you wanted?"

Adrienne noticed the captain's doubtful look, but whatever his thoughts he put them aside and continued. "There's a new recruit here, from Roua," he told her.

"I spoke with the soldier from Roua earlier," Adrienne said.

"Not Freder," Captain Garrett said. "A young recruit. Jeral Rosch. I want you to test him and ascertain his skill level."

"Will he be in the Pen?" Adrienne asked.

"I expect he is. I want you to spar with him, then report back to me on his performance. He's come to Kyrog because we train the best, and the captain at Roua thought he showed promise. We need to know where to start with him."

"Yes, sir."

Adrienne saluted and left in pursuit of Jeral Rosch, forcing herself to block out what had happened with Nissen so that she could focus her full attention where it belonged. On her job.

She found Rosch in the small training yard dubbed the Pen due to its tight position between three neighboring buildings. Rosch was leaning up against one of those buildings, talking to another Yearling whom Adrienne vaguely recognized. Their swords were propped up against the wall beside them, and both seemed completely unaware of her presence.

"Rosch." Her voice cut through their quiet conversation like a knife and caused the young man to jump and spin around.

"You're Adrienne Rydaeg." Though her reputation preceded her, the young soldier seemed more eager than nervous to face her.

"Yes."

"I've heard about you from others who have come to Kyrog to train. They say you're good."

"I am," she said simply. "I'm here to determine your skill level."

Rosch grinned. "I've been training at Roua for two years. One of the lieutenants recommended that I come here, and my captain—"

"We'll spar. No weapons."

He looked over to where his sword rested. "I guess I'm ready, then."

Adrienne unbelted her own sword and set it on the ground. She moved into the center of the pen, feeling the crunch of dried grass beneath her feet, and Rosch followed. He had a height advantage of more than a foot, and his fighting stance was confident as he faced her.

Adrienne had no doubt who would win.

They circled each other for only a minute before the Yearling made a move, lunging for Adrienne. She could see evidence of training in that move, but also a lack of finesse, and she sidestepped it easily. They repeated the maneuver again and again until Adrienne tired of the game. She ducked under a wild swing from Rosch and landed a hard punch to his gut. He doubled over and barely avoided catching her knee on his chin.

He staggered upright and back a few steps, and Adrienne kicked out high, her foot stopping a bare six inches from the Yearling's throat.

Rosch stood frozen, the arm he had moved instinctively to block her kick only halfway raised.

Adrienne lowered her leg, planting both feet firmly on the ground with her weight balanced on the balls of her feet in a fighter's stance that was as natural to her as breathing. "That kick would have crushed your windpipe," Adrienne told the boy, her brown eyes hard and a little mean as she studied him.

Rosch was breathing heavily from the short match, and his eyes were wide with shock. Maybe he was surprised that he had lost so quickly, but Adrienne suspected the surprise had more to do with the fact that he had lost to her, a young woman who stood only as high as his shoulders.

A session with her taught new soldiers not to make assumptions about their opponent based on such trivial factors as size and gender, and that was one of the reasons Captain Garrett used her to test out the new recruits.

"I realize that," the young soldier said stiffly, struggling to maintain some dignity despite the sweat dripping down his dark face.

"Maybe you're just slow, then," Adrienne said bitingly. "Or maybe you are too damned naive to realize that female soldiers can be as great a threat as men."

He moved toward her again, apparently intending to take her down through sheer size. She allowed it, falling so that even as she hit the ground she was building momentum to roll. It took Rosch a moment to realize that she was not pinned, and then she was on top of his back, holding his shoulders down with her legs and locking his head with her arms. She held him a few painful seconds longer than necessary before letting go and getting up in disgust.

She took a deep breathe in an attempt to calm herself. She wasn't angry with the boy. It was the lieutenants and captains that had handed him a sword and deemed him fit to fight that disgusted her. "You need to learn to control your body. If you don't, you're likely to end up with an Almetian knife where your throat used to be."

Adrienne turned on her heel and left the recruit and the crowd that had gathered to watch her work. She moved with the sleek, predatory moves of a panther, her thick black braid swishing behind her like the tail of an angry cat. She was distantly aware of the bustle of soldiers and working civilians around her. Kyrog was always full of people, but she paid them no mind as she made her way once more to the captain's quarters.

She welcomed the anger she felt over the soldier's ineptitude. It helped to push away memories of what Lieutenant Nissen had tried to do earlier, before Ricco had chanced upon them.

Her anger at the Yearling's lack of skill was very real. With the constant threat from Almet to the north and groups of bandits roaming the plains of Samaro looking for travelers or defenseless villages to plunder, it was up to men like Rosch to see that the land did not devolve into lawlessness.

Although there had been little more than skirmishes with Almet in the last decade, everyone in Kyrog knew that Almet would soon bring its large military force against Samaro. Not only would Rosch and soldiers like him be useless against the soldiers from Almet, he would be a liability to the men fighting alongside of him.

Her anger carried her back to Captain Garrett's office. The captain looked up from the stack of paperwork on his sturdy wooden desk and nodded to her.

"I finished sparring with Rosch."

He raised an eyebrow. "And?"

Adrienne began to stalk around the small space, and Captain Garrett's lips twitched with humor in response to the temper rolling off her. She cut a figure with the sword at her hip slapping against her thigh with each turn. Her *swa'il*, the snug fitting leather outfit designed for fighting, was dirty and stained with sweat, dirt, and what was likely blood.

"He was horrible," Adrienne said when she finally came to a stop before the captain's desk. Her dark complexion showcased her expressive brown eyes, and those eyes were burning. "We were sparring without weapons, and I had him beat almost before the match began. If this is the best we can expect from the east—"

"Rydaeg," Captain Garrett interrupted, holding up a hand. "He is young. He only recently reached his majority. Roua does not offer the same experience to its soldiers that Kyrog does." He smiled slightly. "And he was probably surprised by your talent."

"I understand that, sir, but—"

"I don't think you do fully understand," Captain Garrett interrupted. "You are an exceptional soldier, and I rely on you as a teaching aid and for your exceptional skills. Part of the reason you are so exceptional is natural talent, but that is not what sets you apart. You have been a soldier nearly your entire life, and that is why you cannot fully understand soldiers like the one from Roua. You have never been where they are. It is possible that the soldier you sparred with this morning can spend the rest of his life training and never reach your level, but that does not make him a bad soldier. Any man brave enough to pick up the sword has my respect."

"Sir—"

"That was not a slight," Captain Garrett said. "I do not fault you because the choice to become a soldier was not yours." He studied her for a moment. "How long have you been training?"

"Sixteen years, sir."

"And how many of those years have you trained at Kyrog?"

"Twelve," Adrienne said, reluctantly following his line of logic.

"Twelve years. Over half of your life has been spent at Kyrog being trained by some of the best soldiers in Samaro, yet you expect a soldier who has trained for less than a handful of years, and spent only a few days at Kyrog, to present a challenge for you?" Captain Garrett's eyes bored into hers, and Adrienne had to force herself not to look away.

"Some of the Yearling recruits have been better," Adrienne said, though she knew it was a weak argument.

"And others have been worse," Garrett said. "Would you rather no one came to train at Kyrog?"

"Of course not," Adrienne said. "Kyrog has produced some of the finest soldiers in Samaro, and it should continue to do so."

Captain Garrett smiled. "You are worried that recruits such as this latest one will hurt Kyrog's reputation. That our standards will be lowered if we allow soldiers such as Jeral Rosch to train here."

Adrienne struggled with that truth, then sighed. "Yes," she said, her tone taking on a distinctly defensive note. "I am not an elitist, but if we continue to accept soldiers such as this one, how can Kyrog maintain its reputation?"

"Rydaeg, I have no intention of letting Rosch become an instructor here," Captain Garrett told her, his lips twitching slightly. "He, like others before him, will receive a year or two of intensive training at Kyrog before returning to Roua." Adrienne looked about to say something more, but the captain held up a finger to stop her. "Kyrog breeds elite soldiers, but not everyone can train here. To help the larger war effort, we train some soldiers for a short time before they leave to share their increased knowledge and skills with others."

Enough of Adrienne's mad had worn off for the captain's words to sink in. "Is it enough?" Adrienne asked.

There was no hint of a smile on Captain Garrett's lips now. His dark face looked even more tired, his scar more apparent as his mouth hardened. "Every year, men from Kyrog go to the borders of

Almet to support the soldiers already stationed there. They fight and die despite their superior skills, and we send more in their place. Almet is large and prosperous; it can summon vast armies. I don't know if our efforts are enough."

It was not what Adrienne had wanted to hear. She had hoped to have her doubts dispelled, not to hear them from her commanding officer. "Do we keep doing what we're doing?" Adrienne asked when the tight feeling in her chest was too much to bear. What they were doing seemed too small, the task too enormous, to make a difference.

"Highly skilled soldiers like yourself are important, but numbers matter. A hundred Jeral Roschs would make a bigger difference on the border than one Adrienne Rydaeg, if your task was to fight. You have spent your life training and learning to be the best. Do you wish to simply leave Samaro to its fate?"

"No." Adrienne didn't need to think about it. "I will fight to my last breath to defend our country."

Captain Garrett looked as though he had expected no less from her. Following her mother's death, Adrienne had been enlisted into one of the private armies by her father, who hadn't been able to afford four children. Soldiers had become her new family, and Samaro was the cornerstone of that family. Losing one meant losing the other, and Garrett would know that giving up soldiering was not an option for her.

"Then we continue on and hope that something turns the tide in our favor." He looked down at the stack of papers on his desk. Adrienne saw that the paper on top of the stack was a page from an old manuscript, the age revealed as much by the language it was written in as by the yellow, cracking paper. The text was Old Samaroan, a rare sight outside of a library.

"Do you have a translation?" Adrienne gestured toward the page. She moved subtly closer so that she could better see it without being obvious. It was hard to read Old Samaroan upside down, and she was unsure of one of the words she saw. *Necromancer?* That didn't seem right.

"I do," the captain said with a nod, snapping her back to attention, though her curiosity about the old text was nearly overwhelming "I won't need you to translate for me this time. You're dismissed, soldier."

Despite her frustration at not being able to read the text, Adrienne straightened, saluted, and left. She did not head immediately to her barracks, nor to the grounds where the experienced soldiers drilled. Instead she headed back to the Pen.

For the most part, Adrienne had always regarded the Yearlings as a nuisance: a waste of space, resources, and the time experienced Kyrogean soldiers spent training them when they should be sharpening their own skills. But after talking to Captain Garrett, she felt she now understood the Yearlings' purpose in the larger efforts to keep Samaro a country free from Almetian rule. Kyrog could elevate those inexperienced soldiers in a way few other camps could.

"Jeral Rosch!" she shouted in a loud, commanding voice that filled the training yard.

All movement—all sound—in the Pen stopped. Most of those present had already fought Adrienne during their short stay at Kyrog and knew that she had a reputation even amongst the veteran soldiers for being hard and having a temper that could flare at the least provocation. After the demonstration she had given just that morning, no one wanted to call attention to himself and risk her wrath.

Adrienne caught movement out of the corner of her eye. She turned and very nearly smirked as she saw three soldiers putting distance between themselves and the newest Yearling.

Rosch's swallow was nearly audible across the intervening yards, but he stepped forward and presented himself gamely. "Yes, uh, sir?" he asked with polite caution.

Adrienne nodded her approval. "Come with me," she said. Men all but leapt out of the way to clear a path for her as they left the yard. She stalked through the crowd of young soldiers, plans coalescing in her mind. When they reached a nearly empty area of the shaded courtyard, Adrienne turned to face Rosch and knew that he was working to control his nerves.

She respected that.

"Why are you here?" she asked.

"You told me to follow you, sir," Rosch said, looking confused.

Adrienne held back a sigh, reminding herself that he was young and hopefully more nervous than stupid. "Why are you here in Kyrog, Rosch?"

"My lieutenant in Roua recommended me to come here and receive more training. He said I was quite talented." He flushed, no doubt remembering their earlier sparring match and his humiliatingly easy defeat.

"Roua is not Kyrog," Adrienne said. "Do you know why we call recruits like you Yearlings?"

"Uh, no, sir. Not really."

Adrienne smiled. "Because you're young and stupid, like yearling stallions." His face fell. "But you're also strong, and able to learn a lot in the short time you are here. If you are serious about wanting to learn, I will teach you." Lieutenant Mylig was in charge of training soldiers in Kyrog, but she doubted he would be opposed to her taking over the training of one Yearling.

Rosch's look of shock did not surprise Adrienne overmuch. Although she made a point to ignore the Yearlings when possible, she still knew what they said about her. She participated in testing the recruits, but she never trained them, and it was well known that she preferred it that way. She was a good soldier, and could contribute positively to a group when necessary, but she was not a sociable sort, and she did not seek out relationships with the recruits.

"What?" Jeral asked. "Why?"

"If you want to be the best, you have to train with the best," Adrienne told him.

"I will not be an easy teacher," she warned. "I have spent years learning what you must learn in months. I will push you hard, every day, and I will expect you to give me everything you have to give." Her eyes narrowed. "I will know if you hold back."

Rosch nodded, his golden-brown eyes dazed by the unexpected turn of events.

"If you train under me, I will see to it that you too become one of the best," Adrienne promised, her eyes locked on his, looking to see the resolve that would be necessary to make her promise come true.

Rosch licked lips gone suddenly dry. This was why he had left Roua: to train at Kyrog under the best soldiers Samaro had to offer. And he was being given a chance no one else ever had. "When do we start?"

For the third morning in a row, Adrienne had Jeral up before dawn. She led the Yearling through her meditative morning routine: a series of slow, controlled movements that flowed from one position to another like a dance. It stretched the muscles, elongated the limbs and spine, and—most importantly—it improved the practitioner's balance.

Adrienne called out the name of the next move in Old Samaroan and Rosch grumbled that he couldn't understand her. An old soldier named Karse had first taught her the moves, and the names that went with them, when she was barely four-years-old, and he had never bothered to translate them for her. She would let Rosch learn as she had—by doing.

Adrienne owed much to Karse, who had taken her under his wing when all the other soldiers were trying to figure out what to do with a little girl who was too young to understand why she was away from her family, too young to help with camp chores or begin any meaningful training.

"Why are we doing this?" Rosch asked, as he had asked the last two days.

Adrienne gave up on the usual explanations and took a new track. "To teach you discipline, which you obviously lack. If you ask again, you won't like the other way I teach discipline."

Rosch fell silent and copied her moves. Adrienne called out another name.

Practicing those moves, teaching them to Rosch, brought back memories of the soldier who had been like a father to her after her own father had given her up. Karse had been a talented soldier, but he'd had the heart of a historian. She knew that without him, she would not have been the person she was. Without him, she might not have made it through those first rocky years after her mother's death. She would have been just another orphan shoved into a world that had no place for her.

She thought Karse would have approved of her decision to train the Yearling, though he would have probably been baffled by it as well. Even as a child she had preferred her own company over the company of others.

Adrienne was amused by Jeral's somewhat pained expression as he tried to copy her moves. The stretches were not easy for him, nor were the five mile runs that followed. But the slow moves would teach Jeral balance and flexibility, and running would give him speed as well as endurance. Both were essential skills if a soldier was hoping for a long life.

Adrienne's arms came down by her sides on her final exhalation, and she opened her eyes as the sun broke over the horizon in a brilliant show of lights and colors.

She was amused somewhat by Rosch's pained expression, and knew that it would not improve during the run that followed.

Though her legs were shorter than Rosch's, she moved in an economical way, using minimal effort to match his pace. Adrienne would have liked to pick up the pace or go on a longer run, but Rosch's body was not ready for that. Adrienne was well aware of the capabilities of the human body, and though she had regularly pushed

Rosch to his limits in the past three days, she had been careful to never cross the line that would lead to injury. An injury would only slow his progress and shake his confidence.

When they arrived back at the camp Rosch was breathing heavily, his face dripping and shirt soaked with sweat.

"Go get breakfast and drink some water," Adrienne told him. "Meet me back in the Pen in one hour."

Rosch nodded. "Okay." His breath was strained from the morning workout, and Adrienne wondered how long it would be before an easy run did not deplete Rosch's reserves so considerably.

After sending Rosch away, Adrienne decided she had best follow her own advice. She went to the mess hall usually frequented by the more senior soldiers, and was pleased to find Ricco eating at one of the long wooden tables.

Adrienne sat beside her friend and grabbed a piece of fruit from his plate. She bit into the sweet, pink flesh of the fruit, chewing and swallowing before smiling at Ricco's disgruntled look. "This is good."

"I know." He chuckled and slid a piece of sausage her way. "Have this; you'll just steal it otherwise. How's the kid?"

Ricco had been amused to find that Adrienne had decided to train one of the Yearlings herself, and liked to ask how "the kid" was progressing. Adrienne had decided to take his comments as a challenge rather than an insult to her training abilities.

"He tires quickly, and doesn't know how to control his body," Adrienne informed her friend, biting into the sausage and contemplating getting a plate of her own.

"Tires quickly compared to other people, or compared to you?" Ricco asked. "We don't all start our days the way you do."

Adrienne frowned. "You can keep up with me, though."

"Sometimes. There's a reason I don't go running with you in the morning." Ricco picked up a piece of sausage, took a bite, and then gestured with it. "And don't get me started on that dancing thing you do every morning. No man should be flitting and twirling about like that."

"You're just unhappy because my moves make me hard to pin in the ring." She grabbed another piece of fruit off of her friend's plate. "Anyway, I think Rosch has promise."

"Really?"

"He's eager to learn and prove himself."

Ricco nodded. "Long as that eagerness doesn't get in the way of him actually learning, the two of you might accomplish something."

Adrienne frowned and reached for another sausage. Ricco slapped her hand away.

"Do I need to get another plate?" he asked, pulling his food farther away from Adrienne and hunching his shoulders over it protectively.

"No, I'll get my own," Adrienne said. "Stay here." Adrienne walked through the line and got a dish of fruit and some oatmeal sweetened with honey. When she returned to Ricco, two other men were just leaving the table.

Ricco turned back to Adrienne after the two men had gone. "Ade, a few of us are getting together for cards tonight," he said. "Want to join?"

Adrienne didn't typically join Ricco and his friends for drinking and games, but she had been so busy with Rosch that she knew she was neglecting Ricco. And she missed him. "Why not?"

"Good. Meet us at Nils' Tavern?"

Adrienne agreed, thinking it had been too long since she had unwound at the tavern with a few pints of ale and a group of friends. "See you there."

CHAPTER TWO

The noonday sun shone down bright and hot on the small sparring ring adjacent to the Yearling training ground. Adrienne had already spent three hours at her own training before meeting up with Rosch to continue his.

And now he was questioning her methods. "I don't understand why we can't use weapons," Rosch grumbled under his breath as he headed back to his side of the ring.

Adrienne heard him anyway. "Your hands and feet, your body, are weapons in their own right. They are the only weapons that cannot be taken away from you. It would be foolish for me to train you with other weapons before you master the ones you were born with."

Rosch felt his face grow hot in embarrassment, but he squared his shoulders and turned to face her. "I know being able to fight without weapons is important," he said. "But I have training with weapons, so I don't see why I can't practice with both. Variation is good, isn't it?"

The young man might have had a point, Adrienne thought, had she not known that he was still participating in practice fights—with weapons—against the other Yearlings. She had no reason to worry that whatever skills he might have obtained in Roua would grow dull through lack of practice. "You will master the tasks I give you before moving on to the next," she said firmly. "In time, we will use weapons other than our bodies. For now, we use what we were born with and nothing else."

Rosch looked unhappy, but he nodded and settled into a fighting stance. The position looked awkward to Adrienne's trained eye. She took her own stance a pace from him, settling into it with the ease of long experience.

"You have to be comfortable," she reminded him impatiently. "Balanced. This is your base, the position you will always come back

15

to. Do you understand?" Rosch nodded and shifted into a slightly more natural position.

"Good." Adrienne took a step forward and shoved him hard in the chest.

He stepped back, groping for balance.

"No, keep your stance. Shift your balance lower and push against me. Never give up ground if your new position will not be a better one."

Rosch resumed his position and Adrienne pushed against him again. She pushed harder, putting her weight behind it, and Rosch pushed back, digging in his feet. Adrienne shifted quickly, grabbed his arm, and pulled hard.

He tripped over the leg she shot out and wound up sprawled on the ground.

"Very good," Adrienne said with the slightest smile for the recruit.

"I still ended up on the ground," Rosch said as he picked himself up off the dusty ground. Dust mixed with sweat and ran in muddy runnels down his dark face and caked his hands.

"I did," Adrienne agreed. "But how?"

Rosch's brow furrowed in a look she had come to recognize well since starting his training. It was the look he wore when he was running over a past event and analyzing it. "You changed your move. You couldn't push me over, so you pulled me down instead," he said as he replayed the incident in his mind.

"Yes. I'm smaller than you, and you outweigh me significantly, but size is only a hindrance if you don't know how to use it."

"I guess you'd know," Rosch said with a grin that revealed straight white teeth.

Adrienne smiled back, pleased with the changes she was seeing. "I've learned to use my size, rather than let it be used against me." She looked over the tall youth from head to toe. "I have a lot of experience, and you can learn from me, but you have to trust what I am doing. Body now, weapons later. Resume your stance."

Rosch sank down and Adrienne began instructing him on how to avoid having his feet kicked out from under him. After a few unsuccessful attempts, which resulted in Rosch falling to the ground repeatedly, Adrienne had him do the kicking.

The Yearling completely lost his base, and his balance, on the first kick, and Adrienne easily sidestepped him as he concentrated on not falling after the unfamiliar move.

"Sink further into your fighting stance," Adrienne instructed. "I didn't tell you that was your base for nothing. Kicking someone's feet out from under them doesn't help if you both end up on the ground."

Rosch shook his head to clear it and was just sinking into his fighting stance when blasts from the warning horns filled the air. "Flaming Abyss," Adrienne swore in disgust. "Follow me." She ran for their things on the edge of the sparring ring.

She picked up her own sword, tossed Rosch his, and they ran toward the western edge of the camp. Soldiers were lined up around the perimeter in various states of readiness. Most of the Yearlings, Rosch included, seemed to be in a mixed state of confusion and alarm, but all of the Kyrogeans were calm and ready for battle, even the man wearing only his smallclothes and holding a bared sword.

"Well done," Lieutenant Nissen announced to the soldiers standing ready near the outer wall of the camp. "Today was a drill, and we had the perimeter defended in less than ten minutes. Excellent job." The self-satisfaction in his voice made Adrienne sick. He wasn't proud of them and the fact that they would be able to defend Kyrog, he was proud that his section had been ready so fast.

It would make him look good for the captain.

"A drill?" Rosch asked, looking at Adrienne suspiciously.

Adrienne looked away from the lieutenant and forced a smile, hiding her reaction to Nissen's presence. She slapped the Yearling on the back in a show of reassurance. "We have drills periodically to test our preparedness. You did well."

"You knew what was going on?" Rosch demanded. "You knew it was a drill?"

Adrienne shrugged and gave a slight shake of her head. "I suspected that it was a drill. The horns would sound the same, and I wasn't warned ahead of time, but I doubt Kyrog will be attacked anytime soon. Even bandits are not so foolish as to attack a fully armed camp as large as ours."

"I didn't know what the horns meant."

Adrienne had never thought to instruct him on camp procedures, and realized as his trainer that she should have done so. Mylig doubtless taught the new recruits camp procedure their first day of training—perhaps he even had them run drills like today's in preparation.

"There are always scouts and horn-blowers on watch around Kyrog, as well as on the walls. If there is ever an enemy force approaching the camp, three long blasts from a horn is the signal to guard the perimeter."

"Like today," Rosch said.

"Yes. I—and by extension you—am assigned to the middle-west edge of the camp. Wherever you are, whatever you are doing, when those horns blow you grab your weapon and get to the perimeter, whether you think it is a drill or not."

Rosch nodded, his eyes serious as he processed her instructions. There had been similar drills in Roua, but he could not remember one ever being carried out with the serious air that this one had. In Roua, drills were simply that. Drills. In Kyrog, drills were treated as seriously as an actual attack.

"Now we need to get back to your training. If it's not a drill next time, I don't want you tripping over your own feet."

Rosch laughed until Adrienne gave him a look that said she hadn't been joking about him tripping. Adrienne ran Rosch through kicking exercises, as well as various maneuvers to hone his jumping and dodging, until her own stomach protested putting off lunch for so long.

"And we're done. Take two hours," Adrienne advised. "And sit with your legs up. They took a beating."

"Yes, sir."

With Jeral gone, Adrienne went in search of lunch and someone she could practice against. It was hard for her to find time to practice against other soldiers when she was devoting so much of her own time to Jeral.

"Adrienne," a too-familiar voice called out, interrupting her search for a likely opponent.

Adrienne cringed, remembering the last close encounter she'd had with this man, but on the surface she was calm and unconcerned as she turned and stood at attention. "Yes, Lieutenant?" she asked, keeping her voice coolly professional.

"I see you have gotten rid of your boy shadow," Nissen said.

Adrienne couldn't stand his eyes on her, and crossed her arms over her leather-clad breasts in an unconscious gesture of defense. "I dismissed Jeral Rosch for lunch, Lieutenant." And she wished now that she hadn't. If she'd waited even a couple of minutes, she wouldn't be alone with Nissen now.

"We never got a chance to talk," he said, glancing around for observers. The street was not deserted as it had been last time, but no one was paying them any attention. "Maybe you should come with me now. I have a lot to say to you. Especially after last time, when we were...interrupted."

Adrienne could not believe that this was happening again. He was not touching her, but she could see in his eyes exactly what he was thinking, and what he would do to her if he got her alone. "I have to go," she said, turning and walking away from him. She pretended that she did not hear him call her name, and kept walking until the lieutenant was far behind her.

"I was looking for you."

Startled, Adrienne looked up in surprise at being caught off guard. It was Ricco, his voice full of the easy confidence that was so much a part of him, his posture relaxed and unconcerned. "I was wondering if you wanted to practice with me."

Adrienne shook her head, trying to rearrange her thoughts.

"No?" Ricco asked, clearly surprised. He gave her a more careful study, wondering what was wrong with her. "You sick or something?"

"What?" Adrienne asked as Ricco's initial question finally registered. "Practice. Right. We should practice."

Ricco looked at her askance. "I would guess the kid got in a lucky punch, but no punch rattles you that much."

Adrienne gave a jerky shrug in response.

"Hey." Ricco scanned their surroundings suspiciously. His eyes narrowed when he saw a familiar figure in the crowd. "What'd he do this time?"

"Nothing," Adrienne answered, too quickly.

"What did that bastard—"

"I can't do this now," Adrienne nearly shouted, her eyes blazing. She regretted the harsh tone almost instantly, but she couldn't talk about it, and she couldn't tamp down the anger entirely. "I can't."

Ricco took a deep breath, and contrary to his nature, he seemed to let it go. "Still want to practice?"

Despite being suddenly tired, Adrienne smiled. Ricco knew her well.

"Yes, please."

Adrienne had planned to practice using swords, but after the most recent incident with Nissen she didn't want to be careful with sharp blades, nor did she want the steel-cored wooden practice swords that could still hit hard enough to break bone. She wanted the feel of flesh on flesh, of bruised skin and torn knuckles, of having her hands on an opponent.

Ricco must have read her mood, because he stripped off his own sword when they got to one of the small training grounds and set it aside. "Any rules?" he asked.

Adrienne shook her head. "No. Let's fight."

Adrienne didn't pull her punches, and neither did Ricco. By tacit agreement they didn't hit each other in the face. The bruises and swollen skin where fists connected with flesh were left for less visible parts of the body.

Her booted foot connected with Ricco's solid thigh in a kick hard enough to send vibrations up her leg, and she felt some of her stress melt away. Ricco grabbed her and threw her to the ground, and her blood fired as she rolled back up to her feet, burning out the last remnants of stress and worry. All that existed was her and Ricco and the battle between them.

A week later, Adrienne knew something was deeply wrong. Tension was not at all unusual in Kyrog, people were being trained for war—to kill or to die—and it was not a restful process, but Adrienne could not remember a time of such sustained tension, and all directed at one person, in her twelve years at the camp. Though no one was directly defying his orders, it was clear that a large percentage of the unranked soldiers at Kyrog had suddenly developed a problem with Lieutenant Nissen.

"What did you do?" Adrienne demanded when she was finally able to corner Ricco after dinner one night. He had been successfully avoiding her for days, even going so far as to cancel their training sessions.

"I don't know what you're talking about."

Adrienne swore, shoving ineffectually at his broad chest. "You know exactly what I'm talking about." She couldn't remember ever being more furious at her friend, and she pushed him again, infuriated that she could barely budge him.

"I had to do something," Ricco said. "You wouldn't tell the captain, and after the second time…"

Adrienne briefly entertained the thought of strangling Ricco. "Then tell me what you did!" Adrienne had told Ricco what had happened because she had trusted him to keep it to himself. It had never occurred to her that he would betray her trust.

"I might have told a couple of men that the lieutenant made some inappropriate comments to you," Ricco admitted, looking over her shoulder rather than meeting her eyes.

"You what?" Adrienne shrieked. It was a surprisingly girly sound coming from her mouth, but the fear and the sliver of shame that ran through her was equally surprising and unwelcome. She glanced around to see who might have heard her, but for the moment they were alone.

Ricco shrugged. "I didn't tell them what happened in the alley…what he did or said," Ricco defended. "I didn't tell them about your reaction." Adrienne took her first easy breath when she realized that the men did not know how shaken she had been, or how her hands had trembled after the encounter. "All they know is that Nissen disrespected you."

She closed her eyes and hoped to recover some of her calm before she gave in to the urge to strangle her friend. Ricco might not have told anyone exactly what had happened, but it wouldn't have been that hard to guess. She comforted herself with the fact that Ricco was right, none of the soldiers would ever guess that Adrienne had been scared. She was known for her ability to stand calm and steady in the face of enemy swords. A woman who could do that would never be seen as the sort of woman to be scared by a man's advances, unwelcome or not.

"Did you tell the men to act like this?" she asked, wondering how that conversation might have gone and what further explanation he might have given.

Ricco shook his head. "No. I didn't expect half of this. But the men here respect you, Adrienne, and if they believe Nissen was out of line then they aren't going to ignore it any more than I am." He shrugged. "Besides, no one likes the bastard anyway. What he said to you is merely an excuse."

Adrienne still couldn't believe that Ricco had told anyone, but it was somewhat heartening to know that so many in Kyrog were behind her without question, even if it meant walking the line of insubordination to treat the lieutenant the way they were. "You're an idiot," she said, "but thanks."

Ricco flashed one of his face-rending grins now that she seemed less likely to pull a knife on him.

Adrienne rolled her shoulders to relieve the tension lingering there. "Any clue when things will go back to normal?" she asked. It was nice that the other soldiers supported her, but she didn't like so much tension in the camp. What would happen if they were attacked? Would the divide between the enlisted and one of the officers put them in jeopardy?

Ricco rolled his eyes. "I didn't know any of this was going to happen," he admitted. "Who knows when it will stop?"

Since it seemed unlikely any action she took would help, Adrienne decided the best course of action was inaction. She would act as though there was nothing unusual about the current mood of the camp and wait for everything to go back to normal. "Want to train with me and Rosch tomorrow?" she asked.

"The Yearling?" Ricco seemed surprised, and Adrienne realized it had been almost a month since she had begun training Rosch, and she had not invited Ricco to so much as observe their training sessions.

"Why not? Besides…there might be some question about how the techniques I am teaching will work against soldiers larger than myself."

Ricco laughed until he realized she was serious. "He said that?" The look of disbelief was gratifying and justified the frustration Adrienne had been feeling at the Yearling's constant doubting and questioning of her methods.

"Words to that effect." She recalled the recent conversation she'd had with the Yearling. "I believe it is my 'short stature' that worries him, like we have progressed far enough in his training that I've refined his moves based on a particular opponent's size and skills."

Before Adrienne worked with Rosch on how to adapt his moves toward different opponents, he would have to internalize the basic moves to the point of instinct. He was still learning the basics, not the fine adjustments necessary to be most effective against people of different sizes and fighting styles. That training wouldn't come until much later.

"How is fighting me going to prove to him that your training is effective?" Ricco asked skeptically.

Adrienne understood the skepticism. Rosch would have no more chance of beating Ricco than he did of beating Adrienne. It was something Adrienne had already considered when planning to pull Ricco into the training program.

"The two of us will spar first," Adrienne said. "Rosch can watch variations of the moves I've taught him, and if you're already tired maybe he can last more than ten minutes."

"I thought you beat him in five," Ricco said. Adrienne couldn't tell if the offense in his voice was feigned or not.

"He's been training with me for weeks," Adrienne pointed out. "And besides, everyone knows I'm a better fighter than you."

"Say that again when I beat you in front of the kid tomorrow."

Rosch stood off to the side, looking on with interest as Adrienne and Ricco faced each other in the training ring. The match was not taking place in the small ring located in the Yearling training grounds, but in one of the larger, nicer rings used by the more experienced soldiers. Adrienne had no problem training Rosch in the smaller ring, but Ricco had insisted on the change of venue. He did not often formally spar with Adrienne, and he wanted their fight to be visible to more than just the Yearlings.

Neither of the two Kyrogeans held weapons. Swords would play no part in determining whether Adrienne or Ricco was the superior fighter. Though Rosch knew that the match had been set up in fun for his benefit, Adrienne was surprised to see the nerves on her trainee's face as she squared up against her larger, more powerfully built friend. Ricco's arms were as large as Adrienne's thighs, and his broad chest would make two of her. His jaw looked hard enough to crush granite.

Adrienne dropped into a low fighting stance, her brown eyes glowing with intensity, and with a wide grin that more resembled a predator's bared teeth Ricco did the same. Adrienne clenched and unclenched her fists in anticipation of the coming match.

Word had spread through Kyrog that Adrienne and Ricco had set up a sparring match, and other soldiers had gathered around to see the demonstration of superior skills. Quite a few of the Yearlings were there, doubtless to watch the female soldier they had all faced and been defeated by go up against Ricco, a soldier with more than six years of training in Kyrog and the scars to prove he'd seen action outside of the relative safety of the camp's training grounds. The more experienced soldiers gathered to see what promised to be an interesting contest between the two superb contenders.

Adrienne and Ricco trained together on a regular basis, but they rarely competed against each other in a formal way, and some men decided to take bets on the outcome.

"Are you sure you want to risk embarrassing yourself this way?" Ricco asked, his voice taunting as they circled each other.

"I'm ready to embarrass you," Adrienne called back.

Ricco's right fist shot out in retaliation.

Adrienne spun back to avoid the punch, and the game began.

Ricco came at her like a bull, head down, relying on size and weight rather than finesse to overwhelm her.

Adrienne's kick caught him in the solar plexus, using his own momentum against him, and had him doubling over long enough for another sweeping kick to take out his legs.

He fell hard, raising a puff of dust, but Ricco was fast despite his bulky appearance. He leapt to his feet, dodged left, then right, to avoid another kick.

He settled into a fighting stance similar to the one Adrienne had so painstakingly taught Rosch, but he didn't stay still for long. A quick step forward brought him close enough to strike, and his fist very nearly connected with Adrienne's cheek. She felt the wind from the near miss brush past her as she threw herself to the right.

They dodged blow after blow, circling and attempting to strike, until Ricco managed to land a punch on Adrienne's chin.

Her head snapped back, and there were cheers and groans from the crowd as she staggered backward, barely managing to keep her feet.

Money changed hands as the first blood was drawn.

"You've a damned hard head," Ricco said, shaking his hand out to alleviate some of the sting.

Adrienne spat out a mouthful of blood from where she had bitten her tongue, circling Ricco warily. Her head was ringing, her vision just a little blurry. If this had been a normal training session, she might have decided to wait for her head to clear before continuing the fight.

Since they were on display, she fought on through the dizziness.

Ricco had her outmatched when it came to upper body strength, and if it came to a grappling match she stood no change, but her legs were strong. Jumps and kicks were something she had that Ricco didn't, and she used them now.

She kept Ricco on the move, twisting and dodging, and he cursed her as fists and feet flew by his head, missing by inches.

He was tiring, and Adrienne took the chance of a flying leap, kicking out toward his head.

She caught him right by the ear, and he went down. Hard.

Adrienne walked over and put her foot on his chest. Ricco made only a feeble attempt to lift it off.

"We can see now who the better fighter is," Adrienne said smugly, pressing down a bit harder on his chest.

There were chuckles from the crowd and more money was exchanged. The fight had not been a long one, but the strikes and evasions had been great examples of skill. The crowd was obviously pleased by the show, and even those who had placed bets on Ricco and lost joked as they handed over their money.

"To the Abyss with that." Ricco's voice was only slightly stronger than his hands were as he tried to displace her foot again, and Adrienne reduced the pressure on his chest. "I can take you any day. Rematch."

The crowd seemed to like that idea, and though Adrienne wouldn't mind another go at Ricco, she shook her head.

"Rosch needs you in one piece," she told her friend. "Maybe after he has a go at you we can give this another try." She removed her foot and offered Ricco a hand to help him get to his feet. He glared at the soldiers who were gleefully collecting money they had won by betting against him.

"Tonight," Ricco said, pointing a finger at Adrienne. "We'll have another go tonight. See who wins then."

Adrienne raised one amused eyebrow, then nodded. "Tonight." She looked toward Rosch, who was watching the byplay with interest. He didn't look ready to step into the sparring ring and face Ricco himself. She actually thought he looked a bit green under his naturally dark complexion.

She took another look at Ricco, who was covered in dirt and sweat with knuckles beginning to bruise, and could understand why the Yearling might hesitate. "Rosch, are you planning to fight today or just watch?"

Rosch started and looked sheepishly at Adrienne. Like Ricco, she looked even more imposing than usual with bruised knuckles and blood on her face. When she crossed her arms over her chest, he felt oddly grateful that it was not her that he was about to face. Though he had no delusions that he stood a real chance against Ricco, Adrienne looked the more dangerous of the two. "I'm ready," he said, turning to take measure of Ricco as he would an opponent rather than a teacher.

"Very good." She stepped away from Ricco and gestured for Rosch to take her place. "Have at him."

"I've seen great improvement in you these last few months," Adrienne said one morning after she and Rosch had completed their run. What had once been a short morning run that would leave the young man breathless had evolved into an easy eight miles that he could finish with energy to spare. They were sitting on a bench just outside of the mess hall, resting before breakfast and their next training session.

Adrienne had pushed him hard in their time together, and his body had adapted just as she had known it would. She knew a day would come where his new strength and endurance would serve him well.

"Thank you," Rosch said. His words were simple, but Adrienne could see the surprise and pleasure warring in his eyes. She was not free with her compliments, and it was rare for him to receive one.

Rosch's mind and attitude had adapted as well. He no longer questioned Adrienne's methods, or pushed to progress faster than she allowed. She knew that weekly practice sessions with other experienced soldiers had helped Rosch better understand and respect her skill, just as she knew that he benefited from having variety in his instruction.

And today she would provide even more variety. "After breakfast, bring a quarterstaff with you to the sparring ring."

"Sir?"

Adrienne could understand his confusion. Despite four months of training, they had not used more than daggers when they were sparring together. She pretended to reconsider her decision. "Unless you don't think you're ready for real weapons."

"No, sir, I'm ready," he said quickly, before Adrienne had a chance to change her mind.

"Then get going."

When Rosch was well out of hearing, Adrienne felt a presence settle into the space beside her on the bench. She turned to see Ricco sitting there looking after the Yearling's retreating form.

"He didn't even complain that the weapon isn't a sword," he said, letting her know he had been close enough to eavesdrop for quite some time.

"Just because you don't appreciate the proper use of a quarterstaff doesn't mean that Rosch is so narrow-minded," Adrienne told her friend.

Ricco snorted. "He'd be glad for any weapon at this point." Ricco was more than a little amazed that Rosch had lasted so long without complaint.

Adrienne bit back her smile. "Do you wish to be excused from the training rotation until we've progressed to swords?" she asked her friend. "Or at least until we are done with quarterstaffs?"

After the first time Ricco had sparred with Rosch, he had started to train with the Yearling once or twice a week. Adrienne was sure that the extra practice Ricco provided was part of the reason Rosch was progressing so quickly. Even when Adrienne could not train Rosch herself, he was being taught by other Kyrogeans. The other Yearlings were still being taught by Mylig and a small group of others, but Adrienne had been able to convince some of the soldiers that they wanted to help her. As she had heard no complaints from Mylig or the captain, she felt comfortable planning Rosch's training as she saw fit.

"Not if that means waiting another four months," Ricco said. Of all the soldiers Adrienne had talked or coerced into practicing with Rosch, Ricco was the one who needed the least convincing. She thought Ricco must enjoy working with the Yearling.

Adrienne certainly did, although she had not expected to. She had wanted to teach Rosch to fight after she had so easily beaten him that first time, but she had not expected to care for the Yearling, or to take such pride in his accomplishments.

Ricco and Adrienne stood up from the bench and got into the mess line, accepting fruit and oatmeal as well as an egg each. Ricco took a thick slab of side pork, but Adrienne declined and went to claim a table that was more removed from the others, where they would be able to talk uninterrupted and without the need to shout over the other men in the mess. Despite the serious nature with which the soldiers devoured their morning meal, they did so in a loud fashion, calling out to each other between mouthfuls of food.

"Not four months," Adrienne assured Ricco when he had joined her. "We were laying ground work then. Two weeks with the quarterstaff should suffice, and then we will move on."

Ricco frowned. "Two weeks?" He took a bite of side pork and half-chewed it before resuming talking. "That isn't very long." Adrienne made a face at the food still in his mouth and he swallowed before speaking again. "I thought you planned to train him to expert level, the way you were going about it."

Adrienne knew that, despite Ricco's dislike of quarterstaffs, he was more than competent with them. And he was right, years could be spent mastering the oft underappreciated weapon.

She picked up a sweet red berry and bit into it, chewing thoughtfully as she considered her response. "He can't become an expert in everything," Adrienne said once she had completely chewed and swallowed the berry, "especially not within our time frame."

"Then why even bother with the quarterstaff?" Ricco asked, shoveling in some of his egg. Ricco ate at the speed with which most soldiers consumed their food, as though they might be called away at any moment.

"You learned the quarterstaff, though you don't use it when given the choice between that or a sword," Adrienne pointed out. "Is the knowledge you have of the weapon wasted?"

"No. If I didn't know how a quarterstaff was used, I wouldn't be able to defend against one." A look of realization dawned on his face and he smiled. "Clever."

"I want Rosch to have that knowledge. A couple of weeks working with the quarterstaff will hopefully help prepare him in that regard."

Ricco gestured vaguely with a spoonful of oatmeal. "Since you're only going to be using the quarterstaff for a couple weeks, you can count me out for training the boy. Try Oliver."

Adrienne shook her head. Oliver might be the most skilled with the quarterstaff in Kyrog, but he was not the best of teachers. "I know enough to teach Rosch the basics."

Ricco shrugged and resumed eating his food, scraping the plate clean and going back for more before Adrienne was halfway done with her own plate.

"Can't you just threaten them with a sword?" Rosch asked. "They won't know you don't want to kill them, and that way no one gets hurt."

Adrienne looked to the sky and wished for patience. Sometimes, when she was introducing a new idea to Rosch, she thought the young man might have come to Kyrog from Roua just to test her. "People are stupid. Remember that." The quarterstaff could be lethal when used correctly, but it was the non-lethal opportunities that it presented which Adrienne liked most about the weapon. "You might know it will be easier on them if they just sit down and shut up, but half the time some stupid, inexperienced civilian is still going to try and get past you. And stupid people are liable to skewer themselves on swords by accident."

"You sound like you have experience with this." Rosch was no doubt hoping for an interesting story.

"I've encountered such things on patrols." She remembered with a pang the foolish farmer who had come at her with a kitchen knife on one of those outings. There had been bandits in the area, and Adrienne had only wanted to check and make sure that everything was all right at the out-of-the-way farm.

The farmer was lucky to have escaped with only the deep gash on his arm, a wound which had probably affected the use of his hand permanently. The injury had been self-inflicted from when he had fallen into her sword while trying to "defend" his pigs. A wild lunge with his knife had forced him off-balance, and he had reached out for support and connected with her bared sword instead.

She had been only sixteen, and it was not a story that she wanted to share. "Just focus on learning how to use a quarterstaff, and worry about when you'll need one later."

Rosch still looked somewhat unsure, but he got into a semblance of his typical fighting stance, facing her.

"No, here." Adrienne put her hands on Rosch's hips, moving him into a slightly more balanced position. "You need to shift your balance a little lower. The power of your strikes it going to come from your core, so it needs to be strong." Another minute adjustment to his hips and she pulled back, putting her hands on his and moving them along the quarterstaff until they were far enough apart. "Range is important with the quarterstaff. For optimal range, you should keep your hands like this whenever both are on the quarterstaff."

After a few adjustments, all of the physical groundwork Adrienne had laid out made holding the general stance easy. The mental groundwork made Rosch more biddable, so that she no longer had to justify every instruction she gave. Adrienne wasn't sure which pleased her more. The skills he was learning would serve him well and keep him alive in the battles he would inevitably face. And he would be an asset to Samaro in a way that he never would have been had he stayed in Roua for the duration of his training.

CHAPTER THREE

Adrienne sat on a wooden bench looking out over the plains from her seat on top of one of the guard towers. She was on duty for the next four hours, and when she saw a cloud of dust in the distance she almost thought it was a result of the heat playing tricks on her eyes. She squinted against the afternoon light and saw that the dust was being kicked up by a lone horse moving quickly down the otherwise deserted road to Kyrog. She signaled to her fellow guardsmen that someone was approaching, then settled back down on her bench to wait.

The wait was not as long as Adrienne had expected, and when the rider finally pulled the horse to a stop outside of Kyrog's gates she saw that the beast was lathered from too many miles covered too fast.

The woman riding the horse looked to be in little better shape. She was slumped over with weariness, and Adrienne recognized the glazed eyes as a mixture of fear and fatigue. A ripple of apprehension traveled down Adrienne's spine as she scanned the countryside for the slightest movement that might indicate a pursuing force. She saw nothing, and motioned toward the guard standing next to the gate mechanism. "Let her in," Adrienne said, climbing down the ladder of the guard tower so that she could speak to the woman.

It took two men to help the woman down without her falling off her mount and even then she had to cling to the footsore horse to keep from collapsing.

"What happened?" Adrienne asked, standing directly in front of the woman so that the exhausted traveler would have something to focus on.

"A group of men," the woman said in a voice devoid of emotion. "They came to my home and attacked. I got away."

30

The woman fell silent, and Adrienne wanted to shake her to get her talking again. They needed to know if Kyrog was in danger.

One of the more patient men on guard duty stepped forward, taking a spot between Adrienne and the stranger. "Ma'am," he said, keeping his voice low and soothing, "where is your home?"

"Pelarion."

Adrienne recognized the name of the village. It was not far to the west of Kyrog. She turned to one of the soldiers who had come to see what the commotion was about. "Tell Captain Garrett that Pelarion has been attacked."

The woman from Pelarion shuddered slightly at Adrienne's raised words, and Adrienne wished she was able to offer some comfort.

"Can you tell us more?" Adrienne asked, moving so that she could see the woman more clearly, trying to imitate the soothing tone of the other guard's voice. From the woman's expression, she was not successful.

"There were so many of them. They came with swords and spears." A tear welled up in one eye and spilled onto her cheek, but the woman seemed not to notice. "They started killing people. My husband…"

It was hard to tell from looking at the woman exactly what had happened. Pelarion was a hard two day ride from Kyrog, and the woman's filthiness could be due to no more than dusty roads and sweating in the dry heat of the Samaroan plains, but there was more dirt on her back and knees than anywhere else, and her skirts were torn.

Adrienne knew enough of the brigands who roamed Samaro to imagine what the man had died protecting his wife from. She pitied the woman, knowing what it felt like to have someone die so that she might live. It was something the woman would never forget, something that would creep up on her during the night and weigh on her soul. But rather than crippling her, the fear and loss had brought her here, to Kyrog, where she could receive help.

"Get some of the serving women to arrange a tent and a hot bath for her," Adrienne told another soldier who had stopped to see what was happening at the gate. "And have someone hot-walk that horse before stabling it. I have to stay here." Adrienne wanted to question the woman more, or speak to Captain Garrett herself, but she was the senior soldier at the gates, and could not leave her station while on guard duty, not without an order from one of the officers.

And there were other people in the camp that could offer better comfort than Adrienne.

She did not have to wait long for new orders to come. Captain Garrett sent for her within the half hour, and she reported to his office immediately.

"Is this about the woman?" Adrienne asked.

The captain's face was serious. "Yes. If Pelarion has been attacked by brigands, they are likely still in the village. I am sending a group of soldiers to deal with the invaders."

Adrienne nodded, hoping that she would be allowed to be part of that group. Captain Garrett knew she had been looking for an assignment outside of Kyrog since before Rosch had arrived. Training the Yearling had superseded that, but she still wanted time away from the camp, time to go out and make a difference rather than just endlessly train. Purging Pelarion of the men who had taken over would be exactly the change she had been looking for. "What can I do?" she asked.

"I want you to lead the group going to Pelarion," Captain Garrett said. "No more than twenty, and I want the names of those men tonight."

"Of course," Adrienne said, hardly daring to believe the captain's words. He'd never had her lead a group on a mission such as this before. "I will make my choices wisely."

"And quickly," the captain told her. "I want you ready to go by dawn tomorrow."

"The village is just a few miles ahead," Ricco told Adrienne and the rest of the group when he rejoined them. The woman from Pelarion had still been nearly incoherent the morning Adrienne and her men had left Kyrog, and had therefore been unable to give a clear report, so Adrienne had sent Ricco ahead to see what challenges they would face in the village. "It doesn't look good."

Adrienne nodded. She had been honored and excited to be chosen by Captain Garrett to lead the group to Pelarion, but she had known that disposing of invaders in a village would not be the same as taking care of outlaws in the countryside. They could not ride in and kill or capture without impunity, their duty was to save who and what they could.

"I didn't expect it would." Adrienne turned to the men she had chosen to accompany her to Pelarion. Rosch was one of the nineteen chosen, and though Captain Garrett had questioned her decision to include the Yearling, Adrienne had been adamant that he was ready to leave Kyrog and the safety of practice in a sparring ring. There would be enough experienced soldiers to ensure that Pelarion would be reclaimed, and Rosch would gain much needed experience. If he wasn't ready for a real fight by now, he might never be. After talking to Mylig, she had selected two of the more experienced Yearlings as well. They would be leaving Kyrog soon, and Mylig wanted them to experience real fighting before they left.

"What do we do now?" one of the men asked, looking off in the direction of the village as though he could see the brigands from where he stood.

There were several suggestions. Some of the men thought that they should wait to go in until nightfall, when they would be able to sneak in unnoticed, while others thought leaving for Pelarion immediately would be the best course of action. They could be in the village by late afternoon if they followed that plan. They knew that the village had already been at the attackers' mercy for several days.

But if they left now, there would not be time to make careful plans for how to take back the village. Adrienne's blood sang for her to act, but years of study had taught her that battles were won by strategy as often as by strength.

Ricco must have read Adrienne's expression and her intention to wait and plan, for he put a restraining hand on her arm. "Ade, what they're doing in there..." he trailed off helplessly.

Adrienne studied Ricco's eyes, so dark they were nearly black, and saw the reflection of the brigands' cruelty etched into the dark orbs. Waiting even a few hours would subject the people of Pelarion to more of the harsh treatment from the lawless men. Pain and death always played a part when villages such as Pelarion were assaulted, and Adrienne knew that the longer they waited, the more likely it was that villagers would be hurt and killed to entertain those who had taken Pelarion.

"We'll move now," Adrienne said decisively.

The flat plains that dominated this part of Samaro made it impossible to sneak up to Pelarion on horseback, so they picketed their horses in a grove as close to the village as they dared ride. The two hour march to Pelarion allowed Adrienne to consider and reject half a dozen plans. Ricco had been able to sneak up to the very edge of the village and observe what was happening. Although a few of the twenty-some men who had invaded the formerly peaceful village stood guard, most were enjoying the opportunities a village like Pelarion presented. There was food and drink aplenty, and women to be made sport of.

"We'll enter in groups of three," Adrienne said, "and encircle the village. We'll come in from different sides and keep the marauders from forming a unified defense."

Adrienne outlined the basic plan as they walked, splitting them into groups of three and one group of two. She, Ricco, and Rosch would approach on the main road, drawing attention away from the groups that would be sneaking in from the sides. When they got within sight of Pelarion, the groups split up, and Adrienne led her group brashly down the road.

Five men were waiting for them when they arrived at the village, and from the leers on their faces when they caught sight of Adrienne garbed in her tight leather *swa'il*, she did not need to guess if they were some of the men who had invaded Pelarion.

"They're armed," one of older men guarding the town cautioned, looking over the swords Adrienne, Ricco, and Rosch all wore sheathed at their sides. He seemed to be the leader of the small group, and intelligent enough to know that three armed people arriving at the village less than a week after it was taken was not mere coincidence. "No telling if they're alone or not. Take care of them, and warn the other men."

Adrienne and Ricco gave the men no chance to do either. They sprang into action, leaping forward. Rosch joined the fight a moment later, when one of the men darted past Adrienne to engage him.

Rosch's moves lacked the grace of Adrienne's or the brutal strength of Ricco's, but all of the practice accumulated in the past months made him more than equal to the talents of the outlaw he was fighting. He fought the man with skill, blocking and parrying with his sword. He tried out one of the riskier maneuvers Adrienne had taught him, but when the brigand evaded it and came back with a powerful blow Rosch lost his grip on his sword.

The sword went spinning out of his hand, and when his opponent swung his sword at Rosch's head, Rosch did the only thing he could: he dove and rolled.

Rosch got quickly to his feet behind the man, and in a move Adrienne had had him practice over and over, he kicked the man's feet out from under him, buying Rosch enough time to recover his sword.

They resumed the fight on equal ground, sword-for-sword, parry-for-parry.

Rosch's moves came faster and faster, pushing his opponent back. A strong slash drove the outlaw's sword up and out with no time to block, and Rosch drove his sword into the man's gut, stealing his life with one brutal stab.

Rosch stared down at the fallen man, unaware of Adrienne's presence until she laid a gloved hand on his shoulder. "You did what you had to do, Jeral," Adrienne told him, not noticing that she had used his first name for the first time. Her grip tightened. "But there is more to be done."

The soldiers, led by Adrienne, reclaimed Pelarion with minimal injuries incurred. Ricco had received a shallow cut on one of his arms while fighting the two men who had targeted him, but it was only one mark amid dozens of other, older scars his skin bore. Another of the Kyrogeans had twisted an ankle in a bad roll, but otherwise the group Adrienne had led to Pelarion was unharmed.

One of the brigands had been captured during the attack and would be left to the justice of Pelarion. Adrienne doubted that he would long outlive his former companions.

"Do we leave now?" Jeral asked Adrienne. The destruction of the village, the dead bodies of outlaws and civilians, the devastated women, the wide-eyed children, made him sick, and he longed for the familiar sights of Kyrog.

Adrienne shook her head. "We will stay and help them with what we can," she told the Yearling. She too had a heavy feeling in her stomach when she looked out at the village, and knew their job was not yet done. The hardest part, dealing with the survivors, had just begun.

No soldiers had been here to stop the brigands before they had invaded the peaceful village, raping and destroying as they went. Now it would be up to soldiers to do what they could for those left behind. There was little Adrienne could do to help with their emotional losses. Growing up amongst soldiers had not taught her the platitudes other women might use to help soften the brutal punch of grief. But she could do other things.

The next three days were spent repairing houses and digging graves. Adrienne enjoyed the physical labor of repairing roofs and walls damaged by fire. The outlaws had set fire to many of the homes and stables to show the villagers how helpless they were. Adrienne felt good helping to right those wrongs.

It was the digging of graves that filled her with helpless rage. That Kyrog could be located so close to Pelarion and other villages, yet leave those villages completely defenseless and open to such senseless cruelty was hard to bear.

Adrienne and Ricco had just finished digging a new grave when the villagers came to the graveyard bearing an open coffin. In it lay a fresh-faced girl of no more than thirteen, her innocent beauty marred only by a scrape on her cheek. Whatever horror had taken place before her life ended was not evidenced by more than that scrape on a face gone smooth and calm with death. Her long black hair had been lovingly washed and combed, and Adrienne had to force herself to watch as a lid was nailed to the top of the box and the girl placed into the ground.

Adrienne could hear the story of the girl's life in the wails of the mourners. The girl had been innocent and brilliantly alive before the raiders had come, and now she had been brutalized and killed for nothing but sport.

Adrienne wanted to go back in time and stop the raiders before they had stolen the life of that innocent girl. She wanted to comfort the mother who had lost her daughter in such a horrible way. She could do neither.

She knew that most people pictured Almet when they thought of soldiers and fighting. The constant battling on the border, waxing and waning but never ceasing, made the threat from Almet obvious. Adrienne herself felt called to go to the lines and fight the Almetian forces, and knew that one day she would likely do just that.

But here, in Pelarion, as she watched dirt cover the box that held the body of the young girl, Adrienne knew that the enemy was not limited to Almet. The countryside itself had enough dangers to occupy Samaroan soldiers for a lifetime.

Ricco came up to her and lay a comforting hand on her shoulder. "We got here as soon as we could."

"Not soon enough."

"This isn't a story, and you are not Almyria. No one expects you to raise the dead."

"Almyria didn't raise the dead," Adrienne said, thinking of the mythical healer. "She got there in time to save the living."

When Adrienne and her men had done what they could to rebuild and restore a sense of safety to the village, she knew it was time to leave. Though soldiers in Pelarion would provide safety, they would also be a constant reminder of what had happened there. They needed to leave and hope that the losses Pelarion had suffered would heal into a scar instead of remaining an open wound and festering.

Ricco and the others were able to laugh on the way home, but Adrienne could not forget the girl who had died before they could get to her, and Jeral too was subdued. He had taken his first life, and

36

Adrienne knew that nothing would ever be quite the same for the young soldier.

"Ricco," she called when they were a half hour's ride from Pelarion.

"Ya?" He trotted his gelding up next to hers.

"Lord Neecham's keep is a week's ride from here."

"Closer to two," Ricco said. "What of it?"

"I was thinking that Rosch and I would go there. No one from Pelarion reported to him about the attack, and it has been awhile since anyone from Kyrog reported to him in person."

"Shouldn't you talk to Captain Garrett before you go visit Lord Neecham? He *is* the captain?"

Adrienne thought for a minute, and then dismissed the notion. "Neecham should know about Pelarion," she insisted. "You can take the men back to Kyrog and tell the captain what Jeral and I are doing."

Ricco didn't look happy about that. "Thinking of dragging me into the trouble with you? Why not take me with instead of Rosch; at least I'd be able to postpone my flogging until *after* we got back."

"No one is getting flogged. Go back to Kyrog. If any lumps need to be taken, I'll take them."

"I'll remind you of that when you get back to Kyrog."

The ride from Pelarion to Red Ridge Keep was interesting for both Adrienne and Jeral. Whatever Jeral had thought he might feel after the first time he killed a man, Adrienne knew the reality would be different. It would take time for Jeral to reconcile causing a death, and the reality that he would do so again.

"It gets easier, Jeral," Adrienne said.

"Is that supposed to be a good thing?" Jeral's tone was bitter and angry.

"You chose to be a soldier," Adrienne said sharply. "It was not forced upon you."

"I didn't think—"

"You didn't think killing someone would feel bad? Did you think it would be easy? I gave you the skills, but I can't give you what it takes to be able to take a life and live with it."

"How do you?"

Adrienne stared off down the road for long enough that Jeral thought she wouldn't answer, but finally she sighed and turned her head to look at him. "I was raised for this. Being a soldier *was* forced upon me. While your mother was singing you to sleep, I was listening to stories of battle. While you were shoveling muck from stalls, I was cleaning blood from armor. I always knew what being a soldier meant."

"How old—"

"I went to my first camp when I was four," Adrienne answered curtly. "That's how long I've been a soldier." She kicked her horse to a faster pace, knowing that was not the question Jeral had asked, but not wanting to answer.

"I was not expecting visitors from Kyrog."

"Excuse us, my lord. I hope that we are not intruding," Adrienne replied formally.

Lord Neecham laughed; a warm, rich sound that seemed a perfect fit for the lord of Red Ridge. He was a man well into his middle years, but still hale by all appearances. His wavy black hair, which he wore down to his shoulders, was receding slightly, and he was closer to having two chins than one, but his eyes were sharply intelligent, and his smile seemed genuine. "Of course not. I've been meaning to send someone to Kyrog for weeks now. How is the camp?"

Adrienne shifted her weight, a rare show of discomfort. "I can give you my opinions—which are positive—but I was not sent here by Captain Garrett."

Neecham's brow crinkled. "Is something wrong with Garrett? I got a letter from him not long ago."

"No, sir. Captain Garrett and the camp are fine. I came here because the village of Pelarion was attacked a couple of weeks ago. I led the party that cleaned it up."

"'Cleaned it up.' That phrase sounds so tidy for such an unsavory matter."

"Lord—"

Lord Neecham held up his hand. "I have shown a lack of hospitality that would shame my lady mother were she to see me now." He grinned boyishly. "I will have rooms and baths made up for you, Adrienne, and—gah, I didn't even get his name."

"Jeral Rosch, sir," Jeral supplied.

"Jeral. Jeral. Well then, Jeral, you and Adrienne can go freshen up and then join me for supper. We will talk about Pelarion and Kyrog then, yes?"

"That sounds wonderful," Jeral said brightly.

"Thank you, my lord," Adrienne said with more dignity.

"I will have servants show you to your rooms and fetch you back for supper."

38

Over a feast of grouse, roasted antelope, fresh baked bread, and a selection of fruits and vegetables such as Adrienne had never seen, she and Jeral filled the lord of Red Ridge Keep in on what had happened to Pelarion.

"I did not realize that there were brigands this close to the keep," Neecham said, "and even closer to Kyrog."

"I don't remember them ever striking so close before," Adrienne agreed.

"You have not been at Kyrog long, not in the grand scheme of things. When my father was a boy, a large group of raiders—there must have been a hundred at least—came to the keep direct. The guard here was not so big then, maybe half the size it is now. They held though, for the three weeks it took soldiers from Kyrog to get here and save the keep.

"I didn't know that."

"You wouldn't. Your parents would not even have been born at the time, and although it was a terrifying three weeks for those here, the rescue mission to Red Ridge was not one for the legends of Kyrog. I expect it was a rather dull affair, all things considered. There is no reason for it to still be told after such a long time."

Adrienne did not know what to say to that, so she said nothing. Jeral had spoken often at the beginning of the meal, but after repeated kicks from Adrienne, he had finally stopped speaking out of turn.

"But that moment, when Kyrog came to the aid of Red Ridge, was the turning point for that particular camp," Lord Neecham reminisced. "It was not nearly so well-funded then. My great-grandfather, and his father before him, had always given Kyrog a stipend, but not a fraction of what my grandfather and father ended up giving. What I give. Kyrog was a small camp, though well disciplined even before the attack on Red Ridge, and it relied greatly on trade and payments for services to stay functioning."

"Payments for services?" Adrienne asked.

Neecham smiled. "When brigands are plentiful and funding is not, it is not unheard of for camps that 'saved' a village to demand payment of some sort afterwards."

"That happened at Kyrog?" Adrienne was horrified at the very idea. She could not imagine asking anyone at Pelarion to pay her after what had just happened.

"Yes. Before Red Ridge began funding the camp, there was no other way to support the soldiers. Having a camp that was more mercenary than army was better than having no camp at all, but for a while there was resentment and even fear between civilians and soldiers. It has faded now, as memories do, but it was real for a time."

"I have never heard any of this," Adrienne said. "And all camps did this?" She wondered why Karse had never told her. Surely someone as interested in history as he would have known.

"I can't know for sure that every camp had the same practices, but to the best of my knowledge Kyrog was—if anything—less mercenary than the others."

"But it is still kept a secret," Adrienne argued, unsettled that the camp she proudly called hers had such an unsavory history.

"Not a secret, but not something that is advertised. People need to trust soldiers, not fear them. Or worse, consider them on the same level as bandits who demand 'protection money' and attack the villages themselves if they are not paid." Neecham took another sip of palm wine. "As well-funded camps like Kyrog and Roua," he tipped his head to Jeral, "grew, the smaller, more mercenary camps disbanded. The soldiers that remain in Samaro are loyal to the country…or as loyal as the lords who fund them…and nothing will be gained by stirring up old memories."

"Why do we have separate armies?" Jeral asked. Evidently Adrienne's warning kicks had a limited effectiveness. "Why not just one?"

"Just one like Almet does?" Lord Neecham seemed amused. "It is one of the things that I asked my father about."

"And?"

"And I never got a satisfactory answer. Almet stayed strong despite the war not coming to an end. It had strong rulers, and did not splinter."

"And Samaro did?" Jeral asked.

Lord Neecham smiled and gave a lazy shrug. "King Burin is my sovereign leader," he said easily. "Who am I to naysay his rule?"

Adrienne hardly heard the rest of their conversation. Something they had said had sparked a memory. She couldn't place why their conversation would bring up such a memory, but she remembered suddenly the Old Samaroan text she had seen in Captain Garrett's office months ago. In her upset, she had not wondered why Garrett, who could not read Old Samaroan, would have the original text out if he had a translation.

And if he needed to check something, why wouldn't he come to her with it? It would hardly be the first time she had served as a translator when dealing with old documents.

And why would Captain Garrett, so stolid and dependable, have in his possession a piece of writing about necromancers?

"Adrienne, are you ready for dessert?"

She snapped back to reality, wondered briefly how long she had been caught up in her own world, and nodded. "Yes, my lord, though after this meal I'm not sure how much room I have left for it.

CHAPTER FOUR

Under normal circumstances, being summoned to Captain Garrett's office did not worry Adrienne. She reported to him on a regular basis about the new recruits she tested, and he had taken a special interest in Jeral's progress over the eight months of the Yearling's training.

Still, when the order had come down that Adrienne was to report to the captain's office, she knew that it was not to go over the latest news about the recruits.

"Adrienne Rydaeg, reporting as ordered, sir," Adrienne said when the page showed her into the captain's office.

"Rydaeg, come in," Captain Garrett said, his face impassive. "Sit, if you'd like."

Adrienne remained standing, as was her habit when in the captain's office.

"How is Rosch's progress?"

Adrienne was momentarily thrown. She had reported to the captain only a few days ago, after she and Jeral had returned from Red Ridge Keep, and they had discussed Jeral briefly at that time. Despite her confusion, she reported. "He is progressing much faster than I would have predicted eight months ago, sir. He has a natural aptitude for swordsmanship that lends itself well to our current training, and he performed well outside of Kyrog." A sudden and unwelcome thought occurred to her. "Captain, despite his progress, if you are thinking of sending him back to Roua at this time I believe that would be a mistake. A few more months of—"

"I value your input," the captain said, cutting her off, "but it is not my intention to cut Rosch's study at Kyrog short. I requested you to come here so that we could discuss you."

42

"What did you wish to talk about, Captain?" Adrienne asked, her stomach clenching nervously. She forced her body and face to appear calm and relaxed, while inside she was running through anything she had done in the last couple of days that might require disciplinary action.

The captain had been pleased with the results of their mission, and surprised that Adrienne had gone to Red Ridge Keep and met with Lord Neecham without being told, but had been only mildly displeased that she had acted outside of her orders.

Ricco's prediction of flogging had not come to pass.

Adrienne could think of nothing she might have done to displease Captain Garrett then or since her return.

"You've been at Kyrog for a long time," Captain Garrett said.

"Yes, sir," Adrienne answered. It had been thirteen years now, a long time for a soldier in any one place. Even longer than it seemed, considering Adrienne was barely twenty-one.

"To my knowledge, you have never asked for higher rank, or wondered why someone of your experience is still a private instead of an officer."

"I am still young, Captain Garrett." She would be lying if she said she had never wondered why the captain had never so much as hinted at a promotion. "I thought my age might be a factor."

"Age is always a factor to be considered, but in your case age was never the obstacle. You became a soldier so young that you have more experience as a soldier than some men—or women—half again your age. Even before coming to Kyrog you had experience."

The lump forming in her throat made it hard for Adrienne to swallow. Part of her thought that maybe, finally, she would become an officer. The hope refused to die, beating madly in her breast, even as a large part of her was imagining Captain Garrett telling her that there was something preventing her from ever making lieutenant.

Worse, the idea that he might ask her to leave Kyrog came to mind and couldn't be dismissed. "May I ask what the obstacle is?" Adrienne forced the words out.

Captain Garrett nodded. "You are, possibly, the best soldier in Kyrog. You are dedicated—to your training, to Kyrog, to Samaro—in a way that few soldiers are. You are an example of what a great soldier should be."

Adrienne knew there was more waiting to be said.

"I have never doubted your soldiering ability, or your commitment. I have known you would be great since you were thirteen, awkward and gangly when crossing the courtyard but completely controlled in the ring. You are a woman, but no one who is in Kyrog more than a week sees that as a liability."

"I assure you that it is not, sir," Adrienne couldn't help but say. She had met female officers before. Adrienne knew Captain Garrett to be a fair man, and she didn't think he would hold her back due to gender.

"Yes. My concern had nothing to do with your gender, or your skill. It is your ability to lead that I have questioned through the years, whenever the question of promoting you came up."

Adrienne felt as if she had been punched in the gut. Worse, because she could not retaliate, or even defend herself from another blow. "I see," she said, struggling to sound calm despite the screaming in her head. That Captain Garrett, a man she liked and respected, should find her lacking in such an important area hurt far more than she could have anticipated.

"Do you? You are very action-oriented, Adrienne. This is a good quality in a soldier, but you prefer to act alone. Though you follow orders, it has not typically been in character for you to take the lead in a group situation. To my knowledge, you have only one true friend here, and only a small group outside of that with whom you choose to socialize."

Adrienne had not realized that Captain Garrett knew so much about her private life, though hearing it now she did not find it surprising. The captain was a very thorough man. If he was considering promoting someone to officer, he would look at all aspects of that person's life, not just ability in the sparring ring or speed on an obstacle course.

"Because you demonstrate the qualities of a loner, I worried that you might not do well in a command situation. A leader needs to know more than just how to fight."

"I understand why you might think that," Adrienne said. She *was* a loner. For all her skill, Adrienne was aware that she preferred to be by herself, with Ricco as the rare exception. Most leaders were more sociable, more charismatic.

"I think that you do understand. However, since you took on Jeral Rosch as your trainee, of your own accord, I have been forced to reconsider my thinking."

"Sir?"

"Training someone, especially with the attention and consistency you have given Rosch for the past eight months, is not an easy task. Although I know you to be a determined individual, I sense that it is not only determination and a sense of commitment that drives you to continue his training."

"No, sir," Adrienne said. "I enjoy training Rosch, watching his progress, adapting my own methods to best suit him."

"The results are proof of your dedication," Captain Garrett said with approval. "Ricco reported to me after Pelarion and told me how Rosch performed. From what Ricco said, Rosch is now a far superior fighter compared to the recruits who arrived when he did. He has benefited from the personal instruction he gets from you."

Adrienne had known that, but she was proud that the captain had come to that conclusion as well.

"I am also pleased that you have enlisted some of the others here to help you with training. Although I believe that you still have loner tendencies, it has become apparent in the past eight months that these tendencies did not affect your ability to train Rosch, or your willingness to bring others in on your projects."

"Rosch benefited from practicing with different soldiers," Adrienne said. "I would not deny any trainee that, not if I wanted him to excel."

Captain Garrett nodded. "There was an incident some months ago that also moved me to reconsider your career."

The way he phrased it left no doubt in Adrienne's mind that the captain was referring to what had happened with Lieutenant Nissen. "Captain Garrett, I can explain—"

Captain Garrett held up a hand to stop her. "An explanation is not necessary, nor at this late date particularly welcome." That kept Adrienne quiet. "What interested me was the solidarity amongst the men in response to what happened. The other soldiers regard you as one of them completely, and maybe as something more. The respect those serving here have for you is greater and more true than the respect even some of the more well-liked officers are given."

"Let me apologize for—"

"Apologies, like explanations, we can do without at this time. Unless you wish to make a formal complaint." The captain's eyes made it clear that he did not want one, and it was something Adrienne was not eager to give in any case. She shook her head. "Very well. Respect is earned, Rydaeg. It does not come easily, nor do officers automatically gain respect. You have already earned the respect and loyalty of the men at Kyrog, just as you have shown your leadership abilities with Rosch."

Adrienne waited, barely able to breathe.

"You've grown since you began training Rosch. I had you take the lead in sorting out Pelarion as a test. You chose a solid group of men, Rosch included, and by all accounts you were a good leader. I was further impressed by your impromptu visit to Red Ridge Keep. Although I would have preferred you wait until sent, the fact that it occurred to you to contact our patron and inform him of what had happened at Pelarion proved to me that you have vision that reaches beyond the walls of this camp."

Adrienne said nothing, unsure of what to think or feel. The barrage of emotions, from hope to fear that the captain might find her inadequate, was too much for her to fully process.

"Adrienne Rydaeg, as Captain of Kyrog, I would like to formally offer you the position of lieutenant."

Adrienne gave a mental cry of triumph while limiting her physical response to a nod. Despite her stoic efforts, she was unable to suppress her smile. "Thank you, sir. I would be honored." Her words were heartfelt, and she knew that the captain could see everything she was feeling in her deep brown eyes. Embarrassment could not outweigh her joy, however, and her smile grew to reveal straight white teeth.

Pride that she had reached the goal she had been secretly striving toward for years swamped her.

"In addition to your promotion, I would like to place you in charge of training all of the Yearlings," Captain Garrett said, surprising her enough that some of the euphoria cleared.

"Lieutenant Mylig is in charge of training at Kyrog," Adrienne said. She had heard no rumors that Mylig would be leaving, or worse, retiring. He was too skilled a soldier and teacher to waste his talent growing beans or whatever soldiers did after retirement. He was meant to teach and fight, not succumb to old age on a farm somewhere in the countryside.

Adrienne would rather die in a fight than spend the rest of her years living such a life, and she had always gotten the feeling that Mylig felt the same. He was not the retiring type.

"He will remain in charge of the soldiers who will be staying at Kyrog indefinitely; men who have years to learn and perfect their skills," Captain Garrett elucidated. "In light of what you have been able to do with Rosch, I would like you to continue training him and other soldiers in the same circumstances as he."

Adrienne was surprised at the immediate increase in responsibility that came with her promotion. "I will need to set up a team to help me," Adrienne said, still reeling from the sudden promotion and the new task before her. Excitement, almost like the tense anticipation she often felt before a fight, coursed through her veins as she began making plans.

"Of course. Although a one-on-one mentorship will not be feasible due to the number of recruits, I expect you to assemble a large enough team of experienced soldiers to help with the training of the Yearlings. I want to see the same results with the other Yearlings that I have seen with Rosch."

"I will do my best, Captain," she promised.

"Then you are dismissed, Lieutenant Rydaeg."

News spread like wildfire in Kyrog, and Ricco had already heard of Adrienne's promotion before she had a chance to find him and tell him herself.

"Congratulations on your promotion, Lieutenant, sir." Ricco saluted and his smile was, if possible, even wider than usual as pleasure and pride vied for position on his face.

Adrienne allowed her friend to pull her into a congratulatory hug. His massive arms squeezed the breath from her lungs, and for a few seconds Adrienne worried that Ricco might end up cracking a rib in his enthusiasm, but after a few painful moments he loosened his hold enough to eliminate that danger. "It's about time Captain Garrett moved you up the chain of command," he said, ending the hug with a slap on the back in a manner much more typical of their relationship than the long, close hug had been.

"What about you?" Adrienne asked. Ricco was older than Adrienne, and had already been at Kyrog for six years.

Ricco shook his head vehemently and held his hands up in defense. "I don't want the responsibilities of being an officer."

She laughed and shoved his shoulder. "Good, because you'd make a lousy lieutenant," she joked, causing Ricco to laugh.

"And you'll make a great one." He slung his arm around Adrienne and hauled her up against his side. "This calls for a celebration."

Adrienne smiled. "What have you got in mind?"

Ricco's eyes cut toward her appraisingly. "I suggest a bunch of us go to Nils' Tavern and get drunk."

Adrienne shook her head on a laugh. "I'm a lieutenant now. I have to be responsible. It wouldn't be right to spend my first night as lieutenant getting drunk in a tavern."

Ricco snorted. "Getting drunk is exactly the right way to spend your first night as a lieutenant. This is your last day before taking on more duties. Who knows when you'll have another chance to get ripping drunk?"

She thought it must be overexcitement that made that idea sound so appealing, but Adrienne found herself agreeing with Ricco and planning to meet him at the tavern after the evening meal in the mess.

Hours later, Adrienne was sitting at the bar in Nils' Tavern, one of the few permanent structures in the large camp, surrounded by well-wishers and empty mugs of ale, and was well on her way to meeting Ricco's expectations of drunkenness. She liked the warm glow left by the alcohol and the continuous congratulations she was receiving, and wondered why she did not go out with Ricco more often. Even watching him flirt with the serving women had become more amusing than embarrassing.

"It's about time," a man announced in a booming baritone. Adrienne focused her eyes on Lieutenant Curtis Turric, a man who before tonight she would have said was only a casual acquaintance at most.

"Thank you, sir," Adrienne responded automatically. A smile still came to her face with every congratulation she received, and her response to the dark-skinned lieutenant was no exception.

"Curtis," he corrected with a grin. "Or Turric, if you'd rather. You don't 'sir' a fellow lieutenant." He shifted his drink over to his left hand and extended his right. "I've been wondering when Captain Garrett would get around to promoting you." He motioned for the bartender to supply Adrienne with another mug of ale. "You're one of the best soldiers in Kyrog."

"She damned well is," Ricco agreed, raising his mug in cheers. "She's bloody brilliant."

Adrienne accepted the mug with a smile before turning to Ricco, amused by his current state. The stocky soldier was imbued with a wry humor when sober, but when drunk his joking nature came out full force, and she knew she was not the only person in the tavern being entertained by Ricco's behavior that night.

As for herself, Adrienne didn't like the idea of entertaining anyone, and decided to make the mug of ale from Turric her last one of the night. As it was, she was sure her head would be awful in the morning. Despite the warm glow she was feeling from the alcohol, she wasn't fond of how her senses were already dulled by it. She preferred a clear head.

Adrienne scanned the room, and when she spotted Jeral she gestured for him to come over.

"Congratulations, Lieutenant, sir," Jeral said.

Even through the pleasant haze of alcohol, Adrienne could tell that his words and smile were forced. "What's wrong, Rosch?" she asked.

Jeral seemed momentarily taken aback by her bluntness, as if he had expected the alcohol to affect her perception, but he recovered quickly and answered her question with the honesty she had come to expect from him over the past eight months. "I was wondering if you were still going to be my trainer."

"Of course I will," Adrienne said, forgetting herself and accepting another drink from the barkeep. "Why wouldn't I?"

"Well, I heard you would be training other soldiers now. Other Yearlings."

Adrienne shoved Jeral lightly. "That doesn't mean I'm going to stop training you. I haven't finished with you yet."

Jeral's smile became genuine at the news. "Thanks, Lieutenant."

"Adrienne, I would like a word with you," Lieutenant Nissen said, stepping in front of Jeral as if the boy wasn't there. His expression lacked even the parody of charm that it usually had.

Adrienne's first instinct was to evade the officer. Then she remembered that Nissen was no longer her superior, and she no longer had to avoid a confrontation with him. He could not intimidate her any longer, especially not over drinks in the smoky tavern where people had gathered to celebrate her promotion.

She relaxed back onto her stool, resting an elbow on the bar and taking a slow sip of ale. "Sorry, Craig, I'm having a conversation with Rosch here," she said coolly, using his first name as a subtle reminder that they were equals now. "We will have to talk some other time."

His green eyes went hard and stormy, and his face filled momentarily with surprised anger before he managed to control it. "Very well. I wished to congratulate you on your promotion." He turned and spun away, ignored by the other soldiers who were too busy joking and drinking to care about any one person, even a superior officer.

The man had probably thought Adrienne would be easy prey in her sotted condition. She snorted at the thought. There was not enough alcohol in all of Samaro to make that true.

"Lieutenant?" Jeral asked curiously.

"Go back to the barracks, Rosch," Adrienne advised as she absently finished her ale. "I don't want you tired for tomorrow's training."

Jeral looked around the tavern, probably for someone worth spending time with, then shrugged and headed out as Adrienne had told him.

CHAPTER FIVE

As Adrienne soon found out, her responsibilities as a lieutenant were not limited to training the Yearlings. On top of training the young and often fractious recruits, Adrienne also had to divide the duties of the soldiers under her command and administer discipline when necessary.

As a lieutenant, her opinion was asked for more frequently and given more weight by her superiors and the other lieutenants than it had been when she was merely a private. Even more surprisingly, people came to Adrienne for answers and advice, something that had rarely happened in the past thirteen years, even once she had been old enough and experienced enough to offer such advice.

The responsibilities of being a lieutenant kept her busy, and the job was more difficult than Adrienne had expected, but there were benefits as well. When she had call to interact with Lieutenant Nissen, he no longer tried to intimidate her or make veiled threats. She no longer worried about what would happen if she found herself alone with him. He no longer had any power over her, and there was immense satisfaction in that.

Altogether, being a lieutenant sat well with Adrienne, and as she watched Jeral handily dispatch one of her newest recruits, she was pleased with what she was accomplishing at the camp. Nine months ago, Adrienne had been furious after what she had witnessed when sparring with Jeral for the first time. Now that same young man was helping to train others, and was one of the main reasons Adrienne had been promoted to lieutenant.

"Lieutenant Rydaeg? Captain Garrett wishes to see you," a young man who probably had to shave no more than twice a week interrupted her observation to tell her.

Adrienne smiled. "Thank you, Kyle." Unlike the recruits, who were as green as their ages suggested, Kyle's age was deceiving. He had come to Kyrog at the age of eleven, and five years later Adrienne was employing him and his considerable skills in the training of her recruits on a regular basis. Like Adrienne, Kyle's abilities were often underestimated, to the detriment of his opponents. He was fast, and he was ruthless. More than one recruit had had to be helped from the training ground after a match with Kyle.

Another recruit was stepping up to face Jeral, who had broken a sweat when fighting his last opponent but was nowhere near his limit, and she was about to issue instructions to the pair when Kyle cleared his throat. "The captain said I was to bring you back straight away," Kyle said apologetically.

Adrienne had wondered momentarily why Kyle was doing a job most typically left to messengers, but she realized that Captain Garrett knew her well enough to know that she would be less likely to ignore a soldier with a message than one of the pages usually used as messengers. She studied Kyle and saw a hint of amusement in his dark eyes.

She suppressed a sigh. "Very well," she said to Kyle. In a louder voice, she addressed the recruits. "Break for one hour," Adrienne told them. That should give her more than enough time to discuss whatever the captain had in mind.

Now that she was a lieutenant, it seemed that she was always meeting with the captain about something or other. He usually managed to arrange the appointments for times when Adrienne wasn't busy, but as Captain Garrett was much busier than she, his convenience was more important than hers.

"Yes sir, Lieutenant," was the general chorus as the men scattered. Only Jeral and one of the more experienced Yearlings remained, content to spend their free hour training. Adrienne nodded her approval of their decision before heading to the captain's office, thinking that although not all of the Yearlings had Jeral's promise, there were a few that she thought would make exceptional soldiers, and the rest would be more than passable with proper training.

The page had been waiting impatiently for Adrienne to arrive, and he announced Adrienne's arrival at once, all but pushing her into the small room that was the captain's office. The room had never seemed big enough, considering the importance of the man who inhabited it, but it seemed even smaller now that the captain was not the only other person in the office. He sat behind his desk, as was customary, but there were two unknown men occupying the chairs across from him.

The larger of the men wore a sword low on his left hip, but Adrienne dismissed the idea of him being a proper soldier immediately. He was in his middle years if he was a day, but looked and held himself less like a seasoned soldier than even her rawest recruits. At best he was a merchant's guard.

The other man was more interesting to Adrienne. Dressed simply, he appeared unarmed and utterly nonthreatening. He was short and rather rotund, slouched in his chair with his hands clasped over his stomach. He was balding, and a beard of tight black curls decorated his round face. He did not look wealthy or important, and Adrienne's curiosity was aroused by the necessity of a guard for such an unassuming man. Perhaps he had come here bearing some news important enough to need guarding. Or perhaps he was just afraid to travel the plains of Samaro alone. Many were, with good reason, but one ill-trained guard was unlikely to be of much use if they ran into trouble.

"Lieutenant Rydaeg reporting, sir," Adrienne said with a quick salute, making all appearances of ignoring the men, though she was aware of every move they made.

"What's this?" the large man with the sword demanded. "Captain, we came here to Kyrog seeking your best soldier and you give us this-this slip of a girl!" The man looked about to fly into a rage, something Adrienne could relate to. Adrienne was not a slip of a girl by any stretch of the imagination, standing at attention as she was—wearing her well-used *swa'il* and a sword on her hip—she was every inch a soldier.

Captain Garrett merely quirked an eyebrow at the man's words. "You told me you were on an important mission," the captain said, clearly for Adrienne's benefit, "and that you had come to Kyrog for the best soldier available. You then gave me a list of qualifications, which are mutually exclusive in most people. You wanted a skilled, intelligent soldier with the capability and drive to learn new things. You preferred a soldier of rank, but it was necessary that the soldier also be young."

"If you had no one here who could fit the specifications, you could have told us and saved us time." The guard's fists clenched into balls and his dark face was turning an interesting shade of purple, much like a bruise, as his temper peaked. "This farce is disgraceful for a man of authority!"

Adrienne thought briefly of stepping up to defend Captain Garrett, but she knew that he would disapprove. And she was interested in seeing how the man would react to the insult.

"We do have one person who fits the specifications of the ideal soldier you asked for," Captain Garrett said, his voice turning from genial to icy. "Lieutenant Rydaeg is an exceptional soldier and officer. She is highly skilled in multiple areas of combat as well as tactics. She is naturally intelligent and has the all too rare ability of being able to think on her feet."

"Rare in soldiers, maybe," the guard said. "That doesn't mean—"

Captain Garrett cut him off. "Lieutenant Rydaeg is innovative and always working toward improvement, and has recently been charged with instructing all of the new recruits and is doing a remarkable job of it." Captain Garrett's voice did not warm, but it flowed with smooth assurance and the conviction that what he was saying was absolutely true. "Even without the condition that the soldier be young, I would have considered Rydaeg as a candidate."

"A likely story," the guard scoffed. "I think it more likely you wish to unload this aberrant female soldier on us."

Adrienne ground her teeth together.

The other man, who until this point had remained silent, waved his pudgy hands and gave his guard a placating look. "Perhaps you are being rash, Ilso. This lieutenant might be a capable soldier." His eyes swept over Adrienne, and she had no doubt they were taking in her long black hair and short, curvy body more than the way she wore her sword or how she held herself ready to fight or defend at any second. "It is not totally unheard of for women to be soldiers."

The man named Ilso crossed his arms in front of him and snorted rudely. "Perhaps not, but if Kyrog is all that it's cracked up to be, they should be able to offer more than a mere woman."

Captain Garrett must have seen the fire burning in Adrienne's dark eyes, for he made a small gesture cautioning her to contain herself. "If you would like, you can arrange to test Lieutenant Rydaeg's abilities yourself," the captain said. "However, I promise that you will not find her lacking in skill, and as your mission seems important and time precious, I hope that my vouching for her will suffice."

Ilso seemed about to argue, but the other man stopped him once more. "It was my friend here," he said with a gesture to Ilso, "who advised me to come to Kyrog, and to you, Captain, to find the soldier I seek," he said. "Unlike Ilso, I embrace the unexpected in finding the recommended soldier for our purpose to be a woman."

He turned to Adrienne. "Can you be ready to leave in an hour?"

"No," Adrienne said, earning surprised stares from everyone in the room.

"Lieutenant…" Captain Garrett said in a rising tone of warning.

"You see! Not just a female, but an insubordinate one as well," Ilso snapped.

"I'm not declining to go on this 'mission' of yours," Adrienne said, though she wondered just what the mission would involve. "However, I have responsibilities here, and preparations to make before I depart. The earliest I can be ready is tomorrow morning." Even then, she would have to work hard to see that the training of the recruits was maintained at the high standard she had set.

"Rydaeg, I am sure we can manage without you," Captain Garrett told her. The expression on his dark face revealed his displeasure, though no one who did not know him well could have read it.

Adrienne stood even more at attention, pulling her shoulders back and holding her chin high. "With all due respect, sir, I believe that the transition in training the Yearlings will go more smoothly and yield better results if I am allowed to choose and meet with my replacement before I leave."

"This upstart is the soldier you are saddling us with?" Ilso asked. "If she can't even follow orders—"

"Lieutenant Rydaeg has no problem following orders," Captain Garrett said, "and this matter is none of your business. You may take Lieutenant Rydaeg with you tomorrow morning, or not at all."

Ilso jerked his head in acknowledgement, and the other man bowed out with smiles and thank-yous as they exited the room. Finally, it was just Captain Garrett and Adrienne left.

"Captain, what is the mission?" Adrienne asked for the first time. If the captain told her to go, she would go, regardless of what the mission entailed, but she hoped it was something worthwhile if she had to leave Kyrog in the company of a misogynist like Ilso.

"Have a seat, Adrienne, if I may call you that."

"Of course," Adrienne said, for once actually taking his advice and sitting down, though it was an uneasy feeling. She fingered the cord of her necklace, running her thumb over the pendant. The use of her first name had unnerved her.

"They would not give me the details of their mission," Captain Garrett said. "Tam, the scholar, is in charge, although Ilso seems to be the only one with any experience with soldiers."

Adrienne's hand dropped into her lap and she let out a breath of air that was almost a laugh. "If you could call it experience." It had been obvious by Ilso's total disregard for her and the captain that, whatever Tam believed, the guard was no more familiar with soldiers than he was with the sword he wore so awkwardly at his hip.

Captain Garrett inclined his head. "I believe this is a civilian mission, Adrienne, but they hinted that whatever they are planning would help the war efforts against Almet."

Adrienne's focus sharpened at that information. "What have civilians to do with the war, Captain?" The role of civilians in war was typically restricted to three things: supporting the soldiers, hampering the soldiers, or dying at the hands of enemy soldiers. In Adrienne's opinion, they were good for little else when it came to war.

"I do not know, Adrienne." He tapped an envelope on his desk, one with a broken wax seal that was still unmistakably the seal of the king. "I must trust that King Burin has a plan, even if he is unwilling to share it." He smiled, and his gray eyes were kind. "If you wish, you may call me Luis, as you are temporarily relieved from duty now that you have accepted the civilian mission."

Adrienne felt strangely bereft as his meaning became clear. She was no longer a soldier, at least not for as long as this mission lasted. A major component of her life since the age of four was now gone, and she clung to the idea that it was only temporary. "I would prefer to stick with Captain," Adrienne said. "I'm a soldier at heart, if not currently in practice."

"As you wish," Captain Garrett said. "Now tell me about your plans to keep the recruits' training on track. We don't have much time."

"You can't leave," Ricco said for what must have been the tenth time in as many minutes.

"I have to," Adrienne said, frustrated that she had to explain her decision yet again.

"No, you don't. Blood and flaming death, Adrienne, Captain Garrett didn't order you to go!"

"Ricco," Adrienne said with fraying patience, "listen to me. I have to do this." Leaving Kyrog, the place that had been her home for the past thirteen years, was hard enough. Leaving Ricco, the only true friend Adrienne could remember having, would be even more difficult. Her hand rose to the leather cord around her neck, comforted by the presence of the necklace. The cord was worn, but still tough. It was no weak silver chain, easy to snap, it was good and solid and real.

"You can't leave me in charge of them," Ricco said. She thought she saw desperation in her friend's eyes, and the look tugged the edges of her mouth into a reluctant smile.

The "them" Ricco referred to were the Yearlings. Although he was not a lieutenant, when Adrienne had suggested that Ricco replace her in training the Yearlings, the captain had agreed with her choice. "You know more about their training than anyone," Adrienne told him. "You were the obvious choice."

"That's bullshit and you know it," Ricco said. "You just want me to be miserable while you're gone."

The tension that had filled the room since Adrienne had informed her friend that she was leaving the next day disappeared at the ring of Adrienne's laughter. "You enjoyed working with Rosch and me," Adrienne said once she had regained control of herself. "You enjoy working with the two recruits assigned to you now."

"Yeah, but only because you're in charge," Ricco said. "All I have to do is show up and do what you say."

Adrienne knew that Ricco had never asked for the responsibility, but she also knew Ricco would do it well, because it would be the last thing she asked of him before leaving.

"You'll have help," she assured him. "The other soldiers already in the program will help you, and Captain Garrett said he would talk to Mylig so that you can get some pointers in training if you need them."

"Pointers! I'm going to need more than pointers, Ade. I've never done this before."

Adrienne saw real concern in her friend's brown eyes. His dark face was etched with the same worries, and she had a sudden urge to hug him.

She didn't.

"I'm assigning Rosch to you," Adrienne said, her tone belying none of the more tender emotions she was feeling. "He's the most advanced of the Yearlings, and he'll be able to tell you what steps I've gone through with him."

"Shit," Ricco said. "Flaming Abyss, Adrienne, why do you have to go?"

For the first time, Adrienne saw that it was not only training the Yearlings he was worried about. He looked more tired than angry now, and Adrienne's heart squeezed painfully. "You don't have to worry about me," she said. "It's not as though I'm going to Almet."

"You don't know where you're going," Ricco argued. "And you're going there alone."

"I'm sorry." Her voice was hardly more than a whisper. "But this is something I must do. You'll be fine."

"I don't want to be fine," Ricco said, crossing his massive arms. His lips formed into an expression that on anyone else would have undeniably been called a pout.

Such a childish expression on her fierce-looking friend was an interesting sight, and one that at any other time would warrant merciless teasing, but Adrienne had too much to do before she left tomorrow to become distracted. "I need you to do this for me, Ricco. I've put a lot of time and effort into coming up with a program to train the Yearlings, and you're the only one I trust to run it right."

"To run it like you would, you mean."

Adrienne smiled. "Yes."

Ricco uncrossed his arms and huffed out a disgusted breath. "Fine, I'll do it, but you better hurry back."

Adrienne wished she could say that she would. She didn't know where she was going or what she would be doing. There was too much mystery surrounding the mission, and even though she would be undertaking it as a civilian, not an active duty soldier, she knew as surely as Ricco did that every time a soldier left the training camp there was a chance she might never come back.

She hoped that was not the case this time.

"I'll do my best. I don't want to give you too much time to mess up my recruits."

Ricco looked uncomfortable for a moment, and then he did something that took Adrienne completely by surprise. He hugged her, pulling her up tight against his massive chest. "Be careful," he whispered. "Come back to me."

Then he was gone.

Meeting with Jeral Rosch was almost as hard as meeting with Ricco, though not nearly as confusing. Ricco was her longtime friend, but Jeral was her student, and one of the main reasons Adrienne had finally attained the rank of lieutenant. Jeral was nice, and his admiration and respect for her were always apparent. He was her friend, and Adrienne would miss the shining young man when she left.

"Lieutenant, what can I do for you?" Jeral asked. Adrienne had pulled him from the barracks to take a walk with her around Kyrog. Even at night, the training camp was full of life, but people gave Adrienne and Jeral the space she wanted. Something about the two of them must have indicated that whatever conversation they were having was private, because soldiers that might normally have stopped to greet Adrienne and Jeral kept their distance and gave them what privacy the busy camp allowed.

"Tomorrow morning, you'll join Ricco for training instead of me."

"Okay," Jeral said easily. It was not the first time since becoming a lieutenant that Adrienne had been unable to meet with him in the morning. There had been whole weeks that Adrienne had been too busy to see to his training herself.

Adrienne saw that the Yearling did not understand. "Rosch—Jeral. Ricco is going to be your new trainer."

"What?" Jeral asked, appearing completely blindsided. "What do you mean? Did I do something? I—" Jeral halted his words, pulling himself together. "May I ask why?" he said in a more moderated tone.

"I'm leaving Kyrog," Adrienne told him.

"Leaving?" Jeral's expression made it plain that he still didn't realize what she meant.

"I'm going on a mission, and I'm leaving tomorrow. I don't know when I'll be back."

She watched Jeral process that information. Finally he nodded, and Adrienne was impressed to see that, whatever he was feeling about the news, he was containing himself. She was proud of him for that, and proud of the part she had played in his growth. "I assume you told Ricco," Jeral said.

"Yes." Adrienne smiled. "You'll need to help him. You know everything I've put you through, and you're friends with the newer recruits. He'll need your support, and the others will need you to set an example."

"Ricco will be in charge now?" Jeral asked.

"Yes. I chose him to continue training the Yearlings while I'm gone."

"That's good. He is a good teacher. A good soldier."

Adrienne examined his dark face, his countenance even and unguarded. "So are you," she said. She rarely complimented the men outside of the ring, but she didn't know the next time she would see Jeral, or even if she would. He had already been in Kyrog nine months, and she could not be sure how much longer he would stay. It was strange, to think Jeral might be gone back to Roua before she returned. "Keep working hard, Jeral. I can't wait to see your progress when I get back." She smiled, as if the thought that he might not be there when she got back had never occurred to her. And she knew that if she never saw the full soldier he would become, there would always be an incomplete place inside of her.

Jeral smiled too, but she could see in his eyes that he was as aware of the possibility that this might be their last meeting as she. "I'm going to miss you, Lieutenant. There's no way I can thank you for everything you've done for me."

Adrienne reached out and put a hand on his arm, looking up into his tawny eyes. "There is. Help Ricco, help the recruits. That is all the thanks I require."

"Then consider it done."

When Adrienne left the next day with Ilso and Tam, she was as confident as she could be about the continued training of her Yearlings. Everything she could do in the short time allotted her had been done.

As much to comfort herself as her horse, Adrienne patted the neck of the strong chestnut stallion she rode. Strider was a parting gift from Captain Garrett, and the magnificent destrier had no trouble keeping up with the considerably shabbier mounts Ilso and Tam rode. Strider had been bred and trained for the art of war, and even at rest stood out from the other horses.

Ilso's mount, taller than Strider, had good legs but a shallow chest, and Adrienne thought the mare's bad temper was due as much to Ilso's whip as natural inclinations. The plodding gelding Tam rode was more suited to pulling carts than being ridden, but with the haphazard way Tam sat his horse, Adrienne thought it was probably fortunate that the animal was not more spirited.

Tam and Ilso were as disparate as their mounts. Tam seemed nice enough, if distant, but it was clear to Adrienne that Ilso would never be a friend to her. She had heard him commenting to Tam that they should have requested a different soldier, or gone to a different camp, before agreeing to take Adrienne.

When Adrienne had asked to hear more about the mission, now that she was committed to it, Ilso had told her to wait until they reached their destination to ask any more questions.

If Captain Garrett had given her a command to wait to find out, she would have obeyed because she trusted the man's judgment. Had the captain made such a decision, it would have been because he had good reason to do so. She had no such trust in these men. They would not reach their destination for another three weeks, and Adrienne was not content to simply wait. Since it was Ilso who had rebuffed her first request for information, Adrienne heeled Strider up alongside Tam's shaggy gelding.

Hopefully the scholar would be a more receptive audience.

"I was hoping you would tell me more about this mission," Adrienne said in what she hoped was a reasonable, friendly tone. She tried to keep her face smooth and friendly as well, void of the snarling lieutenant look she had perfected even before she had attained the rank that went with it.

"You don't need to worry about that yet," Tam told her, blinking his owlish, mud-colored eyes at her. "We have a lot of ground to cover once we begin, but it can wait until we reach Kessering."

Adrienne was not familiar with any town or city called Kessering, but that meant little. Much of the countryside was unknown to her. Her interests in geography were limited. It was Tam's words, not the place, that caught Adrienne's attention. "If you mean that there is work for me to do, or things to learn, I would like to start as soon as possible," Adrienne told the older man.

"That really isn't necessary." Tam's smile was kind but distracted. "Three weeks won't make a difference, really."

In Adrienne's experience when it came to training, three weeks could mean the difference between the ability to defend with a sword or the ability to trip over one. "Please, I would like to begin as soon as possible."

Tam sighed, long and weary. "I suppose there is no harm in beginning your instruction now," he told her in a voice completely lacking in enthusiasm. "I know the history as well as any of the scholars in Kessering."

"History?"

"Yes. What you will hopefully become a part of is the result of a commission of scholars—and men and women of influence—who are trying to find a way to end the war with Almet. This conflict has been going on for quite a long time, you know."

"I know all of the pertinent details regarding the conflict between Samaro and Almet," Adrienne told Tam. "If that is the history you are referring to, it isn't necessary to teach me. Not unless you are going back before the Fuirons, but that was centuries ago. Nearly a millennia."

Tam regarded her with some surprise. "Not too many people are that knowledgeable about the long and bloody history between our country and Almet," Tam said. "Are you sure you know more than the popular facts? Many people feel that they know more than they do."

The ongoing conflict and on-again off-again war between Samaro and Almet was the main reason camps like Kyrog existed. Most of the battles Adrienne had studied had involved Almet, and to understand an enemy's battle strategy, one had to understand the enemy. Adrienne had spent considerable time studying the history and culture of Almet, initially under the tutelage of Karse, so that she might have a full vision of the conflict and what influenced Almet's armies. Someday, she planned to ride to the Almetian battle lines and fight that evil herself, and when she did, she wanted to know what her enemy was fighting for.

"I am aware that in the distant past, Samaro and Almet were allied by a mutually beneficial and lucrative trade agreement. Almet was considerably smaller at the time, more of a size with Samaro. Then the Fuirons rose to power in Samaro and abolished slavery. When Almet refused to do the same, the trade agreement with Almet was ended."

Tam seemed impressed, and Adrienne continued with what she remembered from what Karse had told her. "The Fuirons were the ruling family for several centuries after that, and are still regarded as perhaps the best monarchal family Samaro has ever had," Adrienne continued. "However, even after the trade agreement ended, Almet continued to grow in size and power by spreading its influence into the countries surrounding it, and the relationship between Samaro and Almet grew more antagonistic, in part due to the fact that Almet, for all of its size, is landlocked." Adrienne quirked an eyebrow. "Need I continue up to the conflict under King Burin's current rule?"

The doubt that had covered the scholar's face was gone, replaced by a beaming smile than even seemed to brighten his muddy eyes. "I am surprised by your knowledge of the subject. Many people find history boring, though it has always interested me. It is quite impressive that you would know so much."

Adrienne felt it was unnecessary to point out that she was especially knowledgeable due to an old mentor's proclivity for dead languages. Most known texts written in Old Samaroan were from the time when the Fuirons were still in power, and Adrienne had read many of those texts.

"What is the 'commission'?" she asked instead. "You've mentioned it before. Who started it?"

"Why, King Burin started the commission, of course," Tam answered, seemingly delighted to impart that bit of information.

Adrienne wanted to roll her eyes. Since the death of the last Fuiron two centuries ago, no royal family had kept the throne for more than a single generation. Most of the kings and queens since then had ruled for only a handful of years before losing the throne, and often their lives along with it.

King Burin was only the latest in a line of poor or unlucky rulers who paid for a personal guard while all but forgetting the encampments like Kyrog that kept the countryside safe. Were it not for private backers and wealthy lords like Lord Neecham, places like Kyrog would not exist, and Samaro would be overrun by the bandits and rogues roaming the plains long before Almet came to enslave the survivors.

Adrienne remembered again the young girl buried in a grave outside of Pelarion, and wondered if her life might have been saved had King Burin not neglected the armies so.

Tam, however, did not seem to share Adrienne's poor opinion of their current ruler. He was practically glowing with the importance of being a part of King Burin's plan.

"King Burin has decided that, since the old ways have proven unsuccessful when dealing with Almet, it is time to look for an alternative solution."

Adrienne was fairly certain that the king's hope for a successful 'alternative solution' to dealing with Almet had more to do with wanting to keep his head on his shoulders than concern over the conflict itself. "So he put together a commission to find a solution?" Adrienne asked skeptically. "What exactly do you do?"

"I am not a member of the commission, per se," Tam admitted. "The commission asked me to go on this errand for them, as they are all much too busy with their work to leave the city themselves. However, I have been privy to a great many of their discussions and know as much as anyone who is not a commissioner himself."

Adrienne nodded, wondering if the scholar was really as important as he thought himself to be, or if was no more than a gofer to the rich and privileged.

"You see, after it was decided that a peaceable agreement with Almet is not likely at this point, it became apparent that what needed to change was the means of warfare." Tam looked uncomfortable, as if the subject of warfare was distasteful to him, but Adrienne became keenly interested.

Many different strategies had been used in an attempt to finally put an end to the fighting, with the implementation of new technology and strategy being foremost among the changes. Still, the basic means of fighting had always been the same: soldiers armed with weapons versus soldiers armed with weapons.

"Go on," Adrienne urged.

"It was decided that scholars would begin looking through the histories to see if there was an alternative to the current means of warfare employed by the armies."

Adrienne's excitement leached out of her, and Strider tossed his head as if sensing his rider's disappointment. Changes in warfare evolved and improved. There was little use in looking back in the histories to find different means. What use could history be here?

Adrienne had studied battle history almost her whole life, and some of what she had studied had involved battles before bows and arrows—and even cavalry were implemented. Battles where spears were the main weapons, before the invention of swords. Such battles offered great insight into military strategy, but there was nothing there that would change the way that Samaro should fight Almet. Strategies could be learned from studying history, but there was nothing new in the old books and stories.

"I don't know what you could have found," Adrienne said. "War is war."

Tam waved away her comment as if it was of no importance. "It isn't research into war that yielded metaphoric gold," Tam said, his tone a clear dismissal of the importance of the soldiering profession and Adrienne's beliefs. "It is the *tales* that were so important."

"Tales?" Adrienne asked at the same time Ilso called out that it was time to stop for lunch, temporarily halting their conversation.

Adrienne was surprised and a bit disconcerted when Ilso began laying out a fire. "How long are we staying here?" she asked, looking around the open meadow beside the road.

Tam shrugged, apparently unconcerned by the stop. "A couple of hours, I expect. Ilso will probably make a stew. It gives the horses a chance to rest."

Since the horses had been kept at a walk all morning, Adrienne doubted even Tam's gelding needed more than fifteen minutes of grazing and watering, and maybe as much time again to rest. She had discovered in the few hours she had been with them that, despite what they had told Captain Garrett, they did not seem to be in a hurry to return to Kessering. It was more or less that they had wanted to leave Kyrog as soon as possible.

"Perhaps you can tell me about the tales before lunch," Adrienne said after she had unsaddled Strider and rubbed him down. She loosely tied the destrier to a tree branch near the stream, within easy reach of the lush grass that grew there. He lipped over the grass contentedly, too well-trained to move away from the spot his rider put him, even had he not been tied to the branch.

Tam made a "hmm" sound in his throat as though considering the idea. "I really don't know if it is appropriate to begin teaching you," he said at last. "Most of the students in Kessering don't begin their training until they reach the city and are introduced to the commission, you understand."

Adrienne didn't understand. It seemed pointless for her to wait if Tam knew enough to get her started. "But it may be beneficial for me to begin my training early, when my mind will be more focused," she said. "What if I have problems learning the material?" Since Adrienne had never experienced much trouble learning before, she deemed it unlikely that she would have trouble with this, but that argument for beginning her training seemed like it would be most effective with a scholar.

"Yes, I suppose you may have a point," Tam said. "I will have to think on it some more before making a decision."

Adrienne thanked him, wondering how such a reasonable answer could sound so unreasonable. She usually valued someone who took the time to think before making a decision, but for some reason Tam thinking this over seemed foolish. Perhaps what seemed foolish was that he had made the decision that she be the one trained, yet he still needed to think over whether or not to begin that training.

Finally Tam went to pester Ilso about lunch, and Adrienne decided to give Strider a more thorough rubdown. "Well, boy, it seems this trip won't be as easy for me as it is for you," she grumbled. "Tam seems content to let me sit idle until we get to Kessering."

Some of the soldiers in Kyrog had enjoyed time off, time that was their own so that they did not have to practice or engage in any taxing activities. Ricco had always enjoyed a few days of lying around and doing nothing after a big campaign. Adrienne had hated it, and even on the days she did not have practice and drills to run she would always partake in some activity, even if it was just her morning run. The only time she was ever inactive for a stretch of time was when she was injured, and even then she pushed as much as possible without risking re-injury. Activity had been a constant in Adrienne's life since she was four, and she liked it that way.

She grimaced as she checked Strider's legs for swelling and hotspots, pleased to find him sound. Destriers were too valuable to allow them to go lame through negligence. "If King Burin is so eager to get the war over with that he put together a commission for it, you would think he'd want training accelerated, not delayed." Satisfied that Strider had suffered no injuries that morning, she patted his muscled shoulder. "Maybe I can talk Tam around." Strider nuzzled her, a response which Adrienne decided to take as encouragement, before she headed back to camp.

A man throwing balls of fire stood beside a woman who had knives twirling in the air before her. She didn't touch them, yet they moved in the intricate patterns of an expert juggler, and she was smiling as she watched them spin and dance.

One of the balls of flame tossed by the man set a tuft of dry grass on fire, and another man ran over to it and, waving his hand above the smoldering grass, sent a spout of water shooting from his fingers to quench the flames. He shouted something at the man tossing fire, and the woman with the knives sent one flying toward him to come to a playful stop a few inches from his face.

In the background, another woman was walking amongst bleeding and dying people, and where she passed they rose unharmed, lively and laughing together as though nothing had happened.

A man flew overhead.

Adrienne started up from her bedroll with a gasp. The dream had been incredibly vivid, and her heart was hammering.

Tam had told her of the tales that had sparked the commission's research into other paths that would end the conflict with Almet, and some of those tales had been incredible. People who could control fire, or water, and others who could control objects with their minds, or heal wounds and illnesses.

Tam had never said anything about people flying, but after that had been incorporated into her dreams along with the other tales, she couldn't help but wonder if it was possible. In her dream, nothing that had happened had surprised her, and she wondered if there were any limits to the abilities Tam had told her about.

The tales he told had seemed incredible, like the tales she had been told as a child. Karse had told her stories and Adrienne had the vaguest memories of her mother doing the same. But Tam had presented them as being reality, and Adrienne wasn't sure that she could believe that.

People couldn't control the elements, or heal the sick with their minds, and yet—and yet Tam had told her that there were recordings of such events in old tomes found deep in the libraries of Kessering and other old cities. Adrienne knew that there were fairy stories about such things, just as there were fairy stories about King Death and his ghostly court, and the Golden God and his seven sisters that were immortalized in one of the brightest constellations in the sky. But Tam's stories were more along the lines of Amyria the Healer, and he had told her that these books were not written as fairy tales; they were written as fact.

Adrienne settled back down in her blankets, deciding to put the tales out of her mind for the night, but as she started to turn over she heard the sound of a twig snapping underfoot.

Most of her life had been spent in soldiering camps, but Adrienne had been on enough hunts, both for food and other, more dangerous game, that she could interpret the night sounds of the countryside.

That sound had undeniably been the sound of a human walking through the woods. Deer would step on dry twigs, but even the proudest buck would not produce the absolute hush that had fallen over the forest as the night animals froze in response to one of the ultimate predators: man.

She concentrated on keeping her breathing even and quiet, straining to hear another sound that was out of place in the night. When it came, it was in the form of fabric brushing against leafy branches, snagging on one and snapping it back into place as the fabric released the branch.

Adrienne freed herself from her blankets and rolled to her feet in one smooth motion. She drew her sword and called to Ilso and Tam to wake before springing toward the man in the trees.

The light was dim, and she relied on instinct and senses other than sight to find the one who had been creeping into their camp. Her sword proved superfluous, as he was armed only with a knife, and she quickly disarmed him with a chop of her hand to his arm. The knife skittered away into the dry underbrush and the man let out a shout.

"What's this?" Tam asked, bumbling through the forest until he found Adrienne pinning the man to the ground. "Adrienne, what are you doing?"

"This man was sneaking up on our camp," Adrienne told Tam. She relaxed her grip on the stranger slightly, assured that he would not try to escape now that she had defeated him so easily and taken his knife. "From his looks, I hazard he planned to slit our throats and steal our things."

"I didn't," the man stammered, turning first to Tam and then to Ilso with bright appeal in his eyes. "I wanted only to join your camp, perhaps share a meal with you."

Ilso cast Adrienne a withering look, and Tam too looked disappointed in her assessment of the man. "He has no bags," the scholar pointed out. "He was probably hungry, and perhaps cold as well. Company is not an unusual want for a wanderer. It would be natural for him to seek us out."

Adrienne shook her head fiercely. "Then why did he try to sneak into our camp like a thief instead of calling out to us in welcome?" she asked.

"I did not wish to wake you," the man said. "Truly."

Adrienne stood up in disgust. She knew the man to be lying, and that he was a danger to them all, but Tam and Ilso would never allow her to deal with the man in any forceful way. The best she could do would be to take him away from their camp and hope that he did not double back and try again to kill them. "Stand up," Adrienne ordered.

The man smiled uncertainly and did as he was told, brushing the dirt and dry grass off of his clothes.

"You will show me to your camp," Adrienne said. "You will gather your things, and I will see you off in another direction before the hour is up."

"I have no things," the man said piteously, directing his words at Tam.

Adrienne had to give the thief credit for picking his mark well. Tam obviously believed the man wholly. "Adrienne, this man said that he was coming to our camp to share our supplies," Tam reminded her, moonlight glinting off his bald head as he nodded vigorously. "We will let him stay here with us. It is good to have company on a journey, and perhaps learn some news. Where do you come from?"

The thief's small, sly smile made it obvious just how dangerous that would be, but Tam saw no threat from a lone man, and listened attentively as the stranger shared information that he had picked up in the last town. Adrienne was disgusted. The man might be alone now, but she doubted even a man who would murder three people in their sleep would wander the countryside by himself.

"No," Adrienne said to Tam, cutting off his conversation with the man. She met the scholar's eyes levelly. "You may come with me, and when this man shows us to his camp, you will be satisfied that he is a liar and a thief, and we will continue on to Kessering without him."

Tam looked unhappy, Ilso doubtful, but Adrienne stood firm. She knew the thief's mind, knew that he planned to lie and lead them nowhere, but was sure that she could outsmart him.

She gripped his arm hard, and whispered in his ear as Tam made ready to accompany them. "You will not lie to me," she hissed. "Do so, and I will gut you like a boar," she assured him. "I will not hesitate to take my knife and open you belt to breast. Do not deceive yourself that you could kill me first. Now show me to your camp."

"I have no camp," the man said, and Adrienne gripped tighter, tight enough to leave bruises on his arm that went deep into the muscle and would pain him for days to come.

Her face remained calm despite the pain she was inflicting, and she saw a spark of fear light in the man's eyes. "You will show me to your camp," she repeated, her tone hard as steel.

"I'll show you," he promised, and led Adrienne and Tam to where he had stored his goods before seeking to take theirs. When the would-be thief revealed where he had stashed his bags, Adrienne sensed Tam's confusion and disappointment, though he said nothing.

"Can you find your way back to camp?" she asked Tam.

"I should be able to." He looked back the way they had come, and Adrienne had a feeling of trepidation. She had no interest in leading the thief away only to spend the rest of the night searching the forest for Tam.

"Wait here for a moment," she told Tam before dragging the thief off a little ways into the woods.

"Where are your friends?"

"What friends?" Adrienne drew her knife and held it against his stomach. "I could kill you now and no one would be the wiser."

"Ah, those friends. There was a signal I was supposed to give if things went well. When they didn't hear it they would have left."

"I assume you set up a meeting point with them?"

The thief nodded.

"Go there and convince them to leave. Now. If I see any signs of you come the morning it won't be only your belly I'm splitting."

The man looked pathetically grateful as he nodded before scampering away.

She went back to gather Tam so that they could return to camp. Ilso was there waiting with their things, and Tam just shook his head at the other man before returning to his sleeping roll.

Adrienne stayed up the rest of the night listening for signs that the thief had not heeded her warning, and didn't breathe easy until the sun dawned.

Tam handed Adrienne a heavy book. "You're fortunate that I brought this along," he told her. "There aren't many copies, and most of them are in Kessering. It is required reading for anyone being taught what you will be."

Adrienne examined the book. The pages were yellow and curling with age, and when she flipped through them she saw that the writing was small and cramped. "Why?" she asked, wondering if the book contained more of the tales he had told her before.

"So that you can understand the accounts and theoretical knowledge that led to the discovery that people can develop extra-ordinary abilities," Tam said in a way that suggested it should have been obvious to her.

"And why would I believe this book?" she asked, hefting it doubtfully. "Why should I believe what you told me? Saying that the stories I heard as a child are true doesn't make them so."

"You seemed to believe yesterday."

"I listened yesterday," she corrected. "And after last night, I don't know why I should believe anything you say."

"Watch your mouth," Ilso snapped.

"You'd both be dead if not for me," she snapped back. "That man last night—"

"Believing the best of people does not make me wrong," Tam said. "I have seen these abilities with my own eyes. Seen people healed in instants."

"And I've seen men swallow fire and juggle knives," Adrienne said. "Travelling performers, nothing more."

The dream last night had made such abilities seem momentarily possible, but Tam's gullibility when it came to the thief cast a shade of doubt that she could not dispel.

"Read the book," Tam said again. "I have seen many incredible things. More than just people being healed. I've seen blacksmiths forge unbreakable tools, scholars able to read and remember in ways I would have thought impossible."

"You told me all of this yesterday." And yesterday it has fascinated her. Now it just made her tired.

"But I'm not the only one. These abilities are centuries old. The book describes this, and the theories behind it all."

Adrienne felt herself softening. What if she was wrong? And Kessering was still weeks away. "Is knowing the theories necessary? At this point in my training, I mean?"

Tam looked appalled by her question. "It is essential that you know why myself and the other scholars came to the conclusions we did about people being able to learn these abilities. You must understand the process we went through in making this discovery. If not, how can you understand why the training is necessary? How can you understand why anyone needs these abilities at all?"

"Over the years I have learned the process of weapon making," she told Tam, "but I was able to use weapons long before that, and I understood the purpose of weapons even earlier."

"This matter is hardly as simple as swordplay," Tam told her.

The scholar was proving to be an enigma. In many ways he was extremely intelligent. His knowledge of history was greater than that of anyone Adrienne had ever met, and she had even managed to engage him in a philosophical discussion on the second day that had made their long stop for lunch pass quickly. But when it came to the subject of soldiers and fighting, Tam's opinion that they had little purpose and were hardly more than dumb brutes was proving unshakeable.

Adrienne considered defending the intricate nature of swordsmanship to Tam, but she didn't waste her breath. Tam did not respect anything but knowledge gained from books. "I can see the differences," Adrienne said sardonically.

"I realize the mental activity of reading such an old book might be difficult for you, but it is necessary." Tam muttered something more under his breath, but the only word Adrienne caught was "translation."

"What language was this originally written in?" Adrienne asked.

"Old Samaroan," Tam said. "I believe the knowledge to be more apparent in the original, but few besides scholars now know more than a couple words of Old Samaroan, so we must content ourselves with the translation."

"I know Old Samaroan," Adrienne said. She still wasn't sure why she needed to read this book on theory herself, instead of Tam teaching her the pertinent details, but she would show him that she was not stupid. "Mental activity" was not beyond her.

"You do?"

Adrienne nodded and explained how she had come to learn the language when she was just a child. Her explanation was delivered in Old Samaroan, perfect but for a rather rough accent. "I would like to use the translation as a reference," she said in the common tongue, "but if you have a copy of the original, I would prefer to work with that."

Tam looked confused. His response was slow, as if he did not know what to do with the new information. "Ah, yes, I did bring a copy of the original text, though I intended it for my own study." He frowned. "Are you sure you know enough of the language for the book to be useful?"

"Yes."

Tam nodded, then turned to search one of his numerous bags for the book. As he searched his movements became quicker and a smile spread across his face. Whatever doubts he'd had about her, it seemed that the new information had replaced them, at least for the moment. "If you really can read and understand Old Samaroan, I believe this will give you a tremendous advantage." He handed the book over and rubbed his hands together eagerly. "This is marvelous. Incredible."

He smiled at her, and there was no reserve in it. Adrienne thought for the first time that Tam's attitude toward her might not have been intentionally harsh. Unlike Ilso, whose dislike of soldiers seemed real and well developed, Adrienne realized that she could very well be the first soldier Tam had ever been in close and sustained contact with. With no real frame of reference, and with Ilso as his companion, it could be that he had no way to relate to her.

"I'd like to talk to you about it tonight," Adrienne said. She still wasn't sure if she believed him, but there was no reason to antagonize him, or to try and understand the book alone.

"Of course, of course," Tam said, rubbing his hands together. "Of course."

Adrienne left and wandered over to the top of a low hill to begin her studies. Since there was no shade to be found, a view and the chance of a breeze seemed the best choice. After an hour of exhaustive reading she was disheartened to see that she had made only minimal progress. Her only consolation was that the translation was as difficult to understand as the original text written in Old Samaroan. The book had not been written as a manual on theory, as she had supposed, or as instruction on how to develop and use the amazing abilities Tam had told her about. Rather, it was a journal written by an unidentified person—Adrienne thought it was probably a man, but that was only a guess—and abilities such as those Tam had spoken of were often mentioned only obliquely, and rarely in a positive light.

Those who use these unnatural means generally behave as though they are superior to their natural brethren. These people speak of a 'connection with the universe' while simultaneously committing acts that go against the natural laws of the universe. Their high-handedness affronts more pragmatic individuals with true and natural concerns. These people will no doubt lead us into anarchy given the opportunity.

There were some words in the journal that Adrienne needed the translation for, and she hoped that no important nuances were getting lost. She could not be sure how good the translation was, or how the informal nature of a journal might be coloring the reality of the abilities it spoke of.

Many passages in the journal gave incredible insights into the author's desultory nature, in Adrienne's opinion, but little insight into the people who could do these "unnatural" things, and even less about what those things were. They did serve to make Adrienne more curious about the people the author was referring to, however, and she became even more grateful that Karse had taught her Old Samaroan in an attempt to entertain the young girl who had been left primarily in his care.

She had learned that reading Old Samaroan was easier when she fully immersed herself in the reality of the text. As she spent more time reading the journal, Adrienne began to understand why Tam and the commission referred to the people in the book as Talented. How else could she describe people with such amazing abilities, such Talents?

"Connection with the universe" sounded like some of Tam's theoretical knowledge, and Adrienne wondered why the Talented thought they were more closely connected than others. And if they truly were more connected, how did they gain that connection? Was it inborn, or something learned?

Adrienne wished more of the journal was focused on the Talented, rather than chronicling the author's days and beliefs.

After the report of riots to the south came in, there was debate about what the response should be. Some are calling for a military response to preempt an act of rebellion. This show of strength, as some are calling it, might suit the brutish minds of some, but those fools do not understand the real issues. These times require a government led by the enlightened, not by men who think that swords will solve every problem.

If Adrienne had not read his previous entry, she might have been sympathetic to his beliefs, but the "riot" he described had resulted in twenty-one people dead and dozens more injured. His dogmatic beliefs about an "enlightened government" over a military-and-defense minded one were terribly naive.

From what she gathered, the journal had been written before the conflict with Almet. Before the rule of the Fuirons, even, as the author referred to slaves as a part of everyday life. An acceptable part of everyday life. He seemed to have no compunction about punishing his own slaves, even going so far as to write down the punishment he had administered to one of his male slaves.

Yesterday I gave Barimbo twenty lashes for disobedience. He had brought food to one of the women when I had forbidden her to be fed for two days.

Today, a boy came to me telling me Barimbo was too sick to work. I went to his shack myself and pulled him out of bed. There is a plot to be turned, and Barimbo is the strongest of my slaves. If he had wanted to avoid a fever, he should never have made me whip him. I will not allow him to get out of work as a result of his disobedience, or I've no doubt he will grow more disobedient in future.

It does not do to show slaves tenderness. To do that is to encourage them to be lax in their duties.

The accounts of his treatment of slaves made her shudder. Adrienne could not imagine such treatment of a human being as legal, yet she knew that that and worse had been done regularly before the Fuirons came to power. And it was happening even now in Almet.

After reading two tedious pages about the author's mother, whose authoritarian character was "unenlightened" and "unbecoming of an educated woman," Adrienne set the book aside in disgust. It was a waste of time, reading drivel about a long-dead someone's longer-dead parent, but she couldn't risk missing some mention of the Talented. She had so little to go on at present that any mention of them could be important, and the author had more than once scrambled his rants about his parent or the government in with his rants against the "unnatural creatures."

It was only late afternoon, but they had already set up camp for the night. Adrienne could not object to the campsite, as it was well situated on a hill near a quick-flowing stream, but as usual she thought they could have pressed on for a couple more hours.

Adrienne did not complain about the early stop; she was grateful to put an end to their travel that day. It had been two days since she had gotten any exercise, and she thought a run and an hour of stretching and balancing poses would help clear her head and prepare her for reading more of the journal. Too much reading and too little activity besides sedately riding Strider were making her itchy and moody. Without some release, she thought she might turn on her companions in hopes of some excitement.

"I am going for a run," Adrienne informed Ilso and Tam. "I should be back in half an hour."

"What?" Tam asked, regarding her as he would a curiosity. It was his usual response whenever Adrienne pursued any physical activity without need. Even volunteering to collect extra fuel for the fire could be perceived as strange by the man. He preferred studying to all else, which was no doubt the cause of the fat paunch around his middle.

"I won't hold supper," Ilso warned.

"I enjoy the exercise," Adrienne explained to Tam, ignoring Ilso's warning. With a parting look she headed downriver at an easy lope, enjoying the feel of her muscles and ligaments flexing and relaxing with the familiar motions. A feeling of peace such as she had not felt since leaving Kyrog filled her as her mind cleared and she fell into a natural rhythm. There were trees lining the stream, and a breeze relieved some of the sweltering heat.

The only sign Adrienne saw of other people was the remains of a fire at least two days old. She would keep an eye out, but she was not overly concerned by what she saw. Whoever had been camping near the river two days ago would be several leagues away now, even traveling by foot.

Adrienne estimated she had run about four miles by the time she returned to camp, and she waved off Ilso's offer of stew, given grudgingly under the watchful eye of Tam. She was sick of stew, and she had saved some of the berries she had found the day before. Instead of joining the men for supper, she went to the edge of camp and began the routine she had taught Jeral those first days of his training.

She began with her eyes closed, her feet hip width apart and her hands by her sides. She breathed deeply for a few moments, then inhaled even deeper as she raised her arms and tilted her head toward the sky. She folded forward, exhaling and felt her lingering tension fade with the familiar, calming moves. She was aware of Ilso and Tam talking, but it was easy to block out the meaning of the words so that they were no more than background noise.

She was aware of other sounds, too, as she moved smoothly through the familiar moves. Adrienne could hear the quiet rushing of the stream, the wind whispering through the branches and leaves and across her sweaty face. Birds sang occasionally in the hot afternoon sun, and squirrels sent up their mad chatter. The smooth, controlled motions took Adrienne outside of herself, away from her companions' disapproval and the drudgery of the journal she was studying.

When Adrienne finally opened her eyes, she found both Ilso and Tam watching her. Ilso sneered and looked away, but Tam looked intrigued.

"That was very interesting to watch," he told her. "A dance of some sort?"

Adrienne thought about the sounds she had heard that had seemed almost musical, and the feelings and sensations that seemed to move around and through her during her routine. A dance would not be the worst comparison someone could make. "Perhaps."

"I saved you some supper, though Ilso was of a mind to throw it out after you turned it down the first time."

Adrienne remembered the berries she had saved, but now that she was calm and relaxed, more stew did not sound as bad. She had eaten far worse and for a far longer stretch of time. "Thank you," she said. "I am hungry."

"Do you mind if I sit with you?" Tam asked. "I would like to discuss what you think of the journal."

When she had left the camp for her run, Adrienne had not even wanted to think of the horribly dry journal, but she was in a better place now, and willing to discuss it. "The reading is slow going," Adrienne admitted. "It is quite clear that the author did not like or approve of people with special abilities. He had some unusual ideas regarding the government and the role of leaders as well."

"I thought his ideas rather brilliant," Tam said. "However, I must agree that he was not a supporter of more people developing abilities."

"I can see why you thought Old Samaroan was the best way to read the text. Subtleties are lost in the translation." Adrienne had started out checking between the two texts to be sure she was reading it correctly, but it had soon become apparent that she understood more from reading the journal in its original language than from reading the translation. "I do wish there was a copy that eliminated the chaff, such as his disagreements with his mother," she added absently.

Tam looked at her with muddy eyes full of disapproval, his dark pate reflecting the evening light. "Those incidents give us a glimpse into the author's mind. Understanding him helps us to better interpret what he is saying when referring to people with special abilities. To eliminate that would be disadvantageous."

"They weren't random people with abilities, these Talented. I think that they were a community, a group with similar goals and experiences. Similar beliefs ."

"That is an interesting view, but there is no evidence to support such a claim," Tam said. "I advise against thinking about them as a group when there is no evidence but your mind's interpretation. It is always best to stick with facts."

Adrienne didn't agree. The entire journal was an interpretation of events through the author's view, and he viewed them only in light of how those events affected his own life. Her studies of war had meant studying groups, their motivations and beliefs and structures, and she was fairly certain that the book she was reading involved one man's dislike of a distinct group of people, even if he never explicitly referred to them as such.

Had she been discussing this with someone other than Tam, she might have pressed the issue. Instead, she decided that her best course of action was to let it lie and not argue her point. This was obviously not a part of the theory Tam had meant her to learn about, and she doubted Tam would be reasonable about hearing more of her theories.

"I plan to read some more before retiring for the night," Adrienne said, rising from where they sat near the fire. "Good night, Tam."

"Good night, Adrienne," he said, pulling another book from his pack before she had even left the ring of firelight.

As Adrienne made her way to her bedroll, she wished there was someone else she could share this with. Ricco would hate studying the old journal, but he would have thought that the Talented were a group, just like she did. Jeral was so eager to learn that he would have loved all of it. She missed both of her friends now, when she was so alone in her studies and beliefs.

The reading did not get easier, although Adrienne's somewhat dusty Old Samaroan improved greatly. Her dislike of the author, whom she now referred to as "Pele," the name of a soldier she had been bullied by as a child, grew with every page, but her understanding of the Talented also grew. She was even more convinced now that they were a sub-group of the general population, brought together by the desire to possess special talents and the effort it took to gain them. The author spoke derisively of the hours the Talented spent practicing, focusing, and training, all to disrupt what he thought of as the "natural order."

Adrienne wondered if Pele had once had aspirations to become Talented, and had somehow failed in his goal. It would explain his intense dislike of the Talented, which seemed more personal the more she read. She had seen the same behavior in men who had desired to become soldiers, but eventually learned they were not suited for the profession.

While Adrienne exercised her mind studying the old journal, she made sure to exercise her body as well. She resumed her morning runs, and began performing her "dance" at night. When they stopped for lunch, which invariably took an hour if not more, she would run through forms with her sword. Ilso and Tam always seemed displeased by her use of the weapon, but Adrienne refused to give up the regular practice that was so essential to maintaining her skills. She only wished that she had an opponent to practice against, and hoped to find someone in Kessering to train with.

Adrienne was running through the sword forms, and just starting the transition from defensive to offensive moves, when a sense of wrongness trickled through her concentration. It was nothing she saw or felt, no sensory input, but a gut-deep feeling. She scanned the woods around them and the road to their right, straining her eyes and ears for a clue as to what had alerted her. She had experienced this feeling before, and her grip on her sword firmed as she readied herself for whatever was coming.

"Ilso, do you hear something?" she asked in her best lieutenant's voice, still scanning the woods for signs of danger. They had all been grateful for the shade the grove offered, but she wished now they were camped out on the grassy plains, where she would be able to see further into the distance.

"No, why?" Ilso's response to her commanding tone had been automatic. He spit on the ground in disgust. His dislike of her had only grown over the two weeks they had spent in each other's company. Adrienne thought that the frustrated guard was coming to hate her, and the fact that he had felt compelled to answer her would not help that.

But Ilso's feelings toward her were unimportant now, and Adrienne forced thoughts of them aside. He was the only other person around with even rudimentary skill with a weapon. "Something is wrong," she said. "Grab your sword."

"I will not," he objected, glancing over at the sword piled on top of his saddle bags beside the fire.

"Grab your sword and begin saddling the horses," she ordered, her voice velvet over steel. "I am going to check the perimeter."

"Adrienne, dear," Tam said in the patronizing tone he used whenever he felt she was interpreting something wrong in the journal, "do you think perhaps all of that sword practice has made you paranoid? Welcoming such violence into your life cannot be healthy. Neither Ilso nor I heard a thing."

Adrienne's rage boiled over. "I don't know why the two of you wanted to bring a soldier to Kessering in the first place, since you seem to disapprove of me and all other soldiers, but something is wrong!"

As she spoke the last word, two men, unkempt and brandishing wickedly curved scimitars, leapt from the thick forest surrounding them. Ilso fell back as quickly as Tam, moving even further away from his sword in the process, and Adrienne allowed herself a grim smile. Ilso would be of no help to her.

"I'll deal with the chit," the smaller of the two men said. His long black hair was matted, and it was nearly impossible to distinguish where dark skin ended and dirt began. "You can—"

Whatever the taller man could do was lost in his cry of surprise as Adrienne leapt forward suddenly. She darted in and out, the razor edge of her sword leaving a thin line of blood on the man's arm.

"Bitch!" he said, and both men turned away from Tam and Ilso and rushed at her.

Adrienne smiled in anticipation as she watched them run toward her.

The dual assault might have been effective had they come at her from different directions, but they were both rushing her from the front, getting in each other's way in an effort to reach her. The two men were poorly trained, that much was obvious, and in minutes they were lying on the ground. Neither would be getting up again.

"Merciful Creator," Ilso said, staring at the men on the ground in shock. Each of them had outweighed Adrienne by at least sixty pounds, yet she had dispatched them with swift efficiency, her sword moving as an extension of her body.

"Was it really necessary to kill them?" Tam asked once he had found his voice. "Couldn't you have simply disarmed them instead?" His tone was shaky and uncertain, and when he looked down at the bodies there was horror in his eyes.

Adrienne looked away from the bodies of the two outlaws to shoot Tam a look of disbelief. She decided to ignore the ridiculous question. "Saddle the horses," she told Ilso again.

"Surely that is not necessary now that you have…dealt…with these men," Tam said. "Although a spot away from the, uh, bodies might be preferable," he added after looking at the bloody corpses.

"No, not just a different spot," Adrienne said. "We don't know that these men were alone. We should keep on until dark, and keep our guards up."

"You're not in any position to issue orders," Ilso said, his expression dark and angry. "Just because some fool gave you rank back in Kyrog doesn't mean anything out here."

"Saddle the damn horses," Adrienne snapped, her eyes skimming the bodies before traveling up to meet Ilso's.

Ilso's eyes fired, and Tam stepped between the two of them. "Adrienne, I know that you must be upset, but I am in charge of this mission, and—"

"You're in charge?" Adrienne turned her anger on Tam. "I'm the only reason the two of you are not the ones lying dead on the ground." She saw the fear in Tam's eyes as her words hit their mark, but it did nothing to cool her temper. "Maybe my rank in Kyrog doesn't matter here," she said, including Ilso in her scathing words, "but this," she raised her sword, "means that when I say move, you move."

"I—"

Adrienne took a step forward, and Tam took two quick steps back. "I'll start packing up," he said. "Ilso, get the horses ready."

Adrienne stood back and kept an eye on the surrounding forest while the two men worked to pack up camp. When she was reasonably sure that no one was in the woods and that Tam and Ilso were fully occupied with their duties, she gathered up the scimitars, knives, and coin purses from the thieves' bodies and bundled them in with her own possessions. There was no point in leaving the weapons to rust, or the coins to be scattered by scavengers come to feed on the dead.

CHAPTER SIX

Kessering was a small but sprawling city.

The people in the streets wandered every-which-way, and Adrienne thought they lacked the commonality of purpose that most of the people at Kyrog had shared. Adrienne had traveled to other towns and cities before, and had observed in nearly all of them such a separateness of purpose amongst the people there, but it was strange to think that she would remain in such a disorderly place for an extended period of time. The soldiers in Kyrog had training to bind them together, but the people who lived in cities went about their business almost completely independent of each other.

"I can't wait to return to the library," Tam said. "I was not able to bring nearly enough books on this trip." Since he had managed to cram more books into a saddlebag than Adrienne had thought possible, she was not sure that his statement was entirely accurate, but she was too busy studying the city to comment.

The city had no surrounding wall to speak of. In lieu of stone defenses, dry wooden boards ten feet high surrounded the city and gave the appearance of safety, but they would provide no real protection if someone were to try and enter without permission. Fire or even a battering ram would work quickly if invaders were too lazy to climb the low walls.

She turned her attention to the hinges on the gates and realized that they were going to rust despite the dry heat. Adrienne could not help but wonder when the gates had last been closed, or if they even could be closed after so many years of neglect.

The three of them rode their horses through the gates and garnered no more than a passing glance from the one guard set to keep watch.

"If my presence is no longer necessary, I am going to leave," Ilso said to Tam, giving Adrienne a dark look. He had not forgiven her for her actions the day she had killed the brigands a week before, and Adrienne was glad to see him gone. She'd had more than one uneasy moment wondering if Ilso might try to harm her in her sleep.

"Of course," Tam said. "If any of the commissioners needs to speak with you, they will be in touch." Tam was practically vibrating with excitement and anticipation, and his gelding snorted and bobbed his head in reaction, showing more spirit than he had since Adrienne had first seen the animal.

"What now?" Adrienne asked, scanning the crowds. There were inns and taverns, storefronts and the occasional vendor selling wares on the street. People went this way and that, some shopping, others with less apparent destinations.

Nowhere did Adrienne see signs of people being trained to unlock special abilities, although she was sure that was what the commission was doing in Kessering. Tam had practically said as much when he was telling her stories of what he had seen. Adrienne did not comment on the lack of noticeable Talents in the city so far. Tam probably thought her too dim to make the connection between what he had said and the reality of what was being done here, and there was no point in disillusioning him at this late time.

Tam's opinions no longer mattered to Adrienne. She was in Kessering now, and she had made her own notes and speculations based on what Tam had said and what she had read in Pele's journal. From now on, she would focus on that.

"Now I must present you to the commission," Tam said. "If you pass their inspection, you will begin your training in earnest."

They dismounted their horses, and as Adrienne walked through the streets she noticed people looking at her out of the corners of their eyes. Some people stared more blatantly, or would look away quickly before looking back. People looked at Tam, too, as people leading horses through the streets tended to draw attention in a city as isolated as Kessering, but they did not look at Tam with the same wary look in their eyes as when they watched Adrienne. Their eyes never failed to take in the sword at her hip or the snug fitting leather *swa'il* that she wore. It made the hair on the back of her neck stand up.

Adrienne and Tam passed carts selling trinkets and baked goods, and she was tempted to stop and buy a meat pie, a change from the stew they had been eating for the past weeks. Now wasn't the time, but she marked the placement of the food cart for future reference. Children ran underfoot shrieking and laughing, and there were more women on the streets than men. It would take her awhile to adjust to the changes between camp life and city life.

When they reached the library where the commission met, Adrienne and Tam handed off their horses and received promises that both horses and baggage would be taken care of. Adrienne pressed instructions on the groom, who seemed happy to take care of such a magnificent animal as Strider. Adrienne was pleased to receive at least a few good words after three weeks of criticism, even if those words were only about her horse.

"Time to move, Adrienne," Tam said when she started instructing the stable boy on Strider's shoes and inquiring after a farrier. "The commission is waiting."

Adrienne knew as soon as they were shown to the commission that the majority of the people on the commission were scholars, and no doubt delighted—as Tam was—by the tomes surrounding them. On the way in she had noticed that the back of the library looked more like living quarters than a place for books, and she wondered how many scholars lived in the library as well as spent their days there.

"Tam, welcome home," an elderly man said after a clerk had announced them. "I see you found someone who might be suitable?" Though she kept her face carefully neutral and her stance relaxed, she noted the skeptical look in his eyes and had to force herself not to speak.

"Yes, Elder Rynn. May I present to the commission Adrienne Rydaeg?"

"Lieutenant Adrienne Rydaeg," Adrienne corrected, stepping forward and giving a short, quick bow, holding her sword back with a practiced move. "Formerly in charge of recruit training at Kyrog."

"You seem rather young to be a lieutenant," the woman sitting to Elder Rynn's left said. She was the only female commissioner, and Adrienne thought she was probably a noble, not a scholar, and given a place on the commission for political reasons.

"Lady Chessing, I was assured that Ad-er-Lieutenant Rydaeg had a great deal of experience as a soldier," Tam told the noblewoman. "The captain at Kyrog recommended her above all others." He smiled in a way that was no doubt meant to be persuasive, but fell short in Adrienne's opinion. It was obvious he did not believe his own words when it came to her abilities, despite what he had witnessed firsthand on their journey here.

"We will interview her before judging if she is suitable or not," Elder Rynn said. Adrienne knew without being told that he was the leader of the commission. She directed her full attention to him, blocking out Lady Chessing and the rest of the commission for the time being.

Adrienne did her best to answer the commission's questions while maintaining her poise. It was not that the questions bothered her, but rather the fact that many of the questions and their answers seemed inconsequential, such as her favored pastimes and whether she preferred the wet or dry season on the plains. She sensed the same disapproval from the commissioners as she had from Tam and Ilso regarding her profession as a soldier and wondered once again why any soldier had been selected to come back to Kessering. The questions they asked regarding her soldiering skills were vague at best, and they seemed not to know what questions to ask or what answers to listen for.

They may have gone looking for a soldier, but they did not seem to want one.

Only the young man seated at the end of the table seemed to be regarding her without a heavy layer of doubt or dislike. The way he watched her projected interest, not skepticism.

After the commission's questions had been answered to the best of Adrienne's abilities, they held a short, hushed discussion right there at the table. Elder Rynn finally called everyone to attention after the discussion wound down. "The majority have found Lieutenant Adrienne Rydaeg suitable for the commission's purposes. The minority has conceded. She will commence with her training."

His words had a ceremonial ring to them, and she wondered who was there besides the commissioners, Tam, and herself to notice or care. And she wondered about the precedence of this event for it to warrant such ceremony. How many before her had been found suitable to begin training? Tens or hundreds, she could not begin to guess.

And now she was one of them.

"Now, Adrienne, I must ask how much you know about the commission and Kessering," Elder Rynn said in a voice dry as old parchment.

Adrienne told them all that Tam had told her, and all that she had learned from reading the old journal. "My best guess is that this commission is using Kessering as a place to train people to use special abilities, and that these abilities will somehow be used in the war efforts against Almet."

Clearly taken by surprise, the commissioners began to talk excitedly amongst themselves until Elder Rynn slapped his hand loudly on the table and got their attention. He glanced over at Tam, but directed his words at her. "Did Tam tell you this?"

"Not explicitly. I reached this conclusion on my own, based on the purpose of this commission, what stories Tam told, and the information found in the journal." Adrienne could see the doubt on their faces. For once she wished that she was older, and wearing a fine dress instead of the worn leather *swa'il* that was so practical for riding or fighting. If she had come to them without a sword and many days' worth of sweat and dust clinging to her, they might not doubt her intelligence. Had she looked different, a mature lady instead of a young soldier, her reception may not have been as rude.

Such thoughts seemed traitorous to everything Adrienne had ever worked for, and she wished immediately to unthink them. "Your goal is to end the war, once and for all," Adrienne said, making an effort to sound sure of herself. "It would be insanity to think you could do this by the same means that have been used before, but if there is a way for people to develop extraordinary Talents that the other side does not possess..."

"There is," Elder Rynn said. "Over the past five years, we have managed to produce over twenty people with abilities."

The information shook her. For all that she had suspected this to be their goal, and despite what Tam had told her, she had expected to come here and find that they had achieved only limited success at best. She had never really considered the possibility that they had already succeeded with such a large number of people. Visions of people going to Almet, controlling fire and throwing the enemy back with just their thoughts, filled her mind. It would change the war more than any weapon. "That is amazing! Can they really do all that the tales say they can? Even the journal talks about—"

The clearing of a throat cut her off. It was another commissioner, a man slightly younger than Elder Rynn and wearing a mustard yellow jacket. "There is a complication that we did not anticipate when we began training people to unlock abilities," he said in a voice surprisingly effeminate for such a large man.

"That is an understatement, Franklin," Lady Chessing said. "What we have is not a complication, it's a disaster!"

It was clear to Adrienne that Lady Chessing did not take any blame for the disaster herself, but placed it all on the other commissioners.

"What complication?" Adrienne asked, wishing Tam had spent more time explaining what was happening in Kessering rather than focusing on the journal. She hated being two steps behind.

"There are limitations that none of us expected," Franklin of the yellow jacket said. "At first, we tried training the commission members, and then scholars. It seemed wise that such powers be limited to logical and intelligent individuals."

"However, the training did not yield the results we had hoped for," Elder Rynn said, taking up for Franklin.

"Why not?"

"For one, it seems you must be young to develop an ability." He shook his head slightly, as though regretting that limitation.

Adrienne was not surprised to hear that, although she could sympathize with the old man's disappointment. Not only had Ilso and Tam asked for a young soldier in Kyrog, but the author of the journal had often used "older" and "more experienced" synonymously, as he had used "young" and "new," as though there were no older Talented who were not experienced. "That isn't so unexpected," Adrienne said. "Some skills are easier to develop when young."

Karse had been the one to tell Adrienne that.

No one looked happy with Adrienne's observation. "Age is not the only limitation," Elder Rynn said in his dry voice. "Some people seem unable to develop an ability, no matter how hard they try, and those who do develop abilities are not able to use them outside of the individual's usual scope."

Adrienne shook her head, confused and wondering why he did not just say what he meant. Captain Garrett would never have taken so long getting to the point. "Scope of what?"

Elder Rynn gestured for the young man sitting at the end of the table to explain. He did not seem old enough to have a place on the commission, and Adrienne wondered why the explanation was left to him rather than to the elder or Franklin. Even Chessing.

"I was the first to develop an ability," the young man said proudly, answering Adrienn's unspoken question. "I had been studying and trying different methods to do so for nearly two years before anything manifested, but I was finally successful."

"What can you do?" Adrienne asked, giving him a closer study. He did not look different from any of the scholars, except that he was the youngest and the only one who was not looking at her with thinly veiled distaste.

He smiled. "I can memorize."

"Memorize?" Adrienne repeated. Tam had mentioned this, but she had forgotten it in light of all the other, more exciting Talents he'd told her about.

He nodded. "Everything I read, hear, see, I can remember with perfect recall. These memories are chronicled in my brain, perfectly organized like a book or the catalog in a library. It is really quite remarkable. And useful," he added in a defensive tone, crossing his thin arms in front of him. Some of the other scholars looked proud or even envious, but the non-scholars did not look happy, and Lady Chessing looked disgusted.

"A fat lot of good that does us, Ben," Lady Chessing said. "All it means is that you will remember perfectly our utter failure as a commission when the king finds out what's happening here."

"I don't consider it a total failure," the young man said, stung by the woman's criticism. "My ability proved that our methods were effective, and we have been able to improve them since."

"So all you do is memorize?" Adrienne asked.

The man smiled ruefully. "That's all I can do, yes. Other abilities have manifested with different people, but they all appear to be extensions of the person's, well, the person's profession, you might say."

"Like a scholar memorizing," Adrienne said, nodding. "A memory such as you described must be a tremendous asset in scholarly pursuits."

"Exactly so," he said, his smile growing and becoming more genuine. "Other scholars have developed an ability to read with incredible speed, or detect books without having to search the shelves. The abilities really are incredibly useful."

"Just not for the purposes of this commission," Adrienne said with growing understanding. From what she had heard, this commission had one objective, and so far the results were not in their favor. "Have people other than scholars been trained?"

"Of course," Franklin said. "We began training healers after we noticed the pattern in the abilities scholars were developing. Healers seemed to be the best choice," Franklin explained, "as they are intelligent and dedicated to their craft, and seemed unlikely to abuse any abilities they might develop."

"We did not want to give power to people who would use it unwisely," Elder Rynn emphasized. The wrinkles lining his dark face served to emphasize his hard expression, and Adrienne began to see why they had a problem with her, a soldier, being brought in.

Soldiers could be dangerous.

Adrienne supposed that choosing the healers for the reasons they had made a sort of sense, but it also seemed to her that the commission had a somewhat naïve view of the world. Adrienne had met her fair share of healers over the years, there was always at least one in Kyrog, and like members of every profession, there were kind healers and cruel ones, gentle and spiteful. If they were so concerned with people who might misuse their powers, the commission would do better to look at individual personalities, not judge groups as a whole.

"Did any of the healers manifest Talents?" Adrienne asked, setting aside the commission's apparent mistrust of everyone different from themselves. She had grown used to that view since leaving Kyrog. Tam had not trusted her, Ilso had hated her. Even the journal had presented a consistent diatribe against anything foreign.

"Oh, yes," the young man Lady Chessing had called Ben said. He leaned forward, his expression animated. "The younger healers, some of them, developed abilities much more in line with the stories you are now familiar with." Adrienne liked his enthusiasm, so different from the other commissioners' staid dispositions. "They are able to heal wounds that should take weeks to heal, even some that would be fatal if given time."

"Some of them can," Elder Rynn said. "Like the scholars, the abilities differ from healer to healer."

"Yes," the young Talented scholar said, looking somewhat embarrassed to have Elder Rynn correct him. "Some of the healers with abilities can heal wounds like I mentioned. Others can mend broken bones in minutes, or break a fever. The medicine some of the healers make also seems more effective, usually in healers who were more along the lines of herbalists."

Lady Chessing sniffed. "Why anyone would choose to see an herbalist now when you could get healed in minutes by a more skilled healer is beyond me. Why settle for second best?"

Adrienne saw the value in better medicines. A Talented healer would doubtless be preferable when one was on hand, but medicine that was more effective would be a useful asset to someone like a soldier, as medicine could be carried with the person, whereas healers were much less portable. But then, some people did not look at the bigger picture.

"True, but it is still a manifested ability," the young commissioner said.

"And a wonderful ability," Adrienne said. "When it comes to battles, the ability to heal would almost be worth more than being able to cast fireballs." Men died from stab wounds or infections that killed slowly as often, or even more often, than they died quickly on the field of battle.

Several of the commissioners shifted uncomfortably. Lady Chessing huffed, as if she did not believe Adrienne's words.

"Although such abilities are remarkable," Elder Rynn said, ignoring Adrienne's comment as though she had never spoken, "they are still not what we need to put an end to this war."

"Have you tried anyone more multipurpose than a scholar or a healer?" Adrienne asked, thinking that perhaps their careful selection process was what was limiting the commission.

"Of course," Lady Chessing snapped, her bosom heaving. "I myself tried to learn, along with just about every young person in this city, provided we found them of suitable temperament." By appearances, Lady Chessing was probably too old by more than a decade to learn, if Ben was any judge, and from the little Adrienne had seen so far she doubted that her temperament was suitable, but she did not voice her thoughts and instead waited to hear the woman out. "It seems that the only individuals that ever develop any abilities are those that are in one stupid profession or other. Scholars, healers, blacksmiths, even a weaver."

Adrienne wondered what Talent would manifest in a weaver, and if Tam's tale about blacksmiths making unbreakable weapons was true in the present, or if that was another Talent that had not yet been reclaimed. However, the list of people able to learn was more important than the particular abilities at the moment. "Not innkeepers or stable boys or merchants?" she asked.

"No," Elder Rynn said, sounding unhappy, as though those results were a puzzle he had been unable to solve. "Though they were all trained as we had trained the others, not one person in the latter professions developed a talent."

Adrienne thought she understood some of the commonality that Elder Rynn was apparently missing. Those who had developed abilities were in a demanding profession where extensive training and practice were necessary. Healers and blacksmiths typically started as apprentices at a rather early age, and although she did not know much about weaving, she figured it was not a skill learned overnight.

Didn't mothers teach their young daughters to weave? That was an apprenticeship of sorts.

She decided not to share her insight at the moment, though, and from the glint in the young scholar's eyes, Adrienne thought he knew or suspected more than he had revealed to the rest of the commission about this particular limitation. "There haven't been any satisfactory Talents?" she asked.

None of the Talents she had heard about so far would be enough to end the war. The Talent for healing came the closest, but it was not the same as an offensive ability.

"Not of a sort that meshes with the old stories," Franklin said, folding his hands over his potbelly. "The stories talk about healing, of course, but we haven't gotten any of the other sort. Not the kinds of abilities that we were expecting. And once an ability manifests in one area, that's it. A healer might be able to mend a bone, stop bleeding, and get rid of an infection, but she can't move anything with her mind, or find a book in the library without looking it up."

"And I can't do more than wrap a bandage and hope for the best," the young scholar added with an easy if self-deprecating humor.

"This is all interesting to me," Adrienne said honestly, "but I am confused as to why I am here. Why go all the way to Kyrog to find someone else to train?"

"I would think even someone like you could figure it out," Lady Chessing said. "If healers manifest talents for healing, shouldn't you develop a way to kill?"

Adrienne barely kept herself from wincing. She had killed many times, the last just a week ago, and she lost no sleep over the necessary death of an enemy, but she was not a killer. She was not malicious, nor did she go out of her way to harm others.

But her realization that those on the commission saw her as little more than a killer was not enough to outweigh the excitement she felt. She was to be trained as one of the Talented. It was what she had been hoping for. Adrienne did not know what sort of Talent she might develop, but it would not be as cold as what Lady Chessing had implied. A Talent that could kill someone would be like skill with a sword—both could kill, but to say they were only for killing was too simple.

"We tried training some of the city guards for this purpose," Franklin said, "but none of them developed an ability."

Adrienne had noticed the city guards when they were entering Kessering and was not surprised to learn that no Talented had emerged from that stock. The one at the gate had barely given her, an armed soldier, a cursory look when she entered the city. Instead, the guard had seemed bored. They were no more trained and disciplined in their profession than innkeepers or merchants. If they had received much more training than how to strap on armor, she would be surprised. "But you're hoping I do get a Talent."

"I admit that most of us were against the idea of using a soldier," Franklin said, "but it seemed the only logical option left to us. King Burin wants something that can help with the war effort."

"We sent out two other parties in search of suitable soldiers," Lady Chessing told Adrienne primly, looking down her pointed nose at the younger woman, "although I have little hope of any soldier manifesting an ability, no matter how many we attempt to train. I doubt any of you have the aptitude for it. Soldiers aren't exactly known for their high levels of intelligence, after all."

Suddenly, Adrienne couldn't take any more. She was tired. Tired of traveling, tired of everyone acting as though she was stupid, tired of the furtive, suspicious glances every commissioner was casting her way. Defending herself would make no difference, so she didn't bother. "I would like a bath and a hot meal before any training begins," she said, no longer caring if she sounded rude. "I would also like to be shown to the place where I am to sleep while in Kessering."

Some of the commissioners looked appalled, and others looked as though they had been expecting such behavior. Only the young scholar seemed unaffected by her abrupt change in behavior. "Of course," he said. "I will show you around."

He stood and stepped around the table, heading out a side door, and Adrienne followed him into a small corridor. "My name is Ben Ruthford, Lieutenant," he said, extending his hand.

Some of Adrienne's tension eased at the small show of respect, and she took the offered hand in her own. His skin was the same shade as hers, a rich tan, and felt soft against her callused palm. Unlike her own hand, it was devoid of any scars and felt fragile despite its greater size. "You may call me Adrienne," she said. As good as "Lieutenant" felt, she thought having a friend here would be even better. Especially a friend on the commission, and one of the Talented as well.

"Thank you," he said. "You probably want some time to rest, given your recent journey, but I'm afraid we can't grant you more than a day or two." They made a couple of turns down twisting hallways and finally exited the large library via a small side door. "We're putting you up in an inn just there," he said, pointing one of those soft hands toward a moderately sized inn across the courtyard. Its sign proudly proclaimed it The Golden Trumpet. "That inn will be most convenient for you and your trainer."

"And who will my trainer be?" Adrienne asked, hoping it was not one of the pompous old commissioners who had not even spoken at the meeting. Franklin might not be such a bad teacher, except for his unfortunate choice in jackets.

"Well, I was hoping to train you myself," Ben said somewhat shyly. "I have had some success with training others in the past," he hastened to add. "We should know within a couple of months whether the training is effective."

Adrienne thought that a couple of months was a long time to wait to see results, but then Jeral had probably thought the same when she had so carefully paced his training. She would have to trust Ben as Jeral had trusted her. Perhaps something like the friendship she had found with Jeral would develop between her and Ben. "That sounds good," she said. "I should be ready to start in a couple of hours."

Ben looked surprised. "Are you sure you don't want a day to acclimate? If you have really read the book, you are ahead of schedule. I don't want you to burn out." His face was earnest and almost painfully innocent, yet he was not one of the scholars who had cringed away from her.

Was he too innocent to see the dangers that the other scholars did, or was he just more open than they were? Adrienne hoped for the later—innocence was too easily shattered and replaced by something harder and far less kind.

"The trip here was not rigorous," Adrienne assured him. "There is no reason not to begin this afternoon. Perhaps we can discuss the journal then."

"Of course," Ben said with the smile all scholars seemed to get in regards to books, especially old ones. "I will meet you in your room in, say, three hours? Will that give you enough time to freshen up?"

"Yes," Adrienne assured him, thinking that three hours would easily accommodate a meal and a bath, and perhaps even a short walk around the city.

The inn was larger than it had appeared from the outside. The common room was already half-filled with patrons, and the small fire cast light without contributing unduly to the heat that was always present in this part of Samaro. Adrienne was still examining her surroundings when the innkeeper approached her.

A clean white apron stretched across the innkeeper's round stomach as he appraised Adrienne from head to toe. His eyes lingered on the sword hanging casually from her hip. "May I help you?" he asked in a voice completely void of the welcoming tone that was typical of innkeepers. Instead, it seemed to suggest that she find another place to stay.

"I am Lieutenant Adrienne Rydaeg," she said, holding her back straight and head high. "The commission has a room for me, I believe."

"The soldier," he said flatly. Adrienne wondered if every citizen of Samaro had such an aversion to soldiers, and she had been spared the discrimination in other cities because she had always been part of a larger group. She didn't think so.

Although people in other places had occasionally been wary, Kessering seemed unique in its pronounced dislike of people in her profession. The men and women who kept inns and taverns were usually glad when soldiers were present, but this man was looking at her as though she was something particularly nasty stuck to the bottom of his shoe.

"Yes, I am a soldier. Do you have a room for me?" Her gaze dared him to contradict the commission and say no.

The innkeeper gave a brusque nod. "In the back."

Adrienne had slept in far worse places than a small back room in an obviously prosperous inn, and being given an unnecessarily shabby room was almost amusing in its pettiness. "Has my horse been delivered here? And my belongings?"

"Your things are in your room," the innkeeper informed her, "and the horse is in the stables." He wiped his hands on his pristine apron. "Is there anything else I can do for you?" he asked impatiently.

"Yes," Adrienne said, keeping her temper on a short leash. "I am going to see for myself that my horse is being properly cared for, and then I would like a bath—a hot one—and a meal. A real meal, mind, with meat and bread, not just a bowl of stew."

The innkeeper looked like he was going to choke, but whatever he wanted to say to her he managed to hold back, even going so far as to force a tight smile. Adrienne thought that the scholars must do business with the inn often for him to make even that small effort.

"I will see to your bath, and the rest," he said at length.

Adrienne nodded before turning on her heel and heading to the stables. Although her nose told her that the stalls were well-maintained overall, her fears for Strider's welfare were confirmed when she saw that, despite the fact that the stable was only half full, the stallion had been placed in a small corner stall with poor ventilation.

"I would like to speak to whoever is charged with the horses' care," she proclaimed loudly, knowing that someone was likely within hearing range.

Moments later a dark, dirty face peaked down at her from the hayloft. "Can I help you?" he asked. He spied her sword and his eyes widened, but a smile split his face, a far cry from the fearful look Adrienne was growing to expect. "Hey, are you a soldier?" He seemed excited by the prospect.

"I am," Adrienne said. "Can you come down here?"

"Sure," the boy said amiably. He crawled nimbly down the ladder to stand before Adrienne. He was thin despite the childish roundness of his cheeks, and Adrienne judged him to be in his early teens, the age where boys seemed to stretch and grow into strange, gangly creatures.

"You care for the horses?" she asked.

"For two years now," he said with obvious pride. "How long have you been a soldier?"

Adrienne smiled in amusement at the rapidly fired question. "Seventeen years. Why is that horse in the corner?" she asked, pointing to Strider.

"Master Inbaum told me to put him there. Said he's a vicious beast and to keep clear of him." The boy shrugged his thin shoulders. "Don't seem vicious. But how come you don't look old? Seventeen years is a long time." he said, eyeing her critically.

"I'm not old, and seventeen years isn't so long," she said, though it occurred to her that for a boy who hadn't yet seen his seventeenth year, seventeen must be an eternity. "That's my horse in the corner," she said, "and I want him moved to a better stall."

The boy whistled. "He's about the finest horse I ever saw. Guess I was right 'bout him not being vicious, then?"

Adrienne had seen Strider wreck a face with his hooves, but at present he was dozing on three legs as peaceful as any pleasure pony. "Not unless I want him to be."

The boy bobbed his head. "He needs a good brushing-down," he said. "Master Inbaum told me not to bother, before, on account of he was dangerous and all."

Adrienne removed a silver penny from her purse and flipped it to the boy. "I'm asking you to take special care of him," she said, looking into dark eyes that were surprisingly pretty for a boy's, fringed as they were by long dark lashes. "If there are any problems, I want you to tell me straight away. Come to me yourself; don't send a message, understand?" Adrienne wouldn't put it past Master Inbaum to "forget" a message for her, or have one of his other employees do the same.

"Got it," the boy said, pocketing the coin.

"I'm Lieutenant Rydaeg," Adrienne said, offering the boy her hand. He took it with the same pleasure as he had taken the silver penny.

"My name's Thom," he said with a wide, goofy smile. "Hey, maybe if I do a good job, you'll let me ride your horse?"

"Not a chance," Adrienne told him easily.

"Will you let me see your sword?"

"Maybe."

He seemed happy enough with that, and went about relocating Strider to a more suitable stall. Satisfied with the transaction, Adrienne left the stable in a brighter mood than she had entered. A young boy was not much of an ally, but he was better than nothing.

Since Adrienne did not trust any of the suspicious-looking girls in Inbaum's employ to clean her *swa'il* without ruining it, she set to work cleaning it herself and removing what stains she could after bathing and putting on a reasonably dirt-free outfit. She stopped only to eat the meal that was delivered to her room. The pieces of chicken had been overcooked so that what parts of it were not fat were brutally dry, but the crusty bread was good and a nice change from trail fare. She ate the bread in lieu of chicken and was reasonably satisfied.

When Ben came calling, Adrienne was glad to leave the confines of the cramped room and explore Kessering some more.

"I hope your accommodations agree with you," Ben said with no trace of guile.

Adrienne thought about the small room and dry chicken, and the lukewarm bathwater delivered by a scowling maid. "I'm sure they'll do," she replied, not wanting Ben to feel badly. It was clear he did not know or suspect how Master Inbaum was treating her.

"I don't know quite where to start," Ben admitted. "Typically I start by giving my students Asmov's journal to read, but you have already read it."

"So his name was Asmov," Adrienne said, a bit disappointed to learn Pele's real name. The memory she had of the disagreeable Pele had fit the author so perfectly that it seemed wrong to think of the author as anyone else.

"Yes. Asmov Petrovicz. I'm a bit concerned about how much of the book you understood. Usually I guide whomever I am training through the text, so that I know if they have any problems with it."

"It was a bit dense, but I believe I understand as much about developing abilities as I can from one journal not dedicated to the topic," Adrienne said. "I understand more after today, of course."

"What do you mean?"

"What I heard today helped me connect some of the dots," Adrienne said. "Age, professions, it makes sense to me now. And why I am here, of course."

"Explain," Ben asked, looking surprised. It was clear that most on the commission thought of soldiers as brutes, capable only of killing. To think that one could learn and reason as well as a scholar was probably unfathomable to most.

"The age 'limitation' is no real surprise," Adrienne said. "As I told the rest of the commission, many skills are best learned young. As for my being here, there has to be a good reason behind it. It's no secret that no one in Kessering has a fondness for soldiers."

Ben kicked a pebble with his soft leather shoe. "You noticed that?"

"It would have been hard not to," Adrienne said.

Ben turned to face her more directly. "It is hard for people who rely on intellect to entrust someone who operates and lives with such a violent lifestyle."

Adrienne had to laugh at such a ridiculous comment. "Perhaps that excuse works for scholars, but not for everyone else.

"What do you mean?"

"This isn't the first city I've been to," she told him. "Some people might be nervous around soldiers, but that's not what's happening here."

"There was an…incident," Ben admitted. "A long time ago," he rushed to add. "No one living now was alive then, but the memory survives in the stories we're told."

"What stories?"

"There was a garrison near here once. A private one, not one that reports to the king."

Adrienne knew that most of the garrisons and soldiering camps reported to the king in some way or another, but she didn't contradict him. "Of course."

"Well, the garrison asked for money. A lot of it."

Adrienne thought back to the conversation she and Jeral had had with Lord Neecham not long before. "I've heard of such things."

"Well, finally the people of Kessering were tired of paying. They told the garrison that if they wouldn't protect them without fee, they weren't needed."

"So they left?"

"Yes. And a week after they did, the city was attacked."

"That's unfortunate, and it was wrong that the garrison was charging high prices for protection, but you can hardly place the blame for the attack on the soldiers that left."

"You can if some of the attackers were soldiers."

Adrienne shook her head. "What?"

"Stories say that some of the attackers were recognized as soldiers that had been stationed at the garrison, and that they attacked to teach the city a lesson." Ben cast her an apologetic look. "I don't know how much of it is true, but it's what we're taught."

Adrienne felt a sliver of sympathy slide into her, but it did not dispel the anger. "It's horrible what your people went through," she said, "But you can't continue to make such generalizations about soldiers. The commission brought me here because you needed me, yet the lot of you dismissed me as a violent brute before you ever saw me. I am a tactician, and I can read and speak Old Samaroan as well as any scholar."

"We had no way of knowing that about you before meeting you," Ben said. "And I don't believe you to be a stupid. In fact, it's vital that you aren't."

"Why?"

"So you didn't figure out everything after today." He smiled. "You already know that everyone who was able to develop an ability was part of a difficult professions. Now tell me what those professions have in common."

"Discipline."

"And?"

Adrienne hesitated. "It takes continuous effort to improve?"

"Study, yes. And?"

Adrienne thought about it and finally had to admit defeat. "I don't know."

"Intelligence. There are no stupid healers, or scholars. Blacksmiths need to know when and where to strike the metal to get the desired result, and how to quench the metal afterwards. Weavers need to know how to dye wool for the most vibrant colors, and how to work the yarn without weakening it."

"I suppose."

"The training and intelligence needed in these professions is unique. You cannot train yourself to be a healer; you have to learn. And we have discovered that you cannot train yourself to develop these abilities, either."

"You did."

Ben looked embarrassed. "It took a long time, and I wasn't truly teaching myself. I read the journals, developed theories, worked with the other scholars and commissioners. And it was still a miracle that I was able to develop an ability at all."

"Sometimes miracles and luck are enough."

"Paired with dedication. And now that you know more about what it takes to develop one of these abilities, do you think I will I be able to train you?" He looked concerned, and as if he did not realize that his questions could be taken as insults. "It hasn't worked on any of the guards we've attempted to train."

Adrienne barely resisted the urge to show him just how different her skills were from those of the insipid guards she'd seen on the gate. "I've a bit more dedication and training than the guards."

"Very good then. Since you seem to have a good idea of the apparent requirements of developing an ability, maybe it is best to begin the next stage of your training," Ben said. They were nearing the southern end of Kessering, where beyond the city walls civilization gave way once more to grassland.

"How do we begin?" Adrienne asked, willing for the moment to set aside trying to convince Ben that soldiers did not by nature lack intelligence.

"One of the most essential steps in your training will be the ability to enter into a state of Oneness."

"Oneness?" Adrienne asked.

Ben blushed. "That is what I call it. Some of the others with abilities have taken to calling it that as well, although the commission doesn't like us naming things. When you achieve that state, you feel like you are one with everything. The trees, the grass, the sun. Everything just feels…"

"Connected?" Adrienne asked.

"Exactly," Ben said. "How did you know?"

Adrienne nearly rolled her eyes, a habit she had broken years ago but felt coming back now. "Asmov wrote about people with special abilities being connected to the universe. I had wondered what he meant, until you started talking about Oneness. Is it the same thing?"

Ben nodded. "I remember that, of course." He tapped a finger against his temple and laughed. "There was a lot of argument about what Asmov meant there. Some of the commissioners thought that those people must be essentially different than the rest of us; that the connection to the universe couldn't be taught and must have been lost forever over the years. We almost didn't try, but there were some, myself included, that thought perhaps that connection was not inborn but could be learned."

"And it can be," Adrienne said. "You learned." Although his ability was hardly one that Adrienne had thought about, she realized now that Ben truly was one of the Talented. They no longer existed only in her mind and in the pages of an old book. "Tell me more about this Oneness."

"After reading Asmov's journal, Oneness is really the first step in your training. You—"

"Wait, explain this to me first. Why did I have to read Asmov's journal."

Ben seemed surprised by the question. "Because that was the beginning of everything."

"I don't understand. It's hardly about Talents at all."

"But it's the first one we found that talked about them. Without Asmov's journal, we wouldn't know anything about people with abilities, or Oneness, or any of that."

"Even so, the people you're training don't need to know it. You could tell them everything they need to know and more. You know more than Asmov ever wrote about." It was clear from Ben's expression that it had never occurred to him that the people he was training didn't have to read the book. "You're a scholar," she said, "you want to know the history of it all. But it isn't necessary, not for everyone."

Ben looked unconvinced, and she decided to save that discussion for a different day. "Tell me about Oneness."

"You have to focus," Ben said, clearly grateful for the more comfortable topic. "You have to learn to block everything else from your mind until it is just you and nature and nothingness, no intruding thoughts or feelings." Ben's voice took on a smooth, lecturing quality as he spoke. His shoulders were no longer hunched, his voice no longer hesitant. It was amazing how much more confident he seemed in that moment. "It is just you and nature, and eventually you will realize that you are not a separate being; you are one with everything around you."

His eyes had a distant look, as if they were seeing something that was not really there. Adrienne wondered if he was experiencing Oneness at that moment. Surely something had caused such a change.

She pursed her lips in thought. "How do I do all that?" she asked. It seemed like a lot of things to do while trying not to think about anything.

Ben smiled apologetically, his eyes focusing on Adrienne, and he seemed once again to grow smaller; whatever change had occurred slipping away. "I tend to get carried away. You start by just clearing your mind. Most people find that it helps to sit out here, away from the distractions in the city. Try sitting down with your eyes closed."

Adrienne gave a little laugh and went to sit under the lone *pago* tree a hundred feet away. "Just sit here with my eyes closed?" she called. It seemed ridiculous, and a waste of time. Surely there were other means of training.

The thought made her think of Jeral, and the doubts he had voiced about her training methods at the beginning, especially the meditative moves she had made him learn and practice every morning. The young soldier had seen no purpose in them, but he had been wrong, and Adrienne thought she might be unfairly judging Ben as well.

The young Talented scholar had trained others; surely he knew what he was doing.

"Yes. Try to clear your mind," Ben reminded her. "I can join you, or I can leave if you'd rather be alone."

"Since I doubt I'll achieve Oneness in the hour or so before dark, you might as well go," Adrienne said. She'd feel awkward enough without Ben sitting there, waiting to see what happened. If this required concentration, she thought she'd have a better chance of succeeding if Ben was not there watching her.

"I'll see you tomorrow morning then," Ben said cheerily. "Good luck."

Ben left, and Adrienne concentrated on not thinking.

"I can't do it," Adrienne told Ben. She had been working on clearing her mind and achieving Oneness for over a week, and the closest she had come was falling asleep under the thick branches of the *pago* tree. Her mind had been clear then, but there had been no connection to the universe involved.

"You have to give it time," Ben told her. "It takes some people months to reach Oneness for the first time. You've only been at it for nine days."

Adrienne resumed her pacing. They were in Ben's room at the library. The room was much larger than Adrienne's room at the inn, but filled as it was with a desk, overflowing bookshelves, and more books scattered on chairs and stacked on the floor, it seemed much more cramped than her own small room. "I'm not making any progress," she told Ben, her voice sounding perilously close to a whine. "Every time I try, I think more and more." The task of clearing her mind hadn't seemed so hard when Ben had first explained it. How hard could not thinking be?

It turned out to be much harder than Adrienne had anticipated. She would have understood if her progress had been slow—training in various disciplines over the years had taught her that, despite her natural aptitudes, not everything came easily to her. Still, there had always been some sign of progress, no matter how small, to encourage her to train more, study harder. "I don't think it's going to work," she said. "I sit there and my mind runs through different scenarios and my body gets all twitchy." She exhaled hard through her nose. "It's not calming."

Ben was quiet, but his expression was one that Adrienne was familiar with. He wore it when he was thinking hard about something. She hoped whatever thought he was having would be helpful.

At length, Ben turned to her, eyeing her athletic body covered in functional leathers and the sword at her hip. "Maybe all of your training makes it hard for you to just sit with your eyes closed," he said. "You're always looking for signs of trouble, even when you're somewhere safe."

Adrienne stopped her unconscious scan of the room and looked at Ben. She had not even realized she had been checking the room for signs of danger. Doing so was as instinctual as breathing. "So what do I do?" She refused to think that this first setback would keep her forever from reaching her goal. She had never given up before, and she was not about to start now, when supernatural abilities were within her reach.

"Is there anything you do that does clear your mind?" Ben asked. "Maybe sitting is the problem. You never do it."

Since Adrienne was standing now, and typically chose to stand or lean against the wall when she and Ben were talking, she knew he had a point. Adrienne thought about the calm state that settled over her before a fight, that moment when everything ceased to exist but her and her opponent. Time, in that moment, ceased to have meaning. But she knew that was not what Ben meant. Although her mind was calm, void of any emotions or distractions that could interfere with her ability to fight, it was not empty. In that timeless moment before a fight, Adrienne's mind was filled with clear, precise thoughts. It was not Oneness as Ben described it. When she was in that timeless moment before a fight, she was not connected with the universe. She was connected only with her own body and that of her opponent.

She was about to tell Ben no when she remembered the smooth, controlled moves of her morning routine. On the surface, it was the complete opposite of sitting in a field with her eyes closed—every part of her was active as she went through the meditative motions she had learned from Karse in childhood. But when she focused on her breathing, on her balance and the smooth transition from pose to pose, her mind was silent. Despite her eyes being closed, she was always aware of herself and the small changes and steady permanence of her surroundings. "Yes," she told him.

"Yes?" Ben asked, surprise coloring his voice. "You already know how to clear your mind and never mentioned it?" He didn't sound entirely happy, and looked a bit suspicious, as though Adrienne had been purposely keeping a secret from him.

"I do it differently than you describe," Adrienne said in her defense. "I didn't connect the two until just now."

"Then maybe it isn't the same," Ben said, looking much less excited than he had moments ago, but also more relaxed. Ben had always been polite, and at times Adrienne thought they were just on the verge of friendship, but she knew he was ever aware of the sword at her hip. Even without it, Adrienne doubted the Talented scholar would ever forget that she was a soldier. Despite her initial hopes, she didn't foresee a bond like the one she and Jeral had shared forming between her and Ben.

It saddened her that Ben would not trust what she said, but Adrienne had no doubts. She knew now that the Oneness that had eluded her for days was something she had been doing unconsciously for half her life. "I can show you now, if you'd like."

Ben looked around his cluttered room, with precariously balanced stacks of books, loose pages of parchment, abandoned quills and empty inkwells. It was not the most soothing of atmospheres to practice clearing the mind, at least not for the first time. "Here?"

Adrienne shrugged. "Here is fine." She studied the space around her, judging how far she could move in any one direction before she would bump into a chair, the wall, or one of the many stacks of books. Then she closed her eyes.

Her breaths came slowly in and out through her nose. She inhaled as she raised her arms, exhaled as she lowered them and bent at the waist, and then her mind was clear, her thoughts of why she was doing this gone as she moved automatically, adjusting her moves to fit the smaller space without conscious thought, never deviating from the smooth, fluid transitions.

As she began to bend and raise an arm over her head, some instinct told her to change the motion, and she did. More obstacles appeared, felt instead of seen, and her body adapted, twisting and turning but never breaking from the essence of the routine. Adrienne's eyes remained closed through it all.

"That was amazing!" Ben said when Adrienne finally stopped and opened her eyes. "I've never seen anything like it."

Adrienne shifted uncomfortably. She was more used to apathy than admiration when someone saw her run through her routine. "Thank you," she said uneasily. Although she had taught her meditative routine to Jeral and the other Yearlings, it was not widely accepted amongst the soldiering community. Even Ricco had occasionally teased her about the strange habit, and it was unlikely he had kept that part of the program going after she had left Kyrog.

Ben still looked amazed by what she had done. "I kept putting things in your way: my arms, books, rolls of parchment. You just moved around them like you could see them there, but your eyes were closed the whole time. Weren't they?" He seemed suspicious again.

"They were closed. I could sense that something was in the way," Adrienne said. "Not consciously, and I couldn't say what it was, but my body knew and avoided it."

"That's really fantastic," Ben said. "It took me nearly five months to gain that much awareness of my surroundings, and that was after having been able to clear my mind for a month." His excitement was back, and his smile was full of pride for his student.

"I started learning those moves when I was four," Adrienne told him, a small smile capturing her lips as she remembered those days. "An old soldier took me under his wing for a couple of years, and he taught me. He was the one who taught me Old Samaroan as well."

"A soldier taught you all of that?"

Adrienne didn't appreciate the obvious surprise in Ben's voice. She wished there was at least one person in the city who didn't consider soldiers dumb brutes. "I'm a soldier," she reminded him.

"Yes, I know, but you seem…different."

"Different than what?" Adrienne asked, her temper spiking. "Different than all the other soldiers you have met and gotten to know?" Ben wisely said nothing. "How many other soldiers have you spoken to? Seen? Have you ever looked past their weapons and seen them as people?"

Ben's face took on a belligerent look. "I've heard stories. I read a lot about soldiers before you arrived so that I would be prepared."

"You heard the same stories you heard as a child," she said. "You read books that confirmed that bias."

"I didn't."

"So the library here contains a lot of books that supports soldiers? I—" Adrienne clenched her jaw. She didn't speak until she was sure she could control the anger in her voice. "I started training to be a soldier when I was four. I have no family, no friends, except other soldiers. I've never been anything but a soldier," she said, every word a staccato note. "If you don't see me as a soldier, then your view of soldiers is wrong, because I am more a soldier than anything or anyone else."

Adrienne left him standing alone in his room, stunned.

CHAPTER SEVEN

Despite the argument with Ben, Adrienne followed his advice and began entering her morning routines with more purpose than simply balancing her mind and body. The meditation was no longer just for her peace of mind and to keep her body limber, it was the first step in a search for something deeper, a conscious connection to her surroundings. Sometimes it was as simple as closing her eyes; other days she could try for hours without being able to sense anything about her surroundings that she had not seen when her eyes were open. It was frustrating, and she wanted to move on to whatever came after Oneness.

"This training is less exciting than I thought it would be," Adrienne told Strider as she combed out the warhorse's mane. She had taken him out for the first time in days, and she had decided to groom him herself rather than hand him off to Thom. It felt good to do something so easy and uncomplicated, where there were no expectations except the occasional scratching behind Strider's ears. "I just do the same thing day after day," she told the muscular destrier. He might not be able to understand her, but directing her words at the horse made her feel more stable than simply talking to herself.

Strider turned and blew warm air in her face, making her laugh and relieving some of her tension.

"That's a nice sound," a female voice said, and Adrienne turned to see a young, round-cheeked woman standing in the stable doorway.

"May I help you?" Adrienne asked, wondering who the strange woman was and what she was doing there. It was possible that she was one of the inn's patrons, but Adrienne did not think so. Most of the people staying at the inn left the care of their horses to the stableboy, and none of them talked to her.

"You're good to that horse," the woman said, ignoring Adrienne's question. "I didn't expect that."

"Who are you?" Adrienne asked suspiciously.

"Maureen Cassin. A healer. Why are you good to the horse?"

Adrienne took in Maureen's age and the self-assured way she held herself and determined that she was not just any healer. She was Talented. "A horse that is treated well will respond because it wants to please its rider. A horse that knows only the whip will obey out of fear, but he will not put his heart into it, or want what his rider wants."

"So you have found that you get better results with kindness," Maureen said.

"Yes," Adrienne replied, growing impatient with the banal conversation. "Are you planning to tell me that you are not a normal healer, or is that supposed to be a secret?"

"There are not many 'normal' healers left in Kessering," Maureen said, showing no sign that she was disturbed by the change of topic. "You don't mention that you are a soldier, but then, that is obvious." She made a point of studying Adrienne's sword, which hung ever-ready at her hip.

Since arriving in Kessering, Adrienne's sword had either been studiously ignored or watched as though it was a cobra poised to strike. Maureen's study of the sword was different. There was no fear in her gaze, just the calm, steady look of a woman who was not easily unsettled.

"It is also obvious that you did not come here to ask me about my horse," Adrienne said. She appreciated the self-assured nature of the woman, but there was something...uncomfortable about the way the woman was questioning her.

"You're smart," Maureen said approvingly. "I said you must be, to have lasted a month, but not everyone agreed."

Adrienne wanted to ask who 'everyone' was and what right any of them had to judge her, but she had learned from Captain Garrett that staying quiet could often gain more answers than speaking up. As a lieutenant she had practiced that, and found that few people could stand sustained silence for long before they tried to fill it themselves.

Maureen was no exception. "The others with abilities are curious about you, but some of them are nervous."

"Because I'm a soldier," Adrienne said. She accepted the prejudice now—accepted that the crowd would tense when she walked through the market and the common room of the inn grow quiet if she decided to eat there.

"We are not used to soldiers here," Maureen said without apology. "This is a peaceful city. However, if you do develop an ability, it is inevitable that you will associate with others of us with abilities. Therefore, I decided to come and meet you now."

Adrienne studied the woman more carefully. She could detect the nerves now, though they were still kept tightly under control, and she was impressed. Maureen was afraid, but she had come today in spite of her fear. "I am Lieutenant Adrienne Rydaeg," she said, extending her hand.

Maureen took the proffered hand and shook it. Her grip was firm and the underlying strength apparent. This was a woman who was used to using her hands and body. "Perhaps when you are done here, you would like to see what the rest of us do?"

Adrienne nodded and called the stableboy over to finish grooming Strider. Thom was delighted as always to handle the big stallion and waved the two women off happily, assuring Adrienne that the horse would be well taken care of.

"That boy seems to like you," Maureen commented as they left the stables and began heading down a street in the opposite direction of the library. Adrienne had rarely ventured that way before.

"Thom is good with horses," Adrienne told Maureen, "and he doesn't have the same problem with soldiers that many in Kessering do. It's nice to spend time with someone who doesn't think I'm a monster." She pursed her lips, displeased that she had said so much. Maureen was an unknown entity, one that Adrienne was not yet sure she could trust.

"Maybe if you didn't insist on wearing your sword around, people would be more comfortable around you," Maureen said in a stern, disapproving tone that Adrienne was sure worked well with her patients.

Adrienne took exception to the tone. She was neither Maureen's patient nor doing something wrong or foolish. "Maybe if I wore silk dresses and walked like a lady, mothers would stop dragging their children out of my path and men would stop treating me as though I lacked intelligence. I am what I am, no matter what I wear."

"Then surely putting your sword away wouldn't change that," Maureen pointed out. "Kessering is not a dangerous place; it isn't necessary to be armed here."

Maureen's disapproval and naiveté helped Adrienne distance herself from the woman and regard her with more objectivity. Maureen might believe that there was no reason to be armed in Kessering, but Adrienne disagreed. For one, she knew how easy it was for a potentially dangerous person to enter Kessering. She had done so herself barely a month ago with no questions asked. And she knew that people could be stupid, and that her presence had frightened and angered a lot of people. Going without her sword now might cause some to view it as an opportunity to show her that they weren't afraid. She wasn't worried that she would be hurt, but rather that she would be forced to hurt someone else in self-defense. "I will take that under advisement."

Maureen gave a half-laugh. "No, you won't. Keep the sword if that is what you wish, but do not be upset with people's reactions to you when you do nothing to counter them. You are the visitor here; if change needs to be made, it is you who should make it." She made a gesture that seemed to suggest she didn't care one way or the other. "The healer I'm taking you to meet will probably be so absorbed in what she is doing that she wouldn't notice if you walked in wearing full armor. Or naked."

They came to the door of a small building with herbs hanging in the window to denote that it was a healer's shop, and Maureen ushered Adrienne in before entering herself. "Louella? It's Maureen," she called, glancing around the empty front room.

"Back here!"

The voice was low and throaty, which was even more shocking when Adrienne caught sight of Louella. The woman was a few years older than Maureen, in her late twenties, with light skin, golden hair, and sky blue eyes, so rare in this part of Samaro that Adrienne was not sure the last time she had seen the delicate combination. Lieutenant Nissen had pale skin, but his skin was not as pale as this woman's creamy complexion. The woman was also small—nearly as short as Adrienne, and very slender. With the exception of her height, she was the picture of Almet.

"I've just made the most amazing discovery," Louella said in that earthy voice, and she held up a bowl of liquid that, although it looked like it might be wine, Adrienne recognized immediately as blood.

"Did you now?" Maureen asked in a patronizing voice, turning her nose up at the bowl. "I will have to hear about it later. Louella, this is Adrienne Rydaeg, the new trainee."

"The soldier," Louella said, inspecting Adrienne as she might inspect a patient, looking her up and down in a way that was clearly and unapologetically assessing, and no doubt very like the way Adrienne was looking at her. "You must have quite a bit of experience with blood." She didn't seem at all suspicious or accusatory, but more as though she was sizing Adrienne up for something.

Adrienne's lips twitched. "You could say that."

"Did you know blood is made up of many different parts?" Louella asked curiously.

Maureen made a disapproving sound. "Can't this wait?" she asked. "Blood is a rather distressing topic to discuss when you have company."

"The blood will congeal if I leave it sitting," Louella muttered, bending back to her work. "It can't wait."

"I didn't know it was made of parts," Adrienne said, ignoring Maureen and returning to Louella's question. She was as interested in Louella as she was in the topic, and too experienced with blood to be distressed discussing it. "Blood mostly seems the same to me." Adrienne knew of a couple different kinds of blood: the slow seep of a cut, the spurt of a severed artery, the sick smell of blood from a gut wound, but for the most part it all looked alike. "What are the parts like?"

Louella frowned. "I don't know what they do yet," she admitted, staring into the bowl as if it held the answers. "This is pig's blood, fresh from the butcher just an hour past. I can feel the particles, like being able to pick out ingredients in cake batter, but without the pig I can't tell what they do."

"If they do anything," Maureen said. "Honestly, Louella, what does it matter if blood has parts? We can heal cuts now, can't we?"

Louella looked hurt by Maureen's reaction, those big blue eyes clouding. "Well, yes, but what if the different types of particles do something? Knowing about them could make our healing better, more efficient. Besides, don't you want to *know*?"

Maureen threw up her hands, but Adrienne moved closer to the small, blonde woman. "Could you test what the particles do with human blood?" Adrienne asked.

"I think so, but the person would have to be bleeding sufficiently and willing to wait while I—"

Without ceremony, Adrienne pulled up her sleeve, took her dagger, and cut a long, shallow line across the inside of her arm. "Will this do?"

Louella looked momentarily surprised, but she didn't waste any time before beginning the study of Adrienne's living blood. Maureen stared at Adrienne, her expression a mix of disgust and horror.

"Why did you do that?" Maureen asked, aghast, as though Adrienne had just committed a horrible crime.

"She needed someone to study," Adrienne said. The stinging pain from the cut was easy to ignore, and she thought the subtle tingling sensation must be Louella watching—or maybe feeling—what the particles in her blood did. Although Adrienne saw no more than a seeping wound, she was sure that it was more than that to Louella.

"This is a place of healing," Maureen said. "This is not a place to harm yourself. And to what purpose? She probably won't find anything of interest," Maureen said. "The butcher probably got dirt in the blood, and those are the 'particles' she sensed. She spends more time experimenting than healing these days. It's shameful."

Adrienne did not like the derisive tone in Maureen's voice, nor the look in her eyes that betrayed her disgust. "I've seen a lot of men bleed to death," Adrienne said. "Good men that deserved to live. If Louella can learn something useful, I want to help. If she discovers nothing, then she can heal me when she has satisfied her curiosity, and no one is the worse for it."

"Fascinating," Louella said, sitting back slightly from Adrienne's arm, where blood was still flowing slowly from the wound.

"What did you find?" Adrienne asked.

"I'll need more opportunities to study," Louella said, "but it seems that some of the particles—there are different kinds if you remember—help the blood to clot."

"You mean they stop the bleeding?"

Louella nodded. "Yes. I wonder…" The tingling amplified and Adrienne watched the long cut scab over. "I pulled those particles together and sped everything up." She smiled, pleased with herself as she studied the scab.

"Why don't you just finish healing it?" Maureen asked. "She can make it look like there was never a cut at all," the woman told Adrienne. "She doesn't need to leave a scab."

Adrienne couldn't decide if Maureen was more disgusted with her or Louella at the moment. She had probably expected Adrienne to be a barbarian, but a fellow Talented healer was probably held to a higher standard.

"I will finish it," Louella told Maureen. "I just wanted to see if it worked, if this is what scabs are made of. They are, for the most part," she said as the tingling resumed and the cut disappeared, leaving smooth, unblemished skin in its wake.

"That was amazing," Adrienne said, ignoring Maureen's displeasure.

"Thank you for allowing that," Louella said. "Now I know what one type of particle does." She looked immensely pleased by the discovery.

"How many kinds of particles are there?" Adrienne asked.

"Many. I haven't been able to get an accurate count of them.

"Louella, is there any way for you to, I don't know, boost these clotting particles? You know, some kind of…preventative thing, so that if there isn't a healer around the bleeding will stop faster." Adrienne could imagine how useful something of that nature would be in a fight. Blood loss, even if it was not enough to be life-threatening in and of itself, could severely weaken a soldier and make her more vulnerable.

"Maybe," Louella said. "I would have to do more research. There are herbs that promote clotting…" She trailed off in thought for a moment before looking up and grinning at Adrienne. "You make a good study."

Adrienne smiled back at her. "Maybe I can help you again," Adrienne said. "Right now, I would like to meet more people with Talents, and I believe Maureen would like to get some distance from me."

The woman in question made a sound that was not too difficult to decipher, but said nothing, pretending she could not hear them.

"Maureen was one of the first healers to develop an ability," Louella said, ignoring the other healer and focusing her attention on Adrienne. "She's good, and quite versatile when it comes to what she can heal, but I think she sometimes forgets that we were all using poultices and needles not so long ago. She isn't interested in learning more about what we do, as long as we can do it."

Maureen sniffed and left the room, closing the door loudly behind her.

Adrienne watched Maureen's retreating form until the woman had closed the door behind her. "Shall we go?" Adrienne asked, thinking that even if Maureen had still been willing to show her around, she would rather Louella do it. The blonde seemed more real. More genuine.

"Who do you want to see?" Louella asked. "There are more healers…" Louella regarded Adrienne more closely. "No, you would probably like to meet Pieter, one of the blacksmiths."

Adrienne had been hoping to meet a Talented blacksmith since she had first learned of them. From the way the people in Kessering acted toward soldiers, she was pretty sure she would not find a Talented swordsmith here, but a properly balanced dagger, one made with whatever ability the smith could channel into it, would be nice. "Yes, I would like that."

The blacksmith's shop that Louella led Adrienne to was located on the outskirts of the city. The heat and noise made it an undesirable neighbor for many of the other shops, but to Adrienne the familiar sounds were soothing. Smiths and farriers were plentiful in camps like Kyrog.

She picked up her pace until she was standing in the door of the shop, watching the familiar sight of a big, heavily muscled man shaping iron while a boy worked the bellows.

The blacksmith thrust the tool he was working back into the red-hot embers and turned to the door, wiping the sweat from his forehead on the back of his arm. "Louella," he greeted in a booming voice, a smile spreading across his face

"Pieter," Louella's voice seemed even huskier, and Adrienne looked at the woman, wondering about the change. Louella's expression was the same, however, and Adrienne thought she must have imagined it. She directed her attention back to the man. Pieter, Louella had said.

"Can I help you?" he asked, casting an experienced eye into the fire at the half-forged tool. Apparently it had not reached the right temperature yet, because he left the heating metal where it was and returned his attention to his visitors.

"Pieter, this is Adrienne Rydaeg," Louella said.

"The soldier?" Pieter's smile widened. "I wondered if I would see you here. Wondered too when they would think to train a soldier at all." He chuckled, and it reverberated in his broad chest like distant thunder. "It took them long enough."

"Pieter," Louella scolded, "it must not have been an easy decision for the commission to make."

"Why? They are training people to ultimately fight Almet. They should have started with soldiers, not turned to them as a last resort."

Since Adrienne agreed, she felt herself warming to the burly blacksmith. "They think soldiers are too dangerous," Adrienne told Pieter. "Not to be trusted with a Talent unless there is no other choice."

"Dangerous isn't a good reason," Pieter said. "I'm strong enough to crack heads, snap necks, whatever you like, and any healer worth her salt would know enough about herbs to poison as well as cure." He looked at Louella. The small woman with her golden cloud of hair and light skin was a perfect contrast to the large, dark blacksmith. And her look of consternation was impressive on such a delicate face.

"I wouldn't do that," Louella squawked, fisting her hands on her hips as if preparing for a fight.

"And I wouldn't snap someone's neck," Pieter said. "But I could. Everyone is dangerous." He turned his back to them and grabbed a pair of tongs. "Besides, they made no allowance for bravery or a willingness to fight. But that is a different complaint, and I need to finish this, but if you can wait awhile I would like to speak with you."

Louella and Adrienne left to wait outside the blacksmith forge. It was only comparably cooler, but they could talk without shouting over the clang of metal or worrying about sparks flying. "Pieter doesn't like scholars," Louella confided. "He doesn't like the commission at all, I'm afraid."

"I picked up on that."

"He disapproves of their selection process, mostly. Blacksmiths were one of the last groups they tried." Louella shook her head. "I reckon they thought smithing took more brawn than brain, but Pieter has plenty of both."

"He doesn't seem to have a problem with soldiers," Adrienne commented.

"Pieter's father was a blacksmith in one of the soldiering camps to the north," Louella told her. "And I don't have a problem with soldiers either, at least not universally. I began my apprenticeship as a healer when I was twelve. I've helped all sorts of people in all sorts of professions. There are good people and bad people making up the world, and I don't think any job has more of one kind than the other."

"Even healing?" Adrienne asked. It was one thing to hold that opinion of people in other professions, but much harder to look into your own profession and see that unsettling truth.

Louella smiled weakly. "My heart wants to say no, but my head knows better. People become healers for all sorts of reasons, not just because they want to help people and ease their pain."

"The same with soldiers," Adrienne said. "Not everyone joins to serve and protect, and others want nothing more than to do just that."

"May I ask how your training is coming along?" Louella asked, her blue eyes gently probing as she changed the subject. She seemed very different from the intense, almost demanding woman who had been studying a bowl of pig's blood not an hour before. More personable, and much more kind. "Ben is training you, correct?"

"Yes. My training is progressing slowly," Adrienne told her with a weighty sigh. "I can achieve Oneness, but I have trouble consistently reaching the level of awareness of my surroundings that Ben says is necessary."

"You've reached Oneness already?" Louella asked, her eyes growing wide. "It takes most people weeks. Months, even. How did you do it?"

"I read the book before I ever got to Kessering, so that sped the training up," Adrienne explained. "And this 'Oneness' thing is something I've been doing since I was young, I just didn't realize it at the time."

"Really?" Louella asked. "The scholars must have been in a frenzy. After waiting so long to begin training a soldier, it must come as a shock that you're progressing faster than any of us did." Louella seemed pleased by the situation, and Adrienne suspected Louella liked the idea of the scholars being caught off guard.

"I wish I could figure out how to become aware of my surroundings more consistently," Adrienne told her. "I hate that it can be so unreliable."

"You're probably over-thinking the whole thing," Louella told her. "Quit trying so hard, and it will happen."

After an hour of trying and failing to achieve the deep level of Oneness she had first experienced in Ben's office, Adrienne left her small room at the inn and crossed the square to the building where the commission met and Ben lived, though neither were part of her destination today.

Today she was interested only in the library.

The library in Kessering was vast, much larger than Adrienne would have expected of such a small city. Most of the books were organized in an orderly fashion, and there was a man who worked in the library who kept track of where the books were and what could be found in them. It was an amazing skill that Adrienne thought could probably rival Ben's Talent. Yet when it came to the older books that were kept on the lower levels, the librarian had little knowledge.

Her Talent continued to allude her, and both Pieter and Louella had duties that took up much of their time, so Adrienne had taken to haunting the library rather than sitting in her room or wandering streets filled with people who feared her. She stuck to the areas that held the oldest books, hoping to find another book or journal that referenced the abilities she was trying so hard to develop. Ben had shown her a few others, but they were all written after Asmov's journal, when Talents were already fading into the things of story and legend. Surely Asmov's journal could not truly be the best reference.

So far she had found no mention of Talents or anything that might relate to them, but something else had caught her interest the last time she was in the library. The books that she had pulled out were written in Old Samaroan, and she doubted anyone had picked them up in decades except perhaps to dust them off every decade or so, but to her they were infinitely more interesting than any of the newer books. They predated the rift between Samaro and Almet, but something about the writing suggested that tension had been brewing between the two countries even then.

There was a table down at this lower level, long-forgotten but still solid, and Adrienne had piled books on it. She had brought candles with her, as the torchlight was too dim to read by, and she picked up the first book. It was something of a journal, but it was written in a different style than Asmov's had been. This journal, though personal, was more focused. It did not contain the wild anecdotes and tangents that Asmov's had. Instead, it seemed to have been written by the personal servant of one of the Fuiron princes, and focused almost entirely around political events and other things that the writer had deemed important on a large scale. The writer had seemed more interested in chronicling events than capturing his own thoughts, and despite the fact that the dialect was different from what Adrienne was used to, she was interested enough to work through it.

There are rumors coming out of Almet that are troubling. Prince Zuka has confided in me that his father is worried, but that the king would not tell him why. It is not my place to ask, or to try to out-guess the prince, but I suspect it has something to do with the slaves. One of the girls went missing the other day, and there were more questions asked about it than is usual for a runaway slave girl of little consequence.

I mentioned this to my uncle, and he reminded me of the slave uprising some months ago in Almet. It is amazing to me that slaves would rise up and cause the damage that is said to have occurred as a result, and I expressed my concerns, but he said that it is unlikely to happen here. The Almetians are said to treat their slaves like animals, which is no doubt the reason for the uprising and consequent damage.

I tried to ask my uncle more in hopes of satiating my curiosity about why there would be so much interest in the disappearance of one young slave, but he told me not to ask so many questions. He reminded me that it is not our place to wonder why our betters do what they do, but instead to serve.

I will listen for more clues from Prince Zuka, however. I do not always plan to be a servant, and knowledge could make all the difference.

Adrienne had never read a text that explicitly talked about a time when Samaro still had slaves. It was strange to read of it, and to think that people had compared the practices of how two countries had treated their slaves and found one side favorable, when to Adrienne the practice itself was abominable. She wondered how long after this journal entry slavery in Samaro had been abolished, and put the journal into a pile to be read further. She opened another book, and found that it seemed to be a history. The language was formal, not the dialect of an intelligent servant, and the words were drier, but it was the content that had her narrowing her eyes in concentration.

King Ignatio Fuiron decided today, the sixty-seventh day of the eighteenth year of his rein, to confront King Eunice Bell of Almet about the armies amassing just north of the border. The armies are said to number upwards of ten thousand, and some reports say that the soldiers seem to be afflicted by a terrible plague. Three pigeons have been sent to the Almetian king to arrange for a meeting, and a rider has gone out as well, should the pigeons fail to reach their destination.

There is speculation that the armies are linked to the figure the common people are calling the Dark Mage, and that is the matter that King Fuiron will discuss with King Bell at their meeting. At this time, who or what the Dark Mage is remains uncertain, but there has been an unusual amount of migration from Almet into Samaro, a large number of them escaped slaves. This has resulted in King Fuiron temporarily suspending the law that all Almetian slaves are to be returned to Almet if they are found and captured until such time that he can discover the reason for the mass escape.

Rumors that those close to the Dark Mage die in high numbers are unconfirmed but will be addressed by King Fuiron.

It is believed at this time that the Dark Mage is a separate entity from the ruling body of Almet, and King Fuiron has expressed his belief that the situation will be resolved peacefully between the two nations.

The name Ignatio Fuiron was vaguely familiar as one of the Fuiron rulers, but it was not that which had her frowning. She had never heard of the Dark Mage before, and despite her schooling on the conflict between Samaro and Almet, she had never heard of Almet raising armies before the rift between the two countries had formed.

She set that book aside with the page's journal and began looking through the other books for more mention of Ignatio or the Dark Mage. She was just setting aside the third book which seemed unlikely to yield anything interesting when she heard footsteps coming toward her. She looked up and saw Ben coming around the corner, a look of consternation on his face.

"What are you doing down here?" he asked in a tone that was dangerously close to accusatory.

"Reading."

"No one reads these books," Ben said. "They're written in Old Samaroan."

Adrienne didn't bother to sigh or to point out—again—that she could read Old Samaroan as well as any scholar, perhaps better than some after all of her study in the library basement. "I wanted to see if anything else was written about the Talented—about people with abilities," she clarified. For some reason she did not fully understand, she was reluctant to tell Ben about what she was finding in the histories. She did not know if he knew anything about the Dark Mage, but something kept her from asking.

And the lie was true enough. It was one of the reasons she had come back to this section in the first place, though it was no longer the driving force behind her study.

"There's nothing else down here," Ben told her. "The commission looked through all the books before we began training anyone." He picked up the book she had just put down and thumbed through it. "And this book is too recent for mention of abilities anyway."

"I didn't realize," Adrienne said, though she had known that any mention of the Fuirons would have postdated the original Talented by centuries. "Maybe I'll see if I can find some older books." She would rather let him believe the lie than explain the truth.

It was clear that Ben thought that was a waste of time, but he didn't say anything. He was probably grateful that she wasn't out threatening people in the streets. "Fine," he said. "Just put the books back when you're finished."

When Ben had left, Adrienne opened up another book, scanning for mention of slaves, Zuka, Ignatio, or the Dark Mage. She saw fragments here and there, oblique mentions of the situation that seemed to be building. These books, like many others written at the time, had not been written for reading by someone unfamiliar with the what was happening at the time. There were no introductions or explanations to what was written, and Adrienne was forced to make inferences about events that had taken place nearly a millennia ago.

She flipped a page in a book that seemed promising and a folded piece of paper fell out. The paper was yellow and fragile along the lines it had been folded, but it held together. She moved it into better light, but was stumped by what she saw.

The language was not Samaroan, Common or Old. It was strange to her, with only the vaguest similarities between it and Old Samaroan. Yet it had been tucked away in this book, and Adrienne could not ignore the feeling that it could be the key to understanding what she was reading.

She gently placed it back between two pages of the book and reached for another book on the stack. She would come back to it later.

The edges of the sword were razor sharp and pierced the skin of Adrienne's thumb when just the slightest pressure was applied.

Adrienne grunted in approval as she stuck her thumb in her mouth to remove the blood before she began to test the balance of the newly forged weapon. She swung the blade around, testing the resistance, the heft and range of motion.

It felt as comfortable in her hands as her own sword.

Adrienne whipped around and swung the blade deep into the trunk of an old stump. She pulled it out, and it came as smooth as silk from the tough wood without any catching or binding. The strange bluish metal was unblemished, the edges still just as sharp. It was perfect.

"Hmm," she said, examining it once more, narrowing her eyes and looking for the slightest sign of weakness, the slightest imperfection in the long blade.

"You won't need to sharpen it," Pieter told her in his deep voice, breaking into her careful inspection of his work.

"Ever?" She looked up into the brown eyes of the blacksmith who had come to be her friend over the weeks since their introduction.

Pieter shrugged his heavy shoulders. "I never had to sharpen one of my blades yet," he said. "Not since I started using my Talent, anyway. The whet stone does no more to it than that old stump did."

Adrienne ran her fingers up and down the smooth face of the sword blade. Despite the color, which had made her doubtful at first, it was a beautiful sword, perfectly balanced, and apparently indestructible. She looked into Pieter's watchful brown eyes. "It's incredible," she said honestly.

"I'm glad you like it," Pieter told her.

Adrienne liked and respected professional pride, and had no trouble offering praise where it was due. "The sword I have now was a gift on my fifteenth birthday, when I was officially acknowledged as a soldier. It was forged by one of the finest swordsmiths in Samaro." She examined the blue tinged blade once again. Pieter had told her the color was due to the fact that he had used his Talent to forge the weapon, and that the color came along with the other special qualities his Talent lent to his work. "This sword is as good."

"Better," Louella argued, crossing her arms over her breasts.

Adrienne would not know that until she had used the sword against a proper opponent, but she did not argue the fact. If Pieter's Talent had manifested in such an incredible way that he could forge a remarkable sword with no prior practice, she was content to be happy with that and welcome whatever surprises might accompany it.

"Well, this sword is also a gift to you, as you are nearly one of us now," Pieter said.

Adrienne had hardly dared to hope that the sword would be hers, although he had used her old sword as a model, but now that he was offering the weapon to her she did not think she could accept it. "This weapon would sell for a small fortune," Adrienne protested. "I can't accept something of this worth."

"I have money," Pieter said. "And I don't want to sell it. Besides, I was thinking of you as I created it. It won't work as well for anyone else as it will for you."

Pieter correctly interpreted the confusion on Adrienne's face. "When I use my Talent, the tool or object I am creating functions better if I think about the person who will be using it, but it won't work as well for anyone else as it will for its intended owner." He looked as puzzled by the strange side effect of his Talent as Adrienne was.

"What if you don't think of anyone?" Adrienne asked. It seemed that there were limitations and strange turns with just about every Talent she had learned about so far. No one could do quite the same thing in the same way with the same result. It was frustrating, and Adrienne was as fascinated by it as Louella was with blood particles. Every new thing she learned only served to make her more anxious to discover her own Talent.

"My tools still work if I don't concentrate on anyone as I shape them," Pieter said, "and they don't break, and knives and such don't require sharpening, but people tell me they aren't as easy to use as even regular tools unless I fashioned the tool with the user in mind."

"The knives in particular cause problems," Louella said. "I've had to mend cuts from a few of his knives that slipped unexpectedly."

Adrienne knew that knives slipped, but she sensed that the incidents were more than the typical accidents that tended to occur with the use of sharp objects. "Have you gotten any of the tools back?"

Pieter laughed. "Dozens. Now I know to think of the user, and I have made replacements for the people that wanted them. It's all a matter of discovering your Talent and *all* of its effects."

Most of the Talented besides Louella and Pieter avoided Adrienne, including Maureen, so Adrienne spent much of her free time helping Louella with her studies or with Pieter, sharing with him the little she knew about weapons-making while learning more herself.

Studying with Ben took up several frustrating hours a day, and Adrienne had begun teaching Thom basic fighting moves to alleviate some of that frustration. They used no weapons, just hands and body and feet, and Thom had none of the talent Jeral had promised almost from the first, but it was a fun diversion from the rest of what Adrienne was doing in Kessering. Although she had told herself at the beginning that it would be good for the boy to know how to handle himself, she acknowledged now that she got a twisted pleasure from teaching someone in Kessering how to fight.

Thom had been sworn to secrecy when it came to their training sessions, and Adrienne believed he would keep quiet. She had made it plain that the sessions would stop if anyone found out, and the boy liked the lessons too much to jeopardize his chance to learn more.

Adrienne genuinely enjoyed the sessions with Thom. He was bright and entertaining, and his enthusiasm for training helped Adrienne to ward off some of the loneliness she had felt since leaving Kyrog.

She spent a few hours a day working on Oneness, and tried her best to keep busy. Studying the books from the library helped. Whispers about the tension growing between Samaro and Almet and hints at the Dark Mage were intriguing and occupied her mind even after she'd left the library.

Only at night did she allow herself to think of Kyrog, of Ricco and Jeral and how much she missed them.

Adrienne banished the tug of nostalgia and brought herself back to the present, looking down at the magnificent sword still in her hands, then back at Pieter. "I want this, but I wish I could make some sort of payment."

Pieter looked thoughtful for a moment. "I would like your old sword," he said at last.

"What?" Adrienne's voice came out high and tight, and she coughed to loosen her throat. "Why?" she asked in a voice that sounded more her own, if a bit strained.

"To hang in my shop," Pieter said. "I know you are attached to that sword, and I won't sell it, but I would like to have it just the same."

Adrienne was torn by the unexpected request, but finally she nodded and began unbuckling the sword belt from her waist.

"Pieter, people aren't going to like you having a sword in your shop," Louella pointed out. "It might hurt business."

Pieter grunted in acknowledgement of the petite blonde. "If people have such a problem with it, I don't want their business. I don't have a problem with soldiers, and Adrienne is one of us now. If they don't like that, they can find a different blacksmith." He gave Louella a hard look. "Do you have a problem with it?"

Louella's smile was beatific. "Of course not. Adrienne is my friend." She turned her smile on Adrienne. "I would hang something of yours in my shop, but I think it might seem contradictory to have weapons in a healer's shop."

"Thanks anyway," Adrienne said awkwardly, unused to such open declarations of affection. In Kyrog, she might receive a slap on the back or a nod of approval, but Adrienne had never been part of a group that vocalized emotions.

Maybe that was the difference between civilians and soldiers.

Adrienne handed Pieter her old sword in its scabbard, and he unsheathed it and, keeping the sword, handed the scabbard back to her. "I don't need this. I will buy my own."

Adrienne thanked him and put the scabbard back on her belt, then slid the new sword home. It fit perfectly.

Louella clapped her hands together. "Well, I'm getting hungry," she said brightly, breaking the tension the exchange of weapons had caused. "Let's go get some dinner at the inn down the road aways. I'll buy."

Adrienne scanned the grove more from habit than for any other reason. It was clear that no one but she and Louella were around, and from the look of it, Adrienne thought it had been awhile since anyone had visited the small cluster of trees two hours outside of Kessering. The sun was only halfway to its zenith, and the day was already growing insufferably hot. The shade under the trees offered some relief from the heat, but Adrienne was not looking forward to the walk back under the blazing sun.

Louella was down on the ground, combing her fingers through the dry and brittle grass. Adrienne crouched down for a closer look and decided that there might be other plants mixed in with the grass, but she couldn't say what they were. The only forms of vegetation she could identify were plants that would cause rashes or were poisonous to men or horses, and none of those were present here. Most other plants were a mystery to her, and Adrienne was content to let it stay that way.

"What are you looking for?" she asked.

"My pot of *pierna* has reached its limit," Louella said, reaching into the pouch she wore for a small trowel and a stiff leather bag. "I need a fresh plant."

Adrienne did not know what *pierna* was or what it did, but she assumed it was one of the herbs Louella had been planning to collect when she had invited Adrienne to accompany her on her trip outside the city. After too many days spent doing little more than reading centuries-old books, Adrienne had readily agreed to go with Louella on her foray outside of Kessering, even if it was to collect plants in the small grove located on the otherwise featureless plains.

"Don't any of the other healers have some you can borrow?" she asked, looking down at the brittle plants skeptically. The twiggy plant with brownish-green leaves hardly looked worth the effort of collecting.

"It's best if I have my own," Louella said. "*Pierna* is useful for breaking a fever and alleviating aches, especially in the bones and joints, but it works best freshly cut, not dried, so I don't want to borrow any."

Adrienne didn't know what use Louella had for herbs now. With her Talent she had little use for the various medicines used by regular healers, and what Louella could not heal with her Talent, other Talented healers could. "Aren't there other herbs that do that?" Adrienne asked.

"Yes, but I prefer *pierna*." Louella carefully deposited the plant and rootball she had dug up into the leather bag so that it could be transplanted when she returned to her shop. "And you think I'm being ridiculous," she said when she caught the look on Adrienne's face.

"I think," Adrienne said slowly, "that were I to come down with a fever while in Kessering I would find a Talented healer to help me, not have someone dose me with *pierna*."

Louella laughed as she stood up and brushed dirt and grass from her dress. "Yes, I suppose it is habit more than anything that brings me here," Louella said, looking around the grove. "When I was an apprentice healer, the woman I trained under would bring me out here and make me identify each of the plants and their medicinal properties." Louella's blue eyes looked wistful. "I guess sometimes it seems that my Talent is taking away everything I spent years learning."

"Don't think that way," Adrienne admonished. "What you can do now is amazing. Surely you don't want to go back to stitching wounds shut and applying poultices and casts, hoping that it heals clean."

"No, I suppose not," Louella said. "But think about it this way: if you discover a Talent that could be used as a weapon, a highly effective weapon, would you be happy to put away your sword in favor of it?"

Adrienne's hand went to the weapon in question. Just touching the hilt of the Talent-forged sword sent a tingle of power up her arm. The connection she felt to the blade Pieter had forged was palpable, and Adrienne could not imagine giving it up.

Giving up any sword in favor of whatever Talent she might develop seemed inconceivable, yet Adrienne realized that is what Louella and the other healers were doing. Unlike Pieter, who used the skills from his profession along with his Talent to become a better blacksmith, the Talents most of the healers had developed were replacing everything they used to do.

"I don't know," Adrienne said, reluctantly letting go of the sword.

Louella offered a soft smile before heading over to root around under a dense bush, though Adrienne could not imagine what plant of any usefulness would grow in such a dark place. She leaned against a nearby tree and watched as her friend gathered plants that she no longer had a need for.

CHAPTER EIGHT

A faint breeze stirred the hair that had escaped from Adrienne's thick black braid. Even in the open meadow breezes were rare, and Adrienne turned her face into the wind, keeping her eyes closed. She moved slowly through the familiar motions of her morning routine, welcoming the dawn of a new day as she welcomed the breeze.

Her mind cleared, but there was not emptiness. She was aware of more than her own body. She felt the wind, the grass beneath her booted feet, the tree behind her. More than anything, she felt the magnificent blade that Pieter had forged while using his Talent resting several paces away in its scabbard against the tree. It was a beacon, and like a light it shown and brought awareness to everything around Adrienne.

She opened her eyes, but the spell was unbroken. Even with her eyes open and her thoughts racing, she was still aware of everything around her. She could still feel her connection with the universe, the Oneness she had been searching for, like an extra sense. It was thrilling, this level of awareness without effort, and she knew that she was ready to move on to the next step in her training.

Holding on to that sense of connection, Adrienne strapped on her sword and headed back to the massive library where she would find Ben. The same clerk was watching the door as usual, but he did not try to stop her as he had on some of her previous visits. He had learned that she would not be detained by the likes of him. Adrienne could sense the clerk as though he was an extension of herself, and wondered if she could really feel his resentment or if it was only her imagination.

When she got to Ben's study, Adrienne found him hunched over his desk, studying a scroll that was yellowed with age. His delicate features looked irritated when he asked why she was there. Adrienne knew he did not like having his studies interrupted and preferred to send for her when they were to meet outside of their set training times, but she figured that this time would be an exception

"I'm ready to move on," she informed him, smiling. Her connection to the universe was still firm, feeding her sensory input from everything around her. It was an exhilarating experience to feel so much, and she wondered how she had gone so long without feeling this way.

"What?" he asked, blinking owlishly, caught between whatever he had been studying and what was happening around him now.

"I can maintain Oneness now," Adrienne said. "I feel connected to everything, even now, standing here talking to you." She closed her eyes and moved unerringly to the other chair in the room. For once the chair was free of the clutter of books and parchments, and she settled herself into it before opening her eyes. "I'm ready."

Ben shook his head. "You're moving too fast," he told her.

Adrienne leaned forward in the chair, resting her forearms on her thighs. "Ben, this is a good thing," she told him, her eyes burning with intensity. "I'm ready for the next step in my training."

"It's not a good thing," Ben said with a shake of his head. "You've been here less than two months. You will remain at this stage of your training for at least another month," he said with finality.

"Why?"

"The rest of the commission thinks it best to slow your progress. You are learning so fast that some of the other commissioners are concerned that you are missing parts of your training." Ben gave her what was meant to be a placating smile, but she was still in a state of Oneness and could sense the insincerity behind it. "Perhaps in a few more weeks we can work on progressing to the next stage."

Adrienne's temper threatened to snap, and she worked hard to modulate her tone. "Commissioners that I haven't even worked with want to slow my training? Why? If I'm ready then I should be able to move on. It's pointless to hold me back."

Ben laughed, but it was a frustrated sound coming from the normally congenial young man. "The commission is worried about not being able to control you," he said, not bothering to soften the harsh reality. "Having a soldier here is bad enough. The whole city is on edge thanks to your presence, and now you are influencing others with abilities. That sword you wear like a badge, the experiments you're doing with that healer, how do you think that reflects on the commission?" His hands had balled into fists on top of the desk, and Adrienne wondered if he was aware of the anger seeping into him, or if he was ignorant of his own darker emotions. Did he realize that his fists betrayed an inner call to violence not so different from her own?

"I would have expected a scholar to appreciate experiments and serious study, and a commissioner to appreciate people coming together and working cooperatively," Adrienne said coolly.

"Not when it involves cutting yourself, or promoting violence." Ben's voice was pure disgust, and Adrienne realized that not everything he was saying had come down from the commission. The commission might have told him these things, but he was in agreement with them.

"I do not promote violence," Adrienne struggled to keep her voice level as she spoke. "Who has been telling the commission these lies?"

Ben shot her a hard look. "That is none of your concern."

Adrienne didn't need to be told it was Maureen, just as she did not need to ask why he and the commission were opposed to her new sword. The commissioners may have wanted a way to stop the war, but they were against anything that might actually help to fight it. Adrienne could hardly reconcile the fact that the commission could hold such conflicting views with equal strength and conviction, but they did so with fervor.

"So what is the plan now? You'll keep me where I am until the commission...what? Decides that the appropriate amount of time has passed?" She had held her trainees back because she had known they weren't ready to advance, that their bodies were not yet adapted for greater physical challenges, or that they did not yet know enough of the basics to move on. She had never held anyone back based on some preconceived timeline. She had spent four months training Jeral to use his body as a weapon, but some of the Yearlings had been ready to move on only a month after beginning their tutelage. And she had let them.

Training—effective training—had to be adapted to the individual, not uniformly applied.

"You will stay where you are in your training until the commission deems it safe for you to develop an ability," Ben said.

"I'm not dangerous!" Adrienne slammed the flat of her hands down on his desk. The candle flames shuddered at the impact, then shot up a foot in the air, burning a bright, angry red. Ben pushed away from his desk so hard that his chair toppled backward, leaving him sprawled on the floor.

"H-how did you do that?" he stammered, pushing himself to his feet with shaking hands. The color had leached from his face until it was a sickly gray.

"I don't know," Adrienne said, staring at the candle flames that were now back to their normal size and color, as surprised as Ben by what had happened. Then the realization of what she had done sank in and she let out a whoop of excitement. "I guess I don't need your help moving on to the next stage after all," she told him with a triumphant grin.

"This isn't possible," Ben said, his voice shaky. He raised a hand to his face and wiped it. "It must have been a-a fluke. A trick of the light." He swallowed. It had definitely been the light that had changed, but they both knew it had not been a fluke or a trick. Candle flames did not behave that way.

Adrienne stared at the nearest candle. She was still in a state of Oneness, and through that connection with the universe she could feel everything around her. But the flame had a different quality to it. It felt...tangible. As if she could reach out and touch it with her mind.

The flame leapt up in response to her mental touch.

"I don't think it's a fluke," she told Ben, playing with the flame, causing it to dance and shoot up sparks.

"The Creator preserve us," Ben said in a voice barely above a whisper.

"Isn't this what you wanted?" Adrienne asked. As new as her Talent was, its potential uses were immediately apparent. A lifetime as a soldier made assessing any skill second nature, and the possibilities here seemed endless. "Didn't you want someone with powers that can be used against Almet?"

"The commission wanted you to wait," Ben said, and she could see the struggle between pride and worry on his face. "They didn't want a dangerous rogue running loose in the city."

She stopped playing with the fire and regarded Ben seriously. "I'm not rogue," Adrienne said with a false calm. "I've done everything you asked of me, worked to meet every request you've made of me, for the past two months."

Ben ran his hands through his hair, then tugged lightly on the tight curls as she had seen him do before when frustrated or troubled by one of his books. When Ben finally dropped his hands, his eyes were cold and flat as though a barrier had gone up between them. "What do you call this, what you just did, if not going rogue?" he asked, gesturing toward the candle.

"I didn't know that would happen," Adrienne said, trying to force some apology into her voice despite the fact that she felt no remorse for what she'd done. Discovering her Talent was too wonderful a thing to apologize for. "It was an accident. I would have waited and done what you told me." Adrienne wondered if that last was true.

She hoped it was.

Her life had been built around rules and following the chain of command. She had been conditioned to obey her superiors from a very young age, and if that had changed in only two short months, she didn't know what would become of her. Who would she be, if not a soldier? Who would she be, if she could no longer follow command?

Then again, before coming to Kessering, her superiors had by and large made decisions she had agreed with. Decisions that were unprejudiced and served to meet the desired goal. Even commands she had not liked had usually had a solid reason behind them, and Adrienne had followed her leaders because she had trusted them and their judgment. She trusted Captain Garrett with her life.

She did not have the same trust in Ben and the other members of the commission. She knew their fear of soldiers was illogical and that they had a strong and unreasonable prejudice against her that clouded their judgments. She didn't trust them, and she didn't know if she would have listened to Ben, or if she would have tried to progress on her own. It scared her not to know.

"It's too late for that now," Ben muttered. "I must tell Elder Rynn immediately. The commission must meet and discuss what has happened."

"Would you like me to come with you or wait for you here?" Adrienne asked as respectfully as she could manage. Angry or not, she wouldn't make him go alone. She had done this.

"Neither," Ben told her roughly. "Go back to the inn. Speak to no one of this until I tell you otherwise."

"Of course." Adrienne left the room and headed back to the inn to wait for word from the commission.

She didn't know how long they would be, or what they might decide. She sat on her bed, tempted by every flicker of candlelight or lick of flame in the hearth. She wanted to attain Oneness, to reach out and touch the fire. She had never felt desire like the desire she felt to use her Talent again. But the commission would not approve, and she was determined to follow their orders. She was a soldier, and she would do as she was told. She would not lose herself.

So she resisted the urge to try out her Talent, and waited for the commission's decision.

It was three days before a boy came to the inn with a message for Adrienne to report immediately to the commission. She had not gone farther than the stable since Ben had sent her away, and she had refused visits from both Louella and Pieter. She knew her friends were confused and worried, but she was determined to follow Ben's orders.

She was a soldier, not an undisciplined civilian.

And now it was time to meet her fate.

The clerk, who typically let Adrienne have free reign of the library, left his station by the door to show her where the commission was waiting, as though she was too dangerous to leave unattended in the halls. He did not speak to her, and Adrienne did not try to start a conversation, preferring to think ahead to what the commission might be planning for her in response to what she had done. She understood that breaking that chain had to come with consequences, even if she had not meant to go against the commission's wishes. It was the only way to maintain order.

When she entered the room, she saw the commission sitting behind the same table, in the same order, as they had been the last time she had seen them. Their expressions were grim.

Elder Rynn sat in the center, with Lady Chessing and Franklin on either side of him. Franklin was wearing a virulent green coat today in place of the mustard yellow, and Adrienne wondered inanely if all of his clothing was so obscenely colored. Ben was located at the end of the table, and Adrienne wondered how much trouble he was in. Maybe none. Perhaps all the blame had been placed solely on her.

She would not be surprised if they blamed a soldier instead of one of their own, despite the fact that the incident was faultless. She had not meant to disobey Ben or the commission; she had discovered her Talent quite by accident.

"Adrienne," Elder Rynn said, his dry voice filled with his displeasure. "I was wondering if you would come."

Adrienne stiffened at the perceived insult. "Of course I came," she said, wishing he did not address her by their first name. Soldiers were often an irreverent lot, but she was a lieutenant and this was a formal setting. She wanted the respect due someone of her rank.

"Due to recent events, it has come to light that you do not always follow instruction," Elder Rynn said. "Master Ruthford did not give you permission to progress in your training, yet you still saw fit to do so. Why should we expect you to listen today?"

Adrienne looked briefly at Ben and caught the slight shake of his head before turning her attention back to Elder Rynn and answering. "He did not give me permission, no, but neither did I intentionally disobey him or go against the commission's wishes. It was by accident that I happened to develop an ability at that time."

Lady Chessing's smile was reminiscent of a cat anticipating a dish of cream as she leaned forward over the table. "He says that you argued with him about delaying your progress," she said.

"I did," Adrienne said, since there was no point denying it. "I did not understand why the commission would want to hold me back. I got angry."

"And in your anger you lashed out with fire," Lady Chessing said, bosom heaving, face alight with pleasure. Some of the other commissioners looked pleased, too, and Adrienne realized that, far from looking for the truth and a good solution to what they saw as a problem, they were hoping to prove that she was dangerous. They wanted an excuse to stop her training.

Adrienne had not realized their dislike of her ran so deep, or that they could be so short-sighted as to want to stop her training at the moment she developed a Talent that could be of use.

"I did get angry, but I did not lash out," Adrienne told her and the rest of the commission. "I didn't know at the time that I had any control of fire. Had I meant to 'lash out' at Master Ruthford, the action would have been physical in nature, I assure you." Her voice was cool and dangerous, and Lady Chessing sat back in her chair as though Adrienne's words had been a threat against the noblewoman's person.

"I won't deny that I can be dangerous," Adrienne said. "I am a highly trained soldier, but that is why you brought me here. I didn't hurt Master Ruthford the other night, though I could have. Even before I discovered my ability with fire, harming Master Ruthford would have been laughably easy." Several of the commissioners shifted uncomfortably, but Adrienne didn't give them a chance to speak. Her temper was up, and she had no interest in subduing it. "Despite that, I haven't hurt him, or anyone. I have done what you wanted. I have developed an ability that can be used against Almet." Her words rang with authority, and Ben looked uncertainly between her and Elder Rynn, as though wondering if there was a play for power taking place that he was not aware of.

And Adrienne realized in a moment of clarity that it was not only her power that was in question. She saw that Ben, the youngest commissioner, had not been informed of the final decision. He, too, had been left out of the decision making process. Was it because of his youth, or because of how much time he spent with her?

"The other commissioners and I have discussed this situation at length over the past three days," Elder Rynn said. "Although it is undeniable that you are now infinitely more dangerous than you were before the development of your ability, it is also true that you have developed one of the abilities we were hoping for." The creases in his cheeks looked deeper, the bags under his eyes larger, and he did not seem gratified that the hope of the commission had been realized.

Adrienne wanted to ask what their ruling was, but she stayed quiet, wondering what she actually wanted their decision to be. She did not like Kessering with its crowds of civilians and the strong prejudice against soldiers; being sent back to Kyrog would almost be a relief. She had discovered her Talent. Surely she could continue to develop it after she was back in Kyrog.

She thought back to the conversations she had had with Louella. Each Talent was different. Even between the healers who had developed similar Talents there had been enough differences that no two healers could do the exact same things. But Louella had told her that working with Maureen and the others had helped her find the strengths and weaknesses of her own Talent. Even Pieter, with a completely different Talent than Louella, had been able to help her explore what she could do. If she left Kessering now, there was a chance she would never be able to reach her full potential. She needed more training before facing Almet.

"It has been decided that you will remain here in Kessering," Elder Rynn said what seemed a lifetime later. "You will resume your training and learn to control your temper as well as your Talent. It is also hoped that you will learn to obey our orders."

Adrienne lowered her head, an expression of humility that did not come easily to her. "I will try my best."

"See that you do," Elder Rynn said.

"What about her association with the healers and that blacksmith?" Lady Chessing asked, her voice shrill. "What about that horrible sword she carries?"

Adrienne's head snapped up. It took everything she had to keep her voice even and deferential rather than snapping at the woman. "Louella and Pieter are my friends," she said, wondering if she should mention that Pieter had forged her sword using his Talent. She thought that Ben knew, or at least suspected, but she decided against adding more fuel to the fire. She did not want to risk getting Pieter in trouble as well as herself.

Elder Rynn sighed. "Much as I would like to do something about that, the damage is done, Lady Chessing. It would hardly be advisable to keep Adrienne in confinement. We must hope that the common sense of the others prevails."

Lady Chessing huffed out a displeased breath but did not argue.

"Adrienne, I will meet you at the inn in two hours," Ben told her, speaking for the first time since Adrienne had entered the room. "I have things to do before we resume your lessons."

Adrienne bowed slightly. "Thank you," she said and quickly took her leave before anything more could be said or done.

She had two hours, and instead of going directly to the inn, she headed in the direction of Louella's shop. She knew that Louella was concerned for her and would want to know that Adrienne was all right.

"Adrienne!" Louella exclaimed as they almost bumped into each other in the doorway. "I was just going to your inn. I was going to insist that you saw me this time, and not leave until you agreed." She clasped Adrienne's hands in hers with a surprisingly firm grip. "I've been worried." Her blue eyes were big and sincere, and she gave Adrienne's hands an extra squeeze before dropping them.

"I'm sorry I worried you," Adrienne said. "I wasn't supposed to speak with anyone."

Louella frowned and all but dragged Adrienne inside before closing and locking the door behind them. "Sit down while I put on some tea, and then you can tell me the whole story."

Adrienne had not planned to tell Louella everything, but watching Louella as she moved around her small kitchen preparing tea, she felt an urge to tell her all that had happened in the last few days. "I discovered my Talent."

Louella snapped her head around and she abandoned the teacup she had been filling to give Adrienne an excited hug. "That's wonderful! When?"

"Three days ago."

"What?" She let go and took a step back. "Why didn't you tell me?"

"Ben told me not to. I wasn't supposed to develop a Talent so quickly."

"I don't understand. Shouldn't he be happy?"

Adrienne shrugged. "He wasn't. The commission wasn't."

Louella shook her head and turned to fetch the tea and arrange sweets on a plate that she set between them on the table. "They were happy when I developed my Talent," Louella said. "Perhaps a bit disappointed that it was healing and not something more fantastic, but—I never asked! You said you discovered your Talent, but I never asked what you could do."

"Fire," Adrienne answered. "I can control fire." She told Louella about the confrontation with Ben, and what had happened with the candles. Saying it seemed so unreal, and as if she was setting down a burden she had been carrying for days. The only other person she had ever been able to confide in so absolutely was Ricco, and she had missed him terribly during her days of confinement. She had thought that Louella could never be the same sort of friend to her that Ricco was, but she had not been altogether correct.

Louella was not the same sort of friend that Ricco had been, but the difference did not make the friendship bad. She could tell Louella everything that had happened, and the Talented healer would listen in a way that Ricco wouldn't. Louella was empathetic, even passionate, but unlike Ricco, Louella did not try to jump in and solve the problems Adrienne placed before her. She let Adrienne talk, listened as Adrienne unburdened herself, and said nothing.

When Adrienne had finished with her story, Louella shoved herself away from the table with enough force to send the chair toppling to the floor. "I can't believe it. You develop one of the Talents that they have wanted from the start, and when they find out you've accomplished what they have been trying to get the rest of us to do for years they treat you like a criminal. It's disgraceful." She stalked around the small room, scowling at the implements of her profession. Her reaction surprised Adrienne all the more because of the calm way she had listened to the story. "I have half a mind to march over there and tell that commission what I think of their actions."

"Please don't," Adrienne said. "I don't want you to get in trouble, too."

Louella stopped her pacing and gave Adrienne a wry smile. "Don't worry, that is only one half of my mind. The other half of my mind knows doing that will do no one any good."

Adrienne began to breathe easier. "I have to meet with Ben in just over an hour," she said.

"Well, that gives you enough time to show me what it is you can do."

Adrienne raised her eyebrows. "What do you mean?"

Louella sat back down across from Adrienne at the table. "This controlling fire thing. I want to see it."

"I don't know if I can just do it," Adrienne told her friend. "It only happened the other night, and I wasn't trying at the time."

"Have you tried since?" Louella asked.

"No. I didn't think I should."

Louella rolled her eyes. "And they say you don't follow orders," she scoffed. "I would have spent the last three days trying everything I could think of, whether they liked it or not."

Adrienne had no doubt of that. Despite her small size and fair coloring, Louella was anything but the fragile, docile waif she seemed. Adrienne wondered if the commission knew about Louella's fiercer traits, and if they worried about the possibility of the healer being dangerous. Probably not. They had placed all of their fear and mistrust in soldiers, and doubtless never considered what danger a maverick healer could pose.

"I'll try it, but I'm not promising anything," Adrienne said. She breathed deeply and the Oneness, the connection to everything, the connection which had once eluded her, came into her as naturally as air. "Can you move the candle closer?" she asked, looking over at Louella.

Louella grabbed the candle that had been burning on the shelf and set it in front of Adrienne. At first nothing happened. Adrienne could feel the flame, but nothing she did could affect it. She took another calming breath and tried again, visualizing what she wanted.

The flame leapt up a foot, shooting up multi-colored sparks. Adrienne smiled and Louella clapped her hands in delight.

"That was wonderful. What else can you do?"

Adrienne concentrated again, and the flame began to move in distinctive patterns, twirling and gyrating on the wick, occasionally sending tendrils of flame out like arms. It was hard for Adrienne to maneuver the flame in such intricate ways, but she felt that she was nowhere near the limits of her Talent. "Do you still have a fire going in your oven?" she asked.

"A low one," Louella told her, "for boiling tea and such. Why?"

"I want to try controlling a bigger flame."

The hearth fire, while by no means roaring, was much harder to control than the candle flame. It did not act like one flame, but instead Adrienne discovered it was many flames, originating from the different logs and embers that were the source of its fuel. It was difficult for her to force the multiple flames to act as one, or to control several separate flames at a time. Sweat beaded on her temples and dripped down the sides of her face.

"I think this is like the particles you can feel in blood," Adrienne said, her voice strained from the effort of controlling so many separate fires at once. "A fire this size has many separate parts, even though you can't see them when looking."

Adrienne tried a few more tricks before sitting back, feeling both drained and elated. It had been like learning to use a new weapon, exhilarating despite the difficulty. "Wow," she said, unable to describe her feelings more coherently.

"I'll say," Louella agreed, her husky voice sounding strained, as if she too had been hard at work. "It isn't as useful as healing, of course, but the show is quite impressive."

Adrienne laughed.

"Do you think you could create a new fire?" Louella asked. "Like the balls of fire in the stories?"

Adrienne thought about the dream she had had before arriving in Kessering and the man in them who had been throwing balls of fire. She imagined herself doing the same and smiled.

"Not today," she told her friend, rising to her feet with some regret. "I have to go meet with Ben." Although she was not looking forward to the meeting, her practice with controlling the fire had left her with a feeling of accomplishment. No matter what Ben said or did, she knew she could take it.

She was a soldier.

"Good luck," Louella said, pulling Adrienne in for a tight hug. It lasted only a few short seconds, and Adrienne headed back to the inn, mulling all the while about the events of the last few days.

Adrienne beat Ben to her room by only ten minutes, and when he got there he started in with explanations on the commission's decision without bothering to say hello.

"They still believe it was unacceptable that you moved ahead without my consent," he told her, pulling himself up straight so that he could stare down at her from his advantageous full height. In Adrienne's opinion, the fact that he was skinny and appeared slightly off-balance now that he was standing instead of slouching ruined the attempt at intimidation.

"I didn't mean to move ahead against your wishes," Adrienne replied calmly, for what seemed the hundredth time.

"I told them that," Ben said, "but they say that is beside the point. I am surprised the commission didn't expel you from Kessering, though frankly they probably believe that it is best that you be contained here." He was breathing hard, and his frail shoulders had fallen inward, returning him to his typical slump.

"Contained?" The thought that the commission wouldn't let her leave had never occurred to her.

"Don't you understand the implications of your Talent? How dangerous it could be?"

"Of course. But that was the point, wasn't it? It's why the commission finally decided to train soldiers. They needed people to develop Talents that could be used in a fight."

"Yes. And they—*we*—needed time to decide what to do with you if you did develop such a Talent."

Adrienne almost felt sorry for the young man, caught as he was between her and the commission. He was both Talented and a commissioner, and being caught between two pieces of himself could not be a comfortable position.

"Perhaps everything happened faster than you and the other commissioners planned," Adrienne began in what she hoped was a reasonable, reassuring tone, "but that is done and cannot be changed. Now we have to focus on the fact that I have developed one of the abilities that the commission was looking for and move forward."

"Fine," Ben said, though it was clear to Adrienne that she had not heard the last of his complaints. "The first step is figuring out the limits of your power."

Adrienne nodded, knowing that such a priority was two-fold in her case. The commission had tested the limits of every new Talent developed in Kessering, but she sensed that the commission wanted to know as soon as possible how potentially destructive her Talent could be.

"You were angry last time. Do you think it is necessary for you to be angry to use your ability?" Ben asked.

That possibility had never occurred to Adrienne, and it was one that might have worried her had she not already known the answer. "I don't think so," she said, not wanting to reveal that she had just spent an hour experimenting with her Talent.

"Good," Ben said, seeming genuinely pleased for the first time since Adrienne had discovered her Talent with fire. "Let's see what you can do."

Adrienne repeated the exercise with the candle that she had performed for Louella, pleased that Ben seemed impressed by what she was able to do. It seemed that for the moment the scholar in him was stronger than the commissioner, and that he had put aside his personal feelings. Whatever disappointment he felt for her as her teacher was outweighed by his eagerness to see what else she could do with her Talent.

"Do you have another candle in here?" Ben asked.

Adrienne stood up and got the candle from atop the mantle, setting it across from the other candle on the small table her room offered. "What do you want me to do?"

"I want to see if you can light the candle."

Adrienne knew this was a real test of her Talent, and she concentrated hard on the cold wick. The already burning flame from the candle beside it beckoned her, and she knew without trying that she could transfer the first flame to the second candle without difficulty. But that was not what she wanted to do. She needed to know if she could start a fire from nothing.

She stared at the wick for a long time with no result. She could feel no fire there, and was nearly ready to give up when she became aware of her surroundings in a new way. She did not focus on the nearby beckoning candle, but on everything else: the heat in the air, the last rays of the afternoon sun, the energy emanating from her and Ben. With supreme effort she pulled them all together, focused them all into the wick, and the candle lit.

"You did it," Ben said with surprise. "It took nearly an hour, but...you did it!"

Adrienne had not realized how long she had been at it, but she knew that she would be able to light the candle much quicker next time. "I want to do it again," she told Ben eagerly, leaning forward to blow out the candle she had just lit.

"Tomorrow," Ben told her, but his smile was filled with understanding.

Adrienne thought about arguing, but the memory that the commission already viewed her as being disobedient stopped her. Besides, she was tired from working with her Talent, first with Louella and then with Ben. It seemed that although using her Talent was a mental process, the effects were physical. "What time?"

"Noon should be soon enough," Ben said. "Make sure to eat before I get here."

"Of course," Adrienne said. The meals Adrienne got at the inn were considerably better when Ben ate with her, but after speaking with the cook and several of the maids over the course of the last two months, she had finally stopped getting meals that looked as though they belonged in a pig trough. She thought that the cook might almost like her by now.

Ben left, and Adrienne stripped out of her *swa'il*, leaving her in only her skin. She blew out the two lit candles and slipped into bed, falling almost instantly asleep.

Adrienne sat at a table placed in one of the corners of Louella's shop. Her friend was dusting the room, but Adrienne hardly noticed her. She was too intent on trying to form balls of fire in her hand.

The tales spoke of people being able to hurl fire the way others threw balls of leather, but her efforts on that front grew increasingly frustrating. Adrienne knew that fire would be a tremendous weapon if she was able to throw it, but she was having trouble forming a fireball at all, let alone being able to throw one. Lighting candles was easy and seemed natural to her now, but sustaining a fire off of nothing but willpower was a different story altogether. Adrienne could barely get a fireball bigger than a slingshot pebble to form before it winked out of existence, unable or unwilling to burn without fodder.

But the tales Adrienne had heard from Tam and Ben, as well as the accounts in Asmov's journal, said hurling fireballs was possible, and Adrienne was determined to keep trying until she could do so. She was in Kessering to become a weapon, though the commission might deny it, and a weapon she would become.

She looked up briefly when someone entered the room and saw a middle-aged woman standing just inside the door. The woman was holding one arm still with the other, and Adrienne thought perhaps she had broken or sprained it. Since the woman did not appear to be a threat, Adrienne went back to working with fireballs, leaving the woman in Louella's capable hands.

Louella ushered the woman into a chair, asking in a low voice what had happened. Their voices were no more than murmurs, but Adrienne could imagine what was being said. Louella would ask for the woman to tell her what had happened to her arm, and the injured woman would confide the story, likely receiving as much comfort from Louella's soft words as she would from her Talent. The healer was good with people, and would ask other things, things about family and friends, things that Adrienne would never think to ask about, to put the injured woman at ease before she got to work. It was Louella's way.

She focused again on forming a fireball and attempted to ignore Louella and the woman. It was harder than it should have been to ignore them; being in a state of Oneness meant Adrienne was acutely aware of their presence, and she could sense every time the woman looked over at her.

Although Adrienne was aware of the woman's pain through the connection Oneness forged, it was easy to block out. What she did have trouble blocking were the mounting nerves that arose in the injured woman with every sideways glance in Adrienne's direction.

Finally, Louella stood up and came over to Adrienne. She had her small hands fisted on her narrow hips, and looked as disapproving as anyone with such a delicate face could look. "Adrienne, do you think you can stop that for just a few minutes?" Louella asked.

Adrienne raised one dark eyebrow in a questioning arch. "Stop what?"

"Stop with the fire," Louella said. "You're scaring that woman."

Adrienne looked over at the woman, and the woman looked away quickly. Fearfully. "Oh."

"I'm having trouble convincing her to stay," Louella said, her temper sounding sharper than Adrienne had expected. "Now stop with the fire until I mend her arm."

Adrienne nodded and let the glimmer of a flame that was wavering weakly in her palm die out. "Fine."

The woman relaxed when Adrienne's fire did not reappear after Louella returned to her side. Mending the woman's arm was quick work once Louella received some cooperation, and when the woman left with her arm and a variety of small, unnoticed aches and pains healed, Adrienne resumed trying to cultivate her Talent.

She refused to feel guilty for scaring the woman. If her Talent, like the fact that she was a soldier, scared people, that was their problem. Even Louella's big blue eyes could not convince her otherwise.

After tossing and turning in bed for what seemed like hours, Adrienne gave up on the thought of sleep and got dressed. She hesitated over her *swa'il*, thinking of the blouse and trousers Louella had convinced her to buy after Adrienne had adamantly refused to buy a dress. Women did not wear trousers, Louella had insisted, but Adrienne had finally convinced Louella that even the tightest trousers would be more modest than her *swa'il*, though Adrienne found nothing provocative about the leather outfit she usually wore.

Maybe if she showed up at Louella's dressed in the outfit Louella had chosen for her, the healer would be less displeased by the late-night visit.

She dressed quickly and made her way through the dark streets to the healer's shop. She went around to the back door and knocked softly so as not to wake Louella if the other woman was already sleeping.

"Adrienne," Louella said in surprise. "What are you doing here?"

"I couldn't sleep," she admitted.

"Come in, come in," Louella said, stepping back so that Adrienne could enter.

"I'm sorry it's so late," Adrienne apologized.

"I'm glad you stopped by," Louella said, setting a cup full of tea in front of Adrienne before going around the table to sit in her own chair. She took a sip of tea from her own cup and sat back with a sigh. "Have you been busy? I haven't seen you for days."

Adrienne shrugged. "Busy enough. I've been trying to work on those bloody fireballs…" She shook her head angrily. "Ben says to keep trying, but the practice doesn't seem to help much."

Adrienne was sick of working with fireballs. She had grown better at forming them, and could sustain a small ball of light above her palm without too much difficulty now, but throwing the balls still seemed all but impossible.

Her research in the library was no less frustrating, and something that she still hadn't confided in her friend. She saw no point in telling Louella about the hours spent in the library until she understood more of what she was reading herself. For now, Louella could think that all of her frustration was from working with her Talent.

Louella smiled around the rim of her teacup. "I know this isn't what you want to hear, but have you considered that your Talent might not develop that way?"

Adrienne scowled. "My Talent is working with fire. In the stories—"

"My Talent is healing, but I'm no good when it comes to illnesses," Louella said reasonably. "In the stories those who could heal seemed to be able to heal everything from a flu to broken bones to stab wounds, but I cannot. Maureen can take care of sicknesses, but it is much more difficult for her to stop a cut from bleeding, whereas for me it's the opposite. It's all I can do to break a mild fever."

"That's different," Adrienne muttered.

"Why?"

"Because I'm the only one who can use fire," Adrienne said. "I'm the only one with a Talent like this, and I should be able to do what the stories say."

"Maureen was the only one, for awhile. Just because you are the only one now doesn't mean no one else will develop your Talent. Perhaps they will be able to throw fire. You must discover what *you* can do." Adrienne didn't respond, and Louella seemed to realize that the soldier was not in the mood to be reasonable. about the limitations of her Talent. "What else have you been doing? You can't be spending all of your time practicing with fire."

"I'm trying to work on my soldiering skills as much as I can without a partner to practice with," Adrienne told her. It was the truth, if not the whole truth. She did spend a portion of each day training. "I wish there was someone here that I could spar with, but even running through the forms is helpful."

Louella made a sound that could have meant anything, and Adrienne smiled. "And you couldn't care less about sword practice."

"No more than you care about herbs," Louella agreed placidly. "That doesn't stop me from talking about them."

Adrienne tried to think of what she did during her days that might interest her friend. "I've been taking Strider, my horse, out for a few hours each day. He needs training as well."

"What sorts of things do you train him for?" Louella asked.

"He's a destrier—a horse specifically trained for battle—and that kind of work requires skills other horses don't have."

"I guess he's like a soldier of the horse world," Louella said. "Before you came here, I never thought much about what it takes to make a soldier." She had watched, and even attempted, Adrienne's meditative routines, but she had never once watched Adrienne practice with her sword.

"It takes more than a sword." Adrienne's hand traveled to the Talent-forged sword at her hip, but her thoughts were on the commission.

"It must be a complex skill," Louella said. "You wouldn't have been able to develop a Talent otherwise."

Adrienne smirked. "I'm glad at least one person sees that."

Louella's blue eyes clouded. "Maybe I should have said something earlier."

Adrienne knew her friend did not mind the soldiering profession the way most in Kessering did, but Adrienne was not foolish enough to think that Louella was completely comfortable with the reality of it.

Louella's interest in Strider was less complicated.

"A destrier needs to have absolute trust in his rider," Adrienne explained, switching back to the more comfortable topic of her horse. "He needs to be able to pull back, to switch off leads, to turn on his hindquarters when the soldier demands it, without hesitating."

"Why?"

"Battle is a loud and confusing place. A stallion like Strider can become caught up in the energy of it, and he needs to listen and trust absolutely the direction he is given by the soldier riding him. And the soldier needs to know that her horse is going to move when and how he's told, or the soldier won't be able to plan her next block or parry."

"It sounds dangerous," Louella said.

Adrienne thought that Louella seemed more concerned for the horse than the rider in this instance, and her mouth twisted in a wry smile. "It can be, even when horse and rider make a perfect team."

"Is it fair for the horse, do you think?"

Adrienne had never thought of it that way. Horses like Strider were chosen and trained from a young age. But then, Adrienne had been placed in a similar situation herself. "A horse has to show a certain temperament to be trained. Mild-mannered horses aren't taken to war."

"But it still wasn't the horse's choice."

With another person, Adrienne might have gotten mad at the comment, but moral debates with Louella were interesting, not upsetting. "Many men are drafted into war against their will. Some of those men don't last long—mentally, I mean. Some horses, either. Strider has a few physical scars from former battles, but mentally I would say he is as healthy as any horse. There aren't many horses of Strider's ilk, and he would be invaluable to a soldier on campaign."

"But you have him sitting in a stall in Kessering instead," Louella mused. "A bit of a waste, if he's as special as you say."

"He was a gift from my captain when I left Kyrog to come here," Adrienne told her.

Louella's blonde eyebrows pulled together in a frown as she considered this. "If a horse like Strider is so valuable, why were you...that is...you must have been very well thought of," Louella finally said.

"Yes." Adrienne looked down at the empty cup of tea in front of her, lost in thought until Louella took her hand.

"I've upset you. I didn't mean I thought you weren't well thought of before," she said. "It's just that if you were given such a gift, you must have really been special back at the camp." She let go of Adrienne's hand and leaned back in her chair, clearly frustrated. "I'm saying all of this wrong."

"It's not you," Adrienne said, meeting Louella's worried blue eyes. "I'm just thinking of Kyrog. Of home. I miss it."

"I'm sorry. I forget sometimes that you left people behind. I'm not used to dealing with homesickness."

"It's not just the people," Adrienne said, though much of it was. "In Kyrog I am regarded as a skilled soldier." She thought of the hours of hard work she had put in over the years. Of sweating through her leathers under the harsh sun of the dry season, and enduring the wet months that turned the dry ground to mud that sucked at her boots and made every step an effort. She did it all, practiced until muscles and bones went weak with weariness and pain, practiced until she was one of the best. Until no one looked at her and saw a mere woman, or worse, a girl whose father had given her away. "Skills count for a lot among soldiers. And I was a lieutenant—a leader—in Kyrog."

"They must have lost a lot when you left," Louella said, as if it was a revelation. "I never realized...I've spent almost my whole life in

Kessering. My father moved here after my mother died, when I was just a year old. I guess I don't think about life outside of Kessering as life, really. But Kyrog was your home, wasn't it, like Kessering is mine?"

The sympathy in Louella's voice nearly undid Adrienne, and she had to look away from the compassion she saw on her friend's face. "I had friends there," Adrienne said, her eyes losing focus as she saw not the wall in front of her, but a camp many miles and memories away. "Ricco, he was a fellow soldier. And Jeral. I was training Jeral, and had been for nine months, before I left."

"When I was getting to know you," Louella said, "I always just thought about what a great opportunity this was for you. You got to come here, to Kessering, and develop a Talent. I never thought about what you had to give up."

Adrienne pulled herself out of the past and took another sip of her tea, only to find that the cup was empty. "I had to leave a lot behind," Adrienne said, her hand slipping up and stroking the cord around her neck without conscious thought. She wondered not for the first time if she would ever get back what she had left in Kyrog. She wondered if Ricco and Jeral would be waiting for her back in the camp, or if they would be gone, possibly forever. She might have already lost two of her closest friends.

"I'm sorry." Louella forced a smile and grasped desperately for a new topic. "I've noticed the necklace you wear, but I've never seen the pendant. Can I have a closer look?"

Adrienne hesitated, then reached back and pulled the necklace over her head. "It was my mother's." Adrienne held the necklace out for Louella's examination.

"It's beautiful," Louella said, tracing a finger over the intricate design inset on the pendant.

"It's supposed to provide protection," Adrienne told her, looking at the lines of the artful knot.

"That's lovely," Louella said, handing the necklace back. "You must have been very young when you received this."

"I was four." Adrienne ran the cord through her hands. "My father gave it to me before he sent me away." She put the necklace back on, ran her thumb over the pendant once, then tucked it back under her blouse, where it would remain hidden from prying eyes. "I think he gave it to me because he felt guilty sending me away."

"Adrienne—"

The back door opened and Pieter strolled in, interrupting whatever Louella had been about to say. He seemed momentarily surprised by

Adrienne's presence but recovered quickly. "Hello. Adrienne, I didn't expect to see you here so late." He smiled at Louella.

"Adrienne's been too busy to come by lately," Louella said, standing to get Pieter a cup of tea. She passed close to him on her way, and Adrienne thought she saw Pieter's hand brush Louella's golden hair as the slender healer moved past him.

"Yes, she hasn't been by my shop either," Pieter said, taking a seat between Adrienne and Louella. "How have you been?"

"Not so bad," Adrienne said, studying him. "You?"

When Pieter accepted the cup from Louella their fingers brushed together and Louella's face pinked.

Adrienne was not experienced when it came to relationships, but she was not completely blind. She watched her friends with interest.

"I got a commission for barrel hoops," Pieter said when he finally looked away from Louella's flushed face. "An easy job. If I had a proper apprentice, I would give the assignment to him."

Adrienne looked over and found Louella staring at the blacksmith, her teacup forgotten in her hand, as if someone ordering barrel hoops was the most interesting news in the world. Adrienne nearly smiled. They seemed such an unlikely couple, but from the way Pieter had walked right in the back door of Louella's shop—the private entrance—Adrienne got the idea that she was the intruder there, and that Pieter was likely the reason Louella had still been up at this time of night. Which meant it was time for her to leave.

"It's getting late, and I was up early," Adrienne said, standing. "Louella, I'll stop by at lunch tomorrow and see if you're free."

"Of course." Louella and Pieter stood to see Adrienne out, and she almost smirked at their eagerness to have her gone. "Have a good night."

"You, too," Adrienne said, holding back the chuckle until the door was closed behind her.

CHAPTER NINE

"Are you still trying to form fire balls?" Louella asked as yet another ball unraveled as it left Adrienne's hand.

"I'm getting better," Adrienne insisted. She formed another ball in her hand, made a throwing motion, and with a tremendous force of will managed to keep the ball lit until it was nearly a foot from her hand. After that point, nothing she could do kept it from falling apart.

"That's better?" Louella asked skeptically.

"I just need more practice."

Louella shook her head. "I can see the effort it takes you to throw one of those. You're spending too much time and energy doing something that is not natural to your Talent. What you should be doing is practicing things you *can* do."

"But if I could throw flames in battle—"

"I don't know about battle," Louella said, "but I know that if the person has to be that close to you for you to hit them with a fireball, you might as well not be able to throw fire at all."

Before Adrienne had a chance to form a response to what she had to admit was a logical point, Pieter let himself into Louella's kitchen.

"What's going on?" He leaned back against the counter where Louella busied herself with the meal she was putting together. He had come for lunch, as it had become habit for the three of them to eat together whenever possible. It could still surprise Adrienne that she was friends with Louella and Pieter, even after months of knowing them.

But Adrienne had come to realize that she had a special bond with Pieter and Louella. They were not as different from her as Adrienne had assumed the first time she met them. The bond forged between soldiers who trained and fought together was strong—they had to trust each other with their lives—but the bond Adrienne shared with

144

the other Talented was even more exclusive than the bond Adrienne shared with the ranks of other soldiers she'd trained with. Maybe Louella and Pieter had never risked their lives to save hers, but they could relate to her in a way few others could.

"Look," Adrienne said, turning to show Pieter the ball of light. She went to throw it, and it unraveled before it had even left her hand.

Pieter cast Louella a sideways glance, then smiled unconvincingly at Adrienne. "You're getting better."

Adrienne sighed. Perhaps Louella was right. "No, I'm not."

"You will be." Pieter seemed confident that she would improve, and Adrienne was grateful for his support.

"I was telling Adrienne that she should move on from fireballs," Louella told Pieter. "Find new ways to use her Talent."

"It was easier for us," Pieter said. "We more or less knew how to use our Talents. Using fire as a weapon…it will take some thought."

The fact that Louella and Pieter had come to accept Adrienne's purpose here was one of the things she was most grateful for. Adrienne only wished that being a soldier did not distance her from the rest of the Talented. The distance between herself and Ben had grown since the night she had unexpectedly developed her Talent, though they worked together every day trying to find the limits of Adrienne's power. But Ben was not the real problem, nor were the other Talented who avoided her the cause of Adrienne's dissatisfaction. Adrienne was beginning to wonder about the commission's long-term plans. They had not mentioned again what her Talent was to be used for or how she should focus her ability, and there was no sign that another soldier was indeed going to be brought to Kessering. One of the groups that had been sent out to find a soldier to train had returned without a soldier at all, and the other group had yet to return to Kessering, though they had been gone for nearly a year.

Adrienne did not voice her concerns that outlaws had probably found and killed the men sent out into the countryside alone. If the scholar's only protection had been someone like Ilso, it was all too likely that they would never make it back to Kessering alive.

But there was no point in revealing such concerns, and if she told Ben or one of the other commissioners she would no doubt receive a lecture about King Burin's justice, or perhaps a lecture on how the Creator protects the faithful. She wanted neither.

"I made meat pies for lunch," Louella told Adrienne and Pieter, sliding the tray out of the brick oven and setting it on top to cool, "and I have leftover cobbler from last night."

"That sounds wonderful," Adrienne said, redirecting her focus to her friends. She hadn't told her friends about her worries regarding the commission. "What are you working on, Pieter?" She could tell from the lingering smell of wood smoke and ore that he had been at his forge before coming here. "More barrel hoops?"

He shrugged his massive shoulders, tilting his head from side to side to crack his neck. "No. I was asked to make a couple of hinges, easy work, but I'm going to try focusing my energy and Talent on what I want them to do, as opposed to whom I am making them for. If that works it would be a way to use my Talent so that it benefits more than one person, and can be passed from person to person."

Adrienne considered this and nodded. Despite her own developing Talent, Adrienne had trouble fully grasping the extent or limitations of anyone else's abilities, and the feeling seemed mutual when the others tried to understand hers. "I hope that works for you," Adrienne told him sincerely. "It would mean—"

"Adrienne!"

Adrienne recognized the voice and heard the underlying panic. She leapt to her feet and ran into the front room where a flushed Ben was breathing heavily and supporting himself against the doorpost.

"What's wrong?" she asked, surprised to see Ben in such a state.

"I-there-I—"

"Ben!" Adrienne snapped, infusing her voice with officer's steel. "What happened?"

Her command penetrated through the fear clouding Ben's mind. "There are men in the city," he gasped. "Armed men. They're attacking the guards!"

Adrienne came to attention. "Where? How many men are there?"

"They came in the north gate." He was still struggling to bring his breathing under control, but his mind seemed clearer. "Twelve men, but there might have been more that I didn't see." Ben's voice wavered. "They started killing people."

Adrienne cursed ripely. "Louella, start gathering the other healers; we'll need your skills. But be careful going through the streets. Ben, Pieter, I want you to get as many people inside, behind locked doors, as possible." Less victims, she thought. Less chance of hostages or collateral damage. She was halfway out the door before she turned back to see them all standing around uncertainly. "Go!"

She tore out of the small shop and ran toward the north end of the city. The fact that Ben had sought her out meant that the situation was dire, but she was not totally surprised by that. The guards weren't skilled enough to fight off men armed with anything more lethal than sticks. It had only been a matter of time before trouble cropped up that they could not handle.

Adrienne ran down the main thoroughfare. She could hear the clashing of swords in the distance, the terrified screams. The cries of pain.

She turned a corner and saw the battle, if it could be called that. Three of Kessering's guards were lying on the ground; three more were engaged in the fight and losing ground quickly. The rest of the guards stood back, paralyzed by fear and uncertainty, and Adrienne realized one of the downed men was their captain.

"With me!" Adrienne shouted, drawing her blue-tinged sword from its sheath. She caught the attention not only of the shocked guards, but of the enemy as well.

Unlike the city guardsmen who were dressed in their burnished armor, Adrienne wore only her *swa'il*. But the men who had come to Kessering were not without experience, and they quickly recognized her as being more dangerous than any of the men standing around wearing expressions of shock and fear along with their armor.

Two of the marauders who had been hanging back watching the slaughter approached Adrienne cautiously, swords raised.

Adrienne held her sword ready and shifted onto the balls of her feet. She waited for the men to come closer. One part of her mind analyzed them, looking for weaknesses, while another part was focused on her own body. It had been awhile since she had done anything other than run through sword forms, and it would be the first time she used the Talent-forged sword in battle. She couldn't afford to worry about either thing now; all she could do was hope for the best.

The smaller of the two men moved quickly, striking with a sudden burst of speed that she was sure had bled more than one opponent.

Adrienne turned his blade back, twisting her own blade in an attempt to force the sword out of his hand. It twisted his wrist back, and only a quick adjustment of his grip allowed him to keep hold of the weapon.

He was no amateur. Few soldiers could have recovered so quickly.

The bigger man, several inches taller than his companion and as much as seventy pounds heavier, approached Adrienne more slowly, his eyes sharply focused. Adrienne would have preferred to be cautious, to take her time and learn this new opponent with his careful moves and dangerous eyes, but another of Kessering's guards had fallen, and there was no time to wait. She dispatched the large man with her sword, shifted her blade to her left hand, and with a practiced movement pivoted and threw her knife, which stuck in the smaller man's throat.

His hand went to the protruding blade in his throat, and a gurgle of blood left his mouth before he collapsed, as dead as his friend.

She had expected to hit his chest and buy herself some time, and she took a single moment to be pleased with her unexpected luck before turning her attention back to the fight.

The remaining invaders converged around her, paying little mind to the few guards still standing, most of whom were wounded. The rest of the city guards were staying back, well away from the fighting, no more threat than the townspeople locked safely in their homes.

Nine against one were not odds in Adrienne's favor, and her mind raced with possibilities as her opponents inched closer. They were being cautious, having seen her in action, but they had her outnumbered, and they knew it. If the guards had been willing to help, Adrienne thought they might be able to dispatch two or three of the raiders, or at least provide a useful distraction, but she knew better than to count on them to do anything more than stand there and stare.

She swept her sword out in front of her in a semi-circle, trying to keep the men back, but it was futile. There were too many of them.

Adrienne sensed movement behind her, but she did not turn fast enough and felt the white-hot pain of a sword stabbing into her thigh.

She stumbled back and fell to one knee as the men approached. One stepped forward, taking his time, enjoying the moment, and Adrienne felt the heat of temper fill her. She would not die on her knees. With all of her remaining strength she surged to her feet and raised her sword. The blue-tinged weapon caught the light and seemed to glow as she brought it down.

Fire erupted. It ran down the length of her sword and up the other man's. It ran over his hands and arms, catching his clothes on fire. He dropped the weapon, and though the connection with her was lost, it didn't matter. The flame seemed to have a life of its own as it covered the man's body, consuming him.

Even as he screamed in pain, Adrienne turned away from the human torch and brought the fight to the other men. The pain in her leg was pushed aside, her tiredness a thing of the past as anger and power took its place.

Some of the men scattered, but most stayed to fight, rage and blood lust overpowering fear and common sense alike. Between the eager flames that ripped down her sword and the skill that had been bred into her for most of her life, it was only a matter of minutes until all of her enemies were laid at her feet, some burnt until they were little more than ash.

Adrienne stood with her legs apart, blood forming a pool around her left boot, sword tip resting on the ground. She breathed heavily as she took in her surroundings.

Guards and townspeople were on the ground, some twisting and moaning, others ominously still. Men and women walked amongst them, and where they stopped the fallen seemed to revive.

Healers, Adrienne realized as her mind cleared slightly of the post-fight haze and the mind-numbing exhaustion brought on by blood loss. *Talented healers.*

"You're hurt!"

It was Louella. Before Adrienne had a chance to answer, Louella bent to examine the stab wound on Adrienne's thigh. A hot, tingling sensation went up and down Adrienne's leg, and the pain faded. She looked down and saw no fresh blood coming through her blood soaked *swa'il*, though the damage to the leather was irreparable. Through the wide tear in the leather and the blood still on her skin, Adrienne saw smooth, unblemished flesh. "Thank you," she said, aware of how serious the wound could have been without Louella there. "How are the others?"

Louella's light blue eyes were sad. "Three of the guards are dead," she said. "Two more were seriously injured, but they should be okay."

Adrienne nodded.

"Two townswomen are dead," Louella added softly. "Four men. A few more people were hurt...a child." She shook her head and Pieter, who had been standing silently beside her, stroked the healer's golden hair with a large, calloused hand. "Why did this have to happen?" Louella asked.

"It didn't have to," Adrienne said bitterly, though she knew the question was meant to be rhetorical. "If we had better leaders and a central army, maybe no one would have died today. If the commission had been prepared, this could have been prevented. Kessering is a wealthy city. A wealthy city with fine goods that was left poorly defended, with barely a double handful of guards all told. The raiders could have been kings in this city, pillaging and making sport of the people living there."

"Elder Rynn and the others couldn't have known."

"It's their job to know!" Adrienne said. "If they are going to be leaders here, it is their job to protect their people."

"You protected us," Louella said, resting her hand lightly on Adrienne's shoulder.

"You did well," Pieter said. His face was set in grim lines as he took in the carnage that filled the normally peaceful street. Although she knew Pieter and Louella accepted the fact that she was a soldier, she was still surprised by his words.

But Pieter looked serious, and Adrienne realized he was not looking at the men she had killed, but at the innocent people hurt and killed by the those men. "It was the sword," she explained.

Pieter nodded. "I could feel it." Surprise won through Adrienne's exhaustion, and it must have shown on her face, because Pieter continued without her having to ask. "I can't always feel what I've made, not without trying, but when your fire was on it...I could feel the power."

"They're connected," she said. "The Talents seem to amplify when brought together." She had felt the immense power rushing through her Talent-imbued sword when she had run fire down the blade; it had been like nothing she had ever felt before.

"They're meant to work together," Pieter said softly.

Louella broke into their conversation with a gentle voice. "We'll discuss this later," she said. "Adrienne, I believe you need to sit down, have something to drink. Between the fight and your leg..."

"Yes, that would be good." Adrienne couldn't remember ever being so tired after a fight. The first fight in which she had killed a man had been draining emotionally, but this was different. The fight had not been long, yet she felt as though it had taken hours. Usually after a fight there was still adrenaline in her system, boosting her, but now all she wanted was to lie down and sleep. It was more than blood loss. It was using her Talent in that way.

Her leg no longer pained her as it had, but it ached enough to remind her of the recent injury that could have cost her leg, if not her life.

"Come back to the shop with me," Louella coaxed.

"She can't go with you just yet," Ben said, appearing from nowhere. His face was ashen, and he was avoiding looking at any of the bodies. Adrienne was surprised to see him there at all.

"Master Ruthford," Louella said in her firm healer's tone, "Adrienne was badly hurt. She needs to rest now."

Ben looked slightly abashed, but he didn't back down. "I'm sorry, but the commission has asked to see her immediately."

"Maybe the rest of the commission should come down here and see what was done, and then they can determine whether what Lieutenant Rydaeg needs right now is a lecture!" Louella said, her voice rising in pitch as her ire grew. Ben's shoulders hunched up around his ears as he shook his head.

Adrienne was not so tired that she could not feel anger, and that anger bolstered her, giving her the energy she needed to speak. "It's all right, Louella," she said, though it was anything but. "I'll visit you when I can."

Adrienne followed Ben toward the large library in silence. The streets were filling again, but there was no business being done. The talk was of the violence and death that had come so suddenly to the normally peaceful city. The bodies still lay there, and Adrienne wondered idly who would come to remove them.

People fell silent when Adrienne passed them on the street, watching her warily until she was well past them before resuming their hushed conversations. It was beyond even their usual level of fear, which had dissipated only somewhat in the months she had been in Kessering. She caught snatches of conversation, and realized for the first time that her clothes were covered in blood. There was a rip in the sleeve of her *swa'il* that she had not noticed, and her now-healed thigh was bared for all to see by the large, bloody tear the sword had made in the leather before reaching flesh. She lifted a hand to her cheek, and it came away wet from blood. The blood wasn't hers, and she wiped it on her ruined leathers.

To the townspeople, she must finally look the part of the monster they had always imagined her to be. They would have heard by now about how she had used her Talent to kill those men. The fire had just become another weapon, and one they could not defend against or anticipate the way they could a sword. She was surprised that they did not run screaming at the sight of her.

"Don't pay attention to them," Ben said, surprising Adrienne. She had not expected any words of comfort from him. He gave her a reassuring look and she felt some of the tension leave her. When they came to the library and Adrienne took her place before the commission, Ben remained at her side in a show of support rather than taking his place at the table. She felt a warm gratitude for him in that moment.

"We have heard about the fight," Elder Rynn said without preamble. "We also heard that you used your ability against others, resulting in the loss of several lives."

"I used whatever means were available to take out the men threatening the lives of the defenseless citizens of Kessering," Adrienne replied. She squared her shoulders and—though it was an effort to stand upright—refused to show weakness by favoring the leg so recently run through with a sword.

"We never gave you permission to use your ability in such a way," Elder Rynn said, his normally frail voice strong in anger. "The people will panic. There will likely be mass hysteria after this."

"Better they panic about me now that they are safe than be left to panic under the marauders' control," Adrienne argued. "The men who invaded the city had already killed several people before I arrived, and as for using fire…I couldn't take on all the remaining men alone with just my sword." She remembered well the feeling, the pain, of an enemy sword tearing into her flesh, and her anger grew as she remembered that the remaining guards of Kessering had stood there doing nothing while she stared down a blade wet with her own blood.

Her eyes were hard and flat as she stared into the eyes of Elder Rynn. "I did what I had to do to keep more people from being killed. To keep myself from being killed."

"That is why we have guards," the old man replied, not giving an inch. Lady Chessing smiled, looking as if she was relishing every word.

Adrienne opened her mouth to defend herself, but Ben spoke before she had a chance. "Three of the guards are among the dead," Ben told Elder Rynn. "And Adrienne was badly injured during the fight. I believe she did what was necessary."

Elder Rynn nodded. "I had heard that not all of the guards survived," he said, not asking how Adrienne fared now.

"Three guards dead, and two seriously wounded and unable to help," Ben told him. "The others had injuries that were less severe: some cuts, a few broken bones which would have hampered any aid they could have provided Adrienne. Only two of the guards were unscathed." Adrienne was glad that it was Ben speaking, not she. Anything she said to the commission would merely sound defensive.

"Then surely those two healthy young men could have helped even the odds," Lady Chessing said with a smile. "Especially with the wounded helping where they could. If this…woman had not jumped to such extremes—"

"Reports say those two uninjured guards never tried to fight off the attackers," Ben said uneasily. "And she did not use fire until after she herself was stabbed."

Franklin frowned. "What do you mean?" he asked.

"One of the men stabbed Adrienne in the thigh," Ben told him, gesturing to her leg. The blood soaked leather gave the testimony that the smooth skin could not.

"No, not about her leg," Franklin said impatiently. "What do you mean about the guards not helping?"

Adrienne wondered if Franklin would have cared about her leg if she had still been bleeding. She shoved the thought aside and returned to Franklin's question. "The guards froze," Adrienne said, knowing that Ben wouldn't know—or be able to explain—what had happened to the guards. "When their officer fell, the remaining guards froze. They were completely unprepared to face an enemy like the one they did today."

"All of our guards had training." This time it was Elder Rynn who sounded defensive.

"Not enough," Adrienne said. "Not for this. They were sloppy. Their skills were minimal, especially when it came to working as a team."

"That is no way to speak of the dead," Elder Rynn said. The rest of the commission looked similarly outraged. Even Ben looked uneasy at her harsh words and shifted slightly away from her.

Adrienne thought of the fallen men and felt pity, and she looked into Elder Rynn's face and felt more. She knew the pain of losing men in battle. But now was not the time to stop and mourn. And it was not the time to soften the truth to protect the dead. It was beyond ridiculous to put the memory of the dead before the welfare of the living. "I am merely stating the truth. The guards here lack the skill and experience necessary to defend Kessering against the bands of outlaws that roam Samaro looking for rich cities to plunder. And the force of guards is much too small."

"The size of the guard has always been more than adequate," Elder Rynn told her stiffly. "They handle any trouble that arises in the city."

"Trouble like thieving and drunken brawls," Adrienne agreed, "but today Kessering was attacked by a group of men intent on killing, torturing, and looting. Your guards crumbled before them because they were not properly prepared for such an onslaught."

The commission began to disagree, loudly and passionately. Lady Chessing's shrill voice spoke of exaggeration and barbaric soldiers, Franklin said something about the guards regrouping and "routing the invaders." Elder Rynn sat quietly, listening, and Adrienne wished she could know his thoughts.

"Adrienne is right," Ben said, stunning everyone into silence. "There were twelve men, maybe more, who came into the city and started hurting people. Three of our guards died, but they only killed one of the...one of the attackers. If it weren't for Adrienne, for her skills, for the fact that she used her ability to kill those men before they could kill her, everyone who could have defended the city would be dead," his voice wavered slightly. "Only the Creator knows what would be happening now, if not for her."

"It may not have been so bad," Franklin said. "We cannot know what those men would have done. Had we simply allowed them to take what they wanted—"

"They killed six unarmed men and women and injured others, including defenseless children," Adrienne said, ruthlessly driving home each point. "These men would have continued to terrorize your people until they tired of Kessering. Then they would have stolen what they could, destroyed what they couldn't, and left."

"You don't know that," Lady Chessing scoffed, but her dark eyes shifted uncertainly.

"I've met men like those that attacked today," Adrienne told her, told all of them. "I have spent time cleaning up such groups and restoring order to villages that have been ravaged by them." Memories of Pelarion came to her once again. Rarely had any atrocity haunted her so, but the innocent girl laid in a grave refused to leave her mind, no matter how many months had passed since that day.

"'Cleaning up,'" Lady Chessing repeated. "A nice way of saying 'killed.' Isn't that what you mean? That you spent time killing groups of men."

Adrienne raised her chin. "Killing groups of thieves, rapists, and murderers," she confirmed. "Those that we capture are turned over to the proper authorities for judgment, and are hanged for their crimes. But if we kill them, that action is sanctioned by the government, by King Burin, as part of what is necessary to keep his citizens safe." Sometimes the king's name seemed to have an almost magical effect on the commissioners, as if anything the king agreed with was absolutely acceptable. This was not one of those times.

Lady Chessing looked about to respond when Elder Rynn raised his hand. "Violence solves nothing," he said. "Killing solves nothing."

"I disagree," Adrienne said. "I haven't just come to cities to clean them up; Sometimes I've come too late. I've watched cities burn. If I prevented that today, if I saved lives today, I believe that solves a lot. "

Elder Rynn shook his head, but again Ben spoke up in her defense. "Adrienne is right," he said, though he looked uncomfortable supporting her actions in such entirety. "This commission was formed with the purpose of fighting Almet. We must accept that fighting— even killing—is sometimes the only option."

"We were brought together to end the conflict," Elder Rynn corrected. "That does not necessarily entail fighting."

Adrienne suppressed the urge to laugh. An army without a plan was doomed to failure, and she wondered if the scholars on the commission were aware that the more they changed their plans, the more likely the failure of the commission was.

"What would you have had her do today?" Ben asked. "If you could change what Adrienne had done, how would you alter the events? Allow the other guards to be slaughtered, and Adrienne along with them?"

Elder Rynn was silent for a long moment. Whatever he decided, the death of one group would still have been the price of saving the other. "It seems that, despite the crude methods, there was not a better means of dealing with these invaders today," he reluctantly admitted. "Perhaps Adrienne's actions were in the best interests of the city."

"I would like to continue to do what I can to help this city," Adrienne said as a thought began to take shape in her mind. "You will need to replace the guards lost today, and I would like to train them."

"Surely the remaining guards should be in charge of the training," Lady Chessing said, glaring at Adrienne. Adrienne knew she was lucky that it was Elder Rynn, not Lady Chessing, who made the final decisions in such matters.

It was an effort of will that kept Adrienne from telling the woman exactly what she thought of the remaining guards training the replacements. "With their commander dead, that will be difficult," Adrienne said instead. She did not mention that with how poorly trained the guards had seemed that day, any men trained by them could not hope to be much better.

"I also suggest at least tripling, the number of guards the city has." Adrienne thought that sixty guards would be a better number than forty, but if she were to ask for so many, she knew she might as well ask for the moons and stars with them for all the good it would do.

"That won't be necessary," Elder Rynn told her. "Fifteen guards have always been enough. This attack was an aberration that has been taken care of."

"Men like those that attacked today will always set their eyes on places like Kessering," Adrienne argued. "Cities with riches and minimal guards are easy targets. After the outcome of today's fight, Kessering might appear to be more of a challenge, but soon memories of that will fade. For the long term safety of Kessering, I believe a larger, better trained force will be necessary."

"I agree," Ben said. "We should let Adrienne take charge of the guards, and listen to her advice in this situation. It would be the best use of her skills." It was a logical argument, and most of the scholars seemed to be considering it. Ben looked at Adrienne. "Will thirty guards suffice?"

It was fewer than she wanted, but it was a start. "Yes."

"You don't think it will take away from the training time the two of you need?" Elder Rynn asked Ben.

Ben looked between the Elder and Adrienne, who was covered in blood and exhausted from the fight, but still standing there, straight and strong, before the commission. "I don't know how much more instruction I can give her," Ben said honestly. "What she can do, what she did today…it was beyond any hopes I had for her abilities. She has exceeded all of my expectations."

Training the Kessering guards was different than training the Yearlings back in Kyrog. Adrienne was able to handle and influence the guards new to the post, but the men who had already been guards before Adrienne took over the training were belligerent and unwilling to listen to her instructions.

"Okay, let's start from the beginning," Adrienne told the thirty assembled men. "Sheathe your swords."

"Is this really necessary?" asked one of the guards who had been present when the city was attacked. "We know how to handle swords." He looked around at the new additions to the city guard. "Well, some of us know."

Adrienne considered it amazing that any of the guards, new or old, weren't tripping over their own swords. As a lieutenant at Kyrog, her word had been law, and the penalty for disobeying her had been steep. Here, she had no power over the men she was training except for the meager power some of them gave her. In Kyrog, she would have demonstrated exactly how easily she could disarm him right now. Here, she had to rely instead on her less-honed skills of persuasion.

"Not everyone is at the same level," Adrienne explained to the guard with a patience she was not really feeling. "I want to train all of you as a unit, from the beginning, until you are all equally capable of using your weapons effectively. Now sheathe your swords, and we'll start from the beginning."

She ran them through the basic sword maneuvers, both offensive and defensive, at a slow and controlled pace, remembering almost fondly when she had thought Jeral's skill was deficient. She had gone to Captain Garrett's tent full of fire and anger over Jeral's lack of skill, but even then he had been leagues ahead of these men.

She wished she could train the city guard as she had Jeral. Instead of practice sheathing and unsheathing swords, Adrienne would start by teaching them to fight without weapons and build their skills from that most basic level. But in this situation, regardless of what she knew to be best, training them as she had trained Jeral was not an option. The existing guards would never have tolerated it, and even many of the new guards would probably balk at the idea of waiting to get trained with weapons for even a few days, let alone months.

Adrienne had the assembled guards increase the speed of the maneuvers, and watched as the careful synchronicity fell apart. Half of them could not follow the correct form at increased speed, and many of those that could were tiring already. "Good," Adrienne said with false enthusiasm when they completed their forms. "Let's go for a short run before we break for lunch."

"Why?" It was the same guard who had questioned her about sheathing their swords—Charles—and Adrienne wished she could assign him to cleaning the mess hall for a week. It was the least of what he deserved.

"To clear the mind," she told him. She gave him a conspiratorial smile, a we're-on-the-same-side look. "And to see how the new recruits keep up."

Charles nodded wisely. "Of course. Test them out."

Adrienne knew that it would be as much a test for Charles as any of the other men, and the run had never been meant as a test but a way to work on their endurance. She disliked having to turn it into a competition. "Okay, fall in." She started them off at an easy pace, barely faster than a jog. The men were mostly young, but none of them were used to strenuous physical activity.

Adrienne had devised a two mile loop, and by the end of it many of the men were lagging, a few even stopping to walk and catch their breaths. Charles was one of the latter, and Adrienne could see the anger on his face as he realized he had failed the test. "Let's break until mid-afternoon," Adrienne said. "We'll practice sparring then. Meet back here at three."

She would need the extra time to prepare some supplies. She did not trust these men to spar with real weapons and not kill themselves, so she would need some practice swords for them to use.

"You look unhappy," Pieter said. Adrienne was surprised to see the blacksmith at the training ground. Neither he nor Louella had shown much interest in her new assignment other than asking if she was pleased to have it. She had initially said yes, but now she was not so sure.

"I have no authority over the trainees," she told him, gripping her braid in a fist and tugging repeatedly. "How am I supposed to train them right when they can do whatever they want without consequences?"

Pieter looked speculative. "The commission wants you to train them. Won't they give you more control if you tell them it's necessary?"

Adrienne snorted derisively. "The commission hardly wanted me in charge of training at all. If I ask for more control over the guards, they will probably stop the training where it is." She sighed and released the hold on her braid that she had hardly been aware of taking, letting her hand fall back to her side. "Besides, I doubt they would understand the need to slow the pace and make sure everyone is on solid ground before escalating their training."

Pieter's muscular arms bulged as he crossed them. "Doesn't all training start with building a base?" he asked. "I was a blacksmith's apprentice for six months before I got to do more than stoke the fire and pump the bellows."

"Because you might have ruined your master's work, or hurt yourself," she said. "Soldiering is like that: dangerous even during training if you don't know enough. I don't think whatever training is necessary to become a scholar calls for those same checks." Her lips twisted in a wry smile. "All scholars would need to worry about is dropping books on their feet."

He made a noncommittal sound. "Perhaps." He was quiet a minute, studying her. "Are you sure you can't…intimidate them into listening?" he asked. "They don't know the limits of your authority."

Adrienne nearly laughed. "I stopped being intimidating the moment I became a commission-approved instructor," she said bitterly. It had been as though, now that the commission was using her, she was no longer dangerous. Even the citizens of Kessering treated her differently now. Despite her bloody walk through the city after the battle, once the commission had put her in charge of training the guards it seemed she was suddenly considered safe. She'd spent months wishing people weren't afraid of her, but now that they weren't she realized it was almost worse this way. No fear, but also no respect.

Adrienne could tell from Pieter's expression that he saw the problem now, and no easy solution to it. "If there's anything I can do," he offered.

"You can help me find something to use as practice swords," she told him. "They're likely to stab one another if I give them the real thing."

Pieter nodded but didn't move. "I didn't come here to ask you about the training. Or not just that."

"Why then?"

"I helped to bury the bodies today."

Adrienne's face softened in sympathy. "I'm sorry. I know how hard it is."

He moved his big shoulders uncomfortably. "That's not why I'm here, either. I found these." He held out his hand and in his palm were three coins.

Adrienne stepped closer and picked one up to examine it. At first it was foreign to her, but with a stab of shock she recognized the markings. "It's Almetian."

"I know. I showed it to Louella, and she identified it."

"Louella?"

"She has some Almetian coins. From her parents."

"They were Almetian," Adrienne said. She'd thought as much.

"Her mother was born in Almet, her father on the Samaroan side of the border. She doesn't tell people."

Adrienne nodded. Suspecting and knowing were two different things. She looked back down at the coin, then back up into Pieter's face. "What does it mean?"

"I don't know."

Adrienne was thankful that the sparring had been done with practice swords. As it was, the men were bruised and bleeding, and she had needed to call for Louella when one of the men tripped over his wooden practice sword and split his scalp on the hard stone pathway.

Real swords likely would have resulted in multiple deaths.

"You all did well," Adrienne lied. She wanted to curse them out, like she would the Yearlings in Kyrog, but she locked the words down tight. "I saw some of you using the moves I taught you over the last few days."

Far too few had used the moves, and that was the problem. Adrienne had made it a point to have her trainees in Kyrog as familiar with the moves as they were with breathing before they ever began sparring. Jeral had told her once that he would sometimes dream that he was doing those moves at night. There was less danger and more value in sparring when everyone knew what they were doing. What they had done today had been a waste of everyone's time.

"For the rest of the week we will stick with going over forms with real swords before resuming sparring with practice swords next week."

There were grumbles from the men, and the ever-troublesome Charles stepped to the front of the group, his legs widespread, hands on his hips. Ricco favored that stance, but Charles looked pompous rather than formidable in that particular pose. "Why can't we spar again tomorrow?" he asked.

With supreme effort, Adrienne forced her snarl into a smile. "A few days will give your scrapes and bruises time to heal," she said. Waiting for scrapes and bruises to heal was a ridiculous excuse, one that would have had any soldier in Kyrog bent over with laughter, but the assembled men seemed to be considering it. Some even nodded their heads in agreement.

"We could go to the healers," Charles said, jutting his chin forward.

"And you can wait a few days to spar again," Adrienne said firmly, not backing down. Charles was a bully, and if she gave in to Charles on this, she would lose the little control she had over the men.

"If we go to the healers, we won't have to wait to practice more," another man said, apparently emboldened by Charles's words.

"If the minor injuries you sustained today warrant a trip to a healer's shop, perhaps you should consider a different means of employ," Adrienne snapped. "Dismissed."

She left before anyone else could argue with her, and when she was safely out of view she removed her leather gloves and threw them down an alley, disgusted with the men and with herself. She wanted to slap the smile off that smug bastard Charles's face. She wanted to spar with one of them to show them all just how ill-prepared they were. She wanted to scream and rant and rave, but she had no choice but to keep her emotions under tight control.

Adrienne took several deep breaths before going to collect her gloves. As she bent over the second one, she became aware of another presence in the alley.

She turned with a smooth, practiced move and stood to face the young guard at the entrance to the narrow street.

"Ad-er-Lieutenant?" he asked, seemingly unsure how to address her.

"Lieutenant," she confirmed. If anyone in this Creator-blasted city should call her Lieutenant, it was the men she trained.

"Lieutenant, the way you're training us…it's not how you would train soldiers, is it?"

"No," Adrienne said, her answer coming out sharp and impatient. She wanted to escape the fool guards for just a short time, not relive the disaster that was their training by talking about it with one of them.

"Why? That is, I heard you have experience training soldiers, and I'm wondering why you aren't training us like you would train them. Soldiers." Fear and nerves had him stumbling over his words.

"What's your name?" Adrienne asked.

"Flynn, Lieutenant."

"Flynn. My main job in Kyrog was training soldiers from other camps. Those soldiers would come to Kyrog for training with the elite, and I would give them that." She remembered the epiphany she'd had when training Jeral, the moment she'd realized the difference she could make by training even just one soldier. "In Kyrog, months could pass before any of my trainees even touched a weapon."

Flynn frowned. "Then why did you let us spar today?" he asked.

"How long would your fellow guards be content practicing without swords?"

"So you don't think we're ready for swords," he asked, sounding disappointed.

"You're about as ready to use swords as a bunch of children are," Adrienne answered roughly. "Having the lot of you spar is a joke, but the commission will replace me if they're not satisfied with my methods, and I'm the only person in the city qualified to train you."

"I want to be trained right," Flynn said softly, staring down at his scuffed boots with an expression very close to shame.

"What?" Adrienne asked, sure she'd misheard him.

Flynn looked up and locked his determined brown eyes on hers. "Lieutenant, I want to be trained right. The way you would train someone meant to be a soldier."

Adrienne looked the young man over again. He was just under six feet tall, by her estimate, and starting to replace the gangly build of youth with muscle. He was probably a year or two younger than she, around Jeral's age. His eyes were an unremarkable shade of brown, but there was a passion in them that Adrienne recognized. A desire to be the best.

It was something they shared.

"If that's what you want, you should go to Kyrog," she told him. "I can write a letter—"

Flynn shook his head. "I want to be a guard here in my city," he said, "but I want to be...good. Great." He flushed beneath his dark skin. "I heard about what you did with those men who attacked.

161

Before the fire part, when you were just using your sword like a regular sword, I mean. I want to be able to do that."

Adrienne remembered taking out the first two men. She was surprised that anyone had repeated that tale in a complimentary way. That anyone even remembered that part in light of what had come after. "I can train you," she told Flynn. "You'll have to do what the other guards are doing when we practice as a unit, but meet me outside my inn tomorrow morning, half an hour before sun-up, and we'll begin your private lessons."

"Really?" Flynn asked. "Thank you, Lieutenant."

"Don't thank me yet."

CHAPTER TEN

Of the thirty men Adrienne trained every day as guards, six of them had decided to join Flynn for extra training, and only one of those had been a guard before Kessering had been attacked. Edward Witter had been seriously injured in the attack on Kessering, and this time he planned to improve his odds of not getting stabbed in the gut, a wound that would have been fatal in any city that was not home to Talented healers.

"You're all showing a lot of improvement," Adrienne told the seven men engaged in extra training before she released them for breakfast. They would meet again, with the rest of the guards, in just over an hour. "You did a good job today." A brisk five mile run, in addition to the meditative moves and sword forms, had become their morning ritual. Their stamina and balance had improved the most; their ability to handle swords was impressive only when compared to those that did not join them for extra practice, but they were improving just the same.

"I want to thank you for this," Edward said. At thirty-eight, he was also the oldest of the small group receiving extra training, and their unofficial spokesman. "Training us like this, it's as much extra work for you as it is for us."

Adrienne nodded her head, not bothering to deny that truth. "I wish more of the men were willing to put in the extra effort."

It was both frustrating and baffling to her that so many of the guards were not interested in learning more than the basics necessary to deal with the average thief or drunk. It was as if the attack had taught them nothing. Even those who had been guards before and seen firsthand what happened when they went up against more skilled adversaries were not much interested in improving.

163

Training in Kyrog had spoiled Adrienne. She was astounded by the reality that many people would choose ease and mediocrity over the effort it took to become truly accomplished at something. "I'll see you all in an hour," she said.

She made her way through the city streets, and despite the people on the streets, she felt oddly alone. Some of the people meandered through the street with no clear destination, stopping to browse the carts and tables selling wares or to look in the shop windows. Others hurried on their way, blind and deaf to those who made their livings as street hawkers. No one looked at Adrienne.

Adrienne pushed away the loneliness, refusing to feel it, as she instead took in the city as a whole. She had become accustomed to the chaos of Kessering. Not that it was loud and noticeably unruly, Kessering was hardly big enough to have the true noise and bustle of a large city, but it lacked the unity of purpose that Kyrog had. Perhaps that unity was why Adrienne had never felt lonely in Kyrog, even when her friends were out on a mission and she was not. The commission had a mission, and Adrienne was supposed to be a part of it, but she didn't feel like it.

She saw a child running down the street, being chased by two others in what she took to be a game based on the laughter from all three of them. It had taken time, but after half a year in Kessering she had become accustomed to the disorganized nature of civilian life. She might not feel a part of it, but it was familiar now.

Adrienne turned onto Market Street and became aware of a new tension. Individual tensions over pricing and arguments were common on the busy commercial street, but this was…more. It was unified. Something had happened to bring these disparate people into a group mindset.

She had not felt such intense group thought since before she had started training the guards. Before then, as a group, the people of Kessering had viewed her as a dangerous outsider, and they had come together in such a way. But Adrienne knew that this time it was not her that they were reacting to.

Adrienne looked around, but she could not see anything in the crowd of people that would warrant such behavior. She heard no screams or shouts to signal another attack, and it would be nearly impossible to find the source of this tension in the crowded streets. She was suddenly grateful that Kessering was not a typical city where newcomers could fade into anonymity by entering an inn or tavern or moving to a less populated street. In Kessering, all visitors to the city made an appearance before the city leaders sooner rather than later.

She changed directions and headed for the library, no longer meandering through the crowds to pass the time. She cut through the milling people with a clear purpose, wondering what she might discover when she reached her destination.

As she neared the library where the commission convened, Adrienne caught snatches of conversation from the crowd. Most of it was just excited whispering that Adrienne did not stop to listen to, but one word was repeated again and again. M'bai.

Adrienne picked up her pace until she was nearly running through the crowds. People jumped out of her way, and a cynical part of her wondered if she would again be feared for such action, or if the people of Kessering would accept it as normal simply because they expected inappropriate behavior from a soldier.

The clerk waiting at the door of the commission's meeting room didn't bother trying to stop her, but he did rush forward to announce her presence to the commission before she could enter the room herself. "Lieutenant Adrienne Rydaeg," he said stiffly as she brushed past him.

"I hope that your presence does not mean trouble in the city, Adrienne," Elder Rynn said patronizingly. Unlike the guards, or even the uptight clerk, he had never deigned to address her by rank. Instead, his tone often suggested he was speaking to a misbehaved child.

Adrienne ignored him and scanned the room. Ben seemed surprised to see her, no doubt because she had made it a point not to cause trouble since being placed in charge of the guards. Franklin, dressed today in florid orange, looked as though he disapproved of her presence; the faint smile on Lady Chessing's face suggested she was hoping Adrienne got in trouble for barging in the way she had.

But it wasn't the commissioners' varied reactions that held Adrienne's attention. It was the three unknown men standing off to the side that captured her interest.

One of the men was older, perhaps forty, with a tall, slender build. He was dressed plainly in a brown shirt and darker brown trousers. The man beside him was shorter, burlier, with a cudgel at his hip and a longbow strapped to his back. Amazingly, Adrienne thought he could probably use both. The first was a scholar, Adrienne surmised, and the second served as his guard. It was a setup similar to the one Tam and Ilso had had when they had gone to Kyrog looking for a soldier, and she dismissed both men as momentarily unimportant.

It was the other person who captured her attention. He stood slightly apart from the other two, and she knew it was this man who had caused the unified tension in the people of Kessering. The man was tall, well over six feet, with shoulders broad as an axe handle. His short-cropped black hair was tightly curled, and his eyes were a stunning ice-blue in comparison to his ebony skin. Though he was not as heavily muscled as Pieter was, there could be no doubt of his strength.

"No, but there is a problem," Adrienne said heatedly, tearing her eyes away from the stranger to rest the Elder. "You placed me in charge of the city's defense, but didn't tell me when a potential threat arrived in the city." Her eyes shifted from Elder Rynn to the stranger and back again. She clenched and unclenched her hands to keep them from shaking with anger, and knew she would have to speak with the guards who had been assigned to watch the gates. They should have informed her the instant the trio entered the city. She had told the guards to alert her to any group that they thought might pose a danger to Kessering, and they had failed to do so.

"Do you think he is a threat because he is a soldier?" Lady Chessing asked. "A bit hypocritical of you."

Elder Rynn looked irritated by them both. "We do not consider this man to be a threat at this time," Elder Rynn told Adrienne in his calm, dry voice.

Adrienne looked at the stranger again and thought that he just might be the most dangerous man she had ever seen. Sleek as the jungle cats to the south, he stood just as stealthily, watching her and the rest of the room with an unreadable expression.

The weapon that the man held, though unfamiliar to Adrienne, was reminiscent of a spear. The butt of it rested on the ground, but the iron tip which came up to his shoulder was more long-bladed dagger than spear-tip. Though the weapon was strange to Adrienne, the man held it like an extension of himself, much the way Adrienne wore her sword.

"Perhaps he's not a threat," Adrienne said, "but if my suspicions as to why he is here are correct, I should have been informed. I am the only other soldier in Kessering." Adrienne had been awaiting the arrival of another soldier since her first day in Kessering, when she had been told other parties had been sent out to bring back soldiers as well. But she had expected a soldier from another camp, or maybe even a soldier from King Burin's army, not one of the legendary M'bai.

She knew of the M'bai only through stories, but what she had heard of the mysterious tribesmen of the Modabi Mountains had only served to increase her curiosity. Tales said they were giants; that they could disappear in one shadow and reappear in another; that they were not human at all but something more. Whatever the truth about the M'bai was, Adrienne could see for herself that this stranger was no ordinary man.

"We would have contacted you when and if we deemed it appropriate," Elder Rynn said. "We have only just begun our interview process, and have not yet decided if he will qualify." The way Elder Rynn stared at the man, eyes cool and remote in his wrinkled face, sent a shiver down Adrienne's spine.

"Then I ask to be allowed to stay for the interview process," Adrienne said. "I may be able to offer insights."

"You may stay," Elder Rynn said, ignoring Lady Chessing's strangled gasp of outrage. "However, you will remain silent. If you speak out of turn, you will be removed from this room immediately. Understood?"

Adrienne nodded and saw Ben let out a relieved sigh.

"This interview will now proceed." Elder Rynn focused his attention on the tall M'bai man. "What is your name?"

"Malokai Kyzeka." Malokai's voice was like dark velvet, deep and smooth.

"How long have you been a soldier?"

"I am not a soldier."

There was murmuring amongst the commission members, and the scholar who had brought Malokai before the commission leapt to explain. "The M'bai do not have soldiers the way we do," he said quickly, his hands grasping each other at his waist. "He is one of their best fighters, however. I was assured of this fact before I brought him." The man's words tripped over each other as he rushed to defend himself and his choice of soldier—warrior.

Elder Rynn held up a hand to halt any further explanations from the eager scholar. "You can fight?" he asked Malokai.

"Anyone can fight," Malokai responded.

Elder Rynn scowled, causing the brackets around his mouth to deepen so that they looked like gouges carved into charred wood. "I don't appreciate glib answers," he told Malokai.

Malokai's bland expression never changed. "Anyone can fight," he repeated. "If you wanted to know if I was skilled, that should have been your question." His words and tone were lyrical, but they revealed nothing of his thoughts, and there was no sign that he was at all invested in the outcome of this interview. Adrienne wondered who this person was, and why he had agreed to come to Kessering in the first place.

"Are you skilled?" Elder Rynn asked with mounting impatience. "Have you had formal training?"

"Yes."

Elder Rynn seemed dissatisfied by the lack of elaboration. With an impatient gesture, he motioned Adrienne forward. "You will ascertain his skill level," he ordered.

Adrienne knew without testing that Malokai would be well able to handle himself, but she was curious to test her skills against his. "Now?" she asked, looking to the commission for direction. They did not even like to discuss fighting, and she doubted they truly wanted to witness the fight between her and the formidable M'bai warrior. There would be nothing civilized about it, and she doubted that the commissioners like Franklin and Ben were ready to see such a fight.

"Yes," the Elder told her. "There is no use continuing until we know he has the requisite skills."

Franklin coughed nervously and a few of the commissioners shifted in their seats, but no one dared speak against Elder Rynn, and no one left the room.

Adrienne turned to face Malokai. She had fought many men, and the idea of sparring with this one should not have frightened her, yet her heart was hammering in her chest. "No weapons," she told him, unbuckling her sword and scabbard from her belt.

"As you wish." Malokai leaned his strange spear-like weapon against the wall. "Would you like me to place my knives aside as well?" he asked. The musical lilt to his deep voice was a surprising sound coming from the serious looking man.

"No, that won't be necessary." Adrienne placed her sword beside Malokai's spear-like weapon, out of the way of their coming match. Her dagger she kept, though she would not use it in the fight.

Without a word, it began.

Adrienne watched Malokai's feet for a sign that he was slipping into a pattern, his eyes for any sign that he was about to make a move. Still, she did not see the punch that sent her to the ground, her head spinning dizzily from the impact of his fist against her cheek.

She rolled left on pure instinct and avoided a second blow.

Adrienne leapt to her feet, blood humming, more alert now than she had been in months. This was not a fight like the one she'd experienced with the marauders, a fight of life or death. This was a test of skill, and it was thrilling in a completely different way.

He was fast, but no faster than she, and when she faked a punch his instinctive move to block allowed her to land a brutal kick to his left leg. It was not enough to knock him down, but it gave her enough time to plant a hard kick in his short-ribs.

Malokai grunted satisfactorily but did not double over as a lesser man might—as Adrienne had expected him to do. Instead, he moved forward, surprising her, and even as she danced back he made a chopping motion with his right hand that connected with her shoulder and made her left arm numb.

Then they were on the floor, each struggling to remain on top, raining blows on each other. Adrienne thrust her hips upward and was able to roll so that the warrior was below her.

The sound of flesh against flesh mixed with grunts of effort and pain in a way that was purely primal.

When it was over, Malokai had Adrienne pinned to the floor. Everything ached, her ribs protested every breath, and the taste of blood warned that her lip was bleeding.

She felt wonderful.

Malokai's nose was bloodied, and his right eye was starting to swell, but even through the blood and swelling Adrienne thought she saw a glimmer of respect. It brought a smile to her bloody lips.

"He's impressive," she told their audience.

"More so than you, it seems," Lady Chessing said imperiously. Adrienne looked over and saw that, far from the disgust she had expected, there was a light of excitement in the noblewoman's eyes.

Adrienne's focus shifted as Malokai rolled off of her more smoothly than she felt he had a right to move after a round like that, then reached down for her hand. She accepted it and allowed him to help her to her feet.

For a moment she dismissed the commissioners as unimportant and regarded the strange man seriously. "What rank are you?" she asked.

"M'bai have no rank," he told her, his stunning, surprisingly blue eyes holding hers steadily. "I am an M'bai warrior, not one of you lowland soldiers."

Adrienne nodded and turned to face the commission. "Although he may not call himself a soldier, he is a skilled fighter with obvious training and dedication to his craft," she told them.

"You didn't even use weapons," Lady Chessing said disparagingly, though that light had not yet left her eyes. "Any idiot can roll on the floor and throw punches."

"There are many different styles of fighting," Adrienne patiently informed Lady Chessing and the rest of the commission. "I am sure Malokai is as skilled with weapons as without." Adrienne looked at

169

Malokai for confirmation, but he was back to staring impassively at the commissioners as though he was not interested in their verdict.

"I believe we should trust Lieutenant Rydaeg's judgment," Ben said, seeming to be happier about her presence at the commission meeting now that she had proven useful. "She has not yet been wrong when it comes to fighting matters."

Her relationship with Ben had grown more comfortable since the day she had fought the raiders, but the fact that she was pleased by such a tepid compliment worried her. She had been away from people who truly appreciated her skills for far too long if such a comment could mean so much. "You can trust me in this," she assured them.

"In that case, let us continue the interview," Elder Rynn said.

The questions the commission asked Malokai about his history, his beliefs, his skills and experiences, were all answered as succinctly and with as little detail as possible. Even at the end of the extensive interview, Adrienne still felt that she knew nothing about him. He had managed to answer all of their questions without revealing anything meaningful about himself. It was intriguing, and it made Adrienne wonder what he was so carefully hiding.

"Adrienne, you will escort Malokai to the inn," Ben told her. "I will meet with him this afternoon."

"Of course," Adrienne said.

She waited to say more until she and Malokai were well away from the library and the prying ears of the commission. "Who are you?" she asked, stepping in front of him so that he had to either stop or run her down.

"Malokai Kyzeka," he told her, not looking at all surprised or perturbed by her abrupt behavior. He did look a bit frightening, though, with his eye swollen and blood drying on his shirt.

"Of the M'bai," Adrienne added. "A group that no one knows anything about."

"We live in the Modabi Mountains," he said.

That was about all Adrienne did know about the M'bai. They lived in small tribes in the mountains to the northeast, and although that land appeared to belong to Samaro on maps, in truth the M'bai were largely left to self-rule. Tales of their savagery were rampant on the plains, and some stories painted the M'bai as monsters who snuck down from the mountains to abduct children and decimate crops. Adrienne did not believe these stories, but she thought there must be a reason the M'bai were left alone.

She wanted to learn the truth about the M'bai, and was about to ask Malokai another question when she remembered that she was supposed to be training the guards. Adrienne had told all of them to continue without her should she ever not arrive for practice, but she didn't trust that they would.

"Would you like to help me train the city guards?" she asked Malokai. It would be good to have another person with fighting experience there to help her. He would bring a different view and style to the sessions, just as Ricco and other volunteers had done for Jeral.

"You were showing me to the inn," he reminded her, and despite the musical quality to his voice it was clear that he was not interested in more than that.

"Ben won't go looking for you until this afternoon," Adrienne said dismissively. "There is plenty of time."

Malokai shook his head. "The inn," he repeated.

Adrienne's mouth tightened. Although she had been mad at the commission for not informing her of Malokai's presence in the city, she'd still been excited by the fact that she was no longer the only soldier in Kessering.

What she had not expected was such aloofness and lack of interest on Malokai's part. "Fine," she said sharply, increasing her pace as she led him toward the inn. It was irritating that his long legs made it so that he could keep pace with her without effort, and she struggled to control her temper.

"This is the inn," Adrienne said, stopping in front of The Golden Trumpet. "Master Inbaum will have a room ready, I'm sure. I should return sometime this evening."

Malokai nodded brusquely and headed into the inn, ducking his head so as not to hit it on the low doorframe.

Adrienne stared at his receding form in disbelief. He had not asked her a single question, not even what her Talent was, despite the fact that Elder Rynn had revealed that she possessed one. With a sound of disgust, Adrienne headed to where the guards should be training. She thought sparring with them three-on-one would be a good way to work out some of her aggression, and after the workout she had just had, it might even present a challenge.

"Lieutenant!" Flynn called out when she entered the training yard. "We didn't know if you were coming."

Only twenty men were present, and only a few of those were sweating to indicate they had been doing more than standing around. "I have instructed everyone to continue training regardless of whether or not I am present," she snapped. "Where are the others?" After Malokai's brush-off she was especially displeased that some of the guards had disobeyed her.

"They left, Lieutenant," Edward said. "Charles said that training without you was a waste of time, so he and some of the others decided not to stay."

Adrienne's hands curled into fists, her short nails digging into her palms. Though a fight might be satisfying, it would cause far more problems than it would solve. Luckily, she knew of other ways to get revenge. Maybe none quite so satisfying as bloodying the guards, but certainly less likely to get her into trouble.

"Three-on-one sparring today," she announced, knowing the men would enjoy the activity, and that those who had left would be sorry to miss out. "Practice swords, three of you against me."

There was an excited flurry of movement as everyone grabbed their practice swords and broke into groups, planning their strategies.

"Lieutenant?" Flynn asked cautiously as he and two other guards faced her.

"Yes?"

"What happened to your lip?"

Adrienne ran her tongue against the tender inside of the split lip. It stung, but was not nearly as painful as her aching ribs. "I had a warm-up round."

Two soft knocks pulled Adrienne forward several centuries. She shook her head in an attempt to orient herself to the room around her. She had been so immersed in reading one of the old journals that she hadn't noticed the dimming light of the candle burning on the table or the stiffness in her neck. There had been another mention of the Dark Mage, and of an even darker force that gave someone control over the dead.

Another knock sounded.

Adrienne was about to call out to ask who was at the door, but reached out with Oneness instead and felt Ben's unmistakable presence.

She hurriedly took the journal she had been reading and shoved it under her bed with two other books, then folded down the blanket on her bed so that the books were hidden before crossing to the door.

"I didn't know you were coming by," Adrienne said as she opened the door to allow Ben inside.

"I want you to talk to Malokai," Ben told Adrienne. It had been two weeks since the M'bai man had arrived in Kessering to begin his training, and Adrienne did not think he had left the inn at all during that time except to train with Ben.

Adrienne motioned for Ben to come in and sit down, more amused than upset that his greeting would be a demand. She rarely met with Ben anymore. Her Talent had progressed significantly, and her abilities with fire were so different from his Talent for memorizing that they hardly seemed related at all. The two of them sometimes discussed theory, and Ben occasionally tried to start a friendly conversation by asking her how training the guards was going, but it was painfully obvious that the only real connection they had was that the commission insisted her training continue.

When they did meet, it was awkward and uncomfortable for both of them, and the meetings didn't last long. They had too little common ground, and too much that they could not say to each other. Adrienne often thought, during those awkward meetings, of bringing up the studying that she was doing, but something always held her back. At first she had not understood her reluctance, and had thought it was perhaps a small rebellion to counteract the tight leash the commission had on her.

She knew it was more than that now. The more she read, the more she learned about what had started the initial conflict between Samaro and Almet. The exact circumstances were still unclear, but she had determined that there had been trouble with the slaves in Almet, and perhaps a fear of slaves had been growing in Samaro as well, though she could not imagine why slaves would be feared.

And there was the nagging question of who and what the Dark Mage was. He had power, perhaps the horrible power of necromancy, and it was that more than anything that kept her from mentioning any of the history of the conflict to Ben. If he took that information to the commission, would they think that the Talented and their powers might be related to something like the Dark Mage and shut the program down? She wouldn't risk that.

"What do you want me to talk to him about?" Adrienne asked.

"Malokai seems disinterested when it comes to learning," Ben said. "He may do what he's told, but he lacks your...enthusiasm for the process."

Adrienne remembered her "enthusiasm" as having been a problem for the commission, but apparently the commission found a driven soldier better than an indifferent one. Or perhaps they just wanted Malokai to be more like her in general. Better someone they understood, or thought they understood, than an M'bai savage.

She thought it was ironic that after everything that had happened the commission would ask her to be an influence on someone else. "I don't know what I can do about that," Adrienne told Ben.

"The rest of the commission thinks that you can relate to him better than we can," Ben told her. He sat back in his chair, crossed his ankles, and stared down at his folded hands. "We're hoping the two of you will be able to find common ground. He doesn't seem to care for books and knowledge." Ben looked up at her again, his dark eyes displeased.

The critical tone she heard in his voice, the tone that implied that the M'bai warrior was stupid, nearly made her laugh. Although she had hardly spoken to Malokai since the first day they had met, she had sensed an intelligence in him that would probably surprise the young scholar. It was more likely that Ben, young and interested in little outside of the library, was what Malokai did not care for. "He wouldn't have been brought here if he wasn't smart," Adrienne pointed out.

Ben shrugged his thin shoulders. "Who knows how the M'bai measure intelligence?"

If this was the opinion Ben was expressing to the warrior, Adrienne could understand why Malokai wasn't being overly cooperative when it came to his training. "I'll talk to him," she agreed. Perhaps she would be able to learn more about Malokai—and the M'bai people—if she approached him instead of waiting for him to come to her. It would give her something else to do other than train and puzzle over her books. Perhaps talking with someone who was not from Samaro—not really—would give her a new perspective.

Ben smiled and stood to leave. "I will check in tomorrow to see how it goes."

"Tomorrow?" Adrienne asked, catching his arm to hold him in place a moment longer. "I'll need at least a few days to broach the subject."

"Why?"

Adrienne released him and pinched the bridge of her nose, wondering how someone so smart could be so completely lacking in people skills and common sense. "I can't just walk up to him and tell him to try harder," she explained. "We need to build some sort of rapport first."

"Elder Rynn isn't going to like this," Ben said. "He's disappointed in how the commission's work is progressing, and told me to take care of it." For the first time Adrienne could remember, it seemed that Ben had a problem with how the commission was going about its work.

Adrienne just shook her head. The commission did little more than sit around and talk all day, and discussion alone rarely accomplished anything in Adrienne's experience. It wasn't surprising that Elder

Rynn wouldn't be happy with their progress when there wasn't any, and wasn't likely to be any. Ben changing Malokai's attitude about training would not solve the underlying problem. "I will speak with Malokai over the next few days," she said again. "That's the best I can do."

"Good. Perhaps a positive result with Malokai will improve Elder Rynn's outlook on the project."

"Perhaps." Adrienne wondered if the king knew that his commission showed no real signs of assembling a useful force against Almet. Aside from Adrienne, none of the Talents could be used in battle, and although Adrienne's Talent could be useful, they had made no move to begin training her on using it for that purpose. Then again, from what she had heard of King Burin, he probably didn't have the stomach to order a battle that could result in active war between Almet and Samaro. If the conflict turned to war, Burin would have to take a real role.

Ben turned to leave; then turned back and offered Adrienne a weak smile. "Has your ability progressed?" he asked, as though only just remembering that he was supposed to be her instructor, not a commissioner asking her for help in gaining the cooperation of one of his other trainees.

Adrienne held out her hand and a ball of flame appeared two inches above her palm, flickering weakly before dying. Ben's face fell, then lit again as Adrienne flung her hand out and had flame erupting in what had been a cold fireplace.

"I've given up on fireballs," she admitted. "But lighting fire…that I can do."

"Are you sure you can't throw fire?" Ben asked. "That would be useful in…That's what the commission is hoping you can do."

"I've tried, but there was no progress. However…" She pulled her sword from its sheath and held it out. With little more than a thought she sent fire racing up and down the blade. It was not the fury of flame that had engulfed the sword in battle. It was gentler, and left as quickly as it had come. "I think this will accomplish something similar to what the commission was hoping for."

Ben shuddered but nodded. "Yes, that seems like it would be an effective weapon. Perhaps without the distance of fireballs, but…Yes, it should do."

"I'll keep working on it," Adrienne said. "There might still be better ways to use it."

"That's good." Ben looked around her small room awkwardly. "I have things I need to get done today," he said, the hunch of his shoulders becoming even more pronounced as he drew in on himself.

Adrienne reached up and touched the leather cord of her necklace idly. She wished once again that things could have been different between them, that they had been able to develop some sort of friendship. "I understand," she said. "I'll see you soon for more training."

"Yes." Ben looked relieved as he left, and Adrienne sank down onto her bed to think about how she would approach Malokai the next day, forgetting for the moment the book she had been reading.

When Adrienne went downstairs for breakfast the next morning, she saw Malokai sitting alone at one of the tables. She had expected as much.

Like her, Malokai got up with the sun. And being M'bai, an even more dangerous version of a soldier in the eyes of the inn's patrons, there was no one who would dare eat with him, even if they were awake so early in the day. All of which worked in Adrienne's favor.

"What do you think of Kessering?" Adrienne asked as she sat at Malokai's table. He was eating a bowl of lumpy porridge and a piece of bread with a stingy amount of butter. Adrienne was happy she had made friends with the cook, earning her more butter and lump-free gruel sweetened with honey. Good food made the time in Kessering more bearable.

"It's big," Malokai said, barely glancing up from his bowl.

Adrienne was surprised by his opinion of Kessering. As far as cities went, Kessering was not much larger than a decent-sized town. It was far richer than its size indicated due to the abundance of artisans, but most of the goods were traded outside of the city. Kyrog was home to nearly as many people, if the craftsmen, families, and women who flocked around soldiers were included. "Not so big," she said. "Your cities must be smaller up in the mountains than those here."

"There are no cities in the Modabi Mountains," Malokai said, eating another spoonful of porridge. Adrienne had heard that the M'bai were heathens and savages, but she didn't believe they were so uncivilized that they really lived in caves like animals as some stories suggested. Malokai seemed too comfortable indoors for that to be true.

"Surely there must be some," Adrienne said.

Malokai shook his head. "Cities are for lowlanders," he told her. "Tribes live in small villages, not cities. There is no flat land in the mountains for cities, and cities are vulnerable. Weak. Men huddled behind walls like children."

Adrienne wasn't sure what to do with that information, so she let it go and moved on to another topic. "Don't let the fact that the townspeople avoid you bother you," she advised. "Just about everyone here is afraid of soldiers. Or people they view as soldiers," she added, remembering that he was opposed to that term. She recalled clearly him telling her that he was an M'bai warrior, not a soldier.

Malokai finished his piece of bread, chewing and swallowing completely before answering. "I'm not concerned with what they think."

Out of sight under the table, Adrienne rapped her fingers on her thigh in a staccato rhythm. He wasn't answering in monosyllables as he had with the commission, but it was hardly a conversation that could lead to sharing confidences and her giving him advice. "Good," she said, irritated. "If you'd like, I can introduce you to some people today. Other people with Talents."

She thought she saw a glimmer of interest in his intense blue eyes before he banked it. "What of the guards?"

Adrienne nearly smiled. Malokai must have been paying attention to her whereabouts to know that she spent most of her days training the city guards. "They can do without me for the morning."

Malokai nodded. "I will meet these people you speak of," he said. "This must be what Master Ruthford asked you to do."

Adrienne flushed with embarrassment. She hadn't meant for him to know that she was talking to him because Ben had asked. "My introducing you to other Talented has nothing to do with Ben," she said, which was at least partly true. Ben had never mentioned introducing Malokai to other Talented. In truth, Adrienne suspected the commission wouldn't be pleased when they found out what she had done, but she was past the point of caring what they thought. If they ever got the nerve to punish her, she would accept whatever punishment they deemed fit. Perhaps they would decide to send her home. To Kyrog. Day by day she realized that was a punishment she would gladly accept.

"We can leave whenever you're ready," Malokai said, gesturing to Adrienne's half-full bowl.

Adrienne took her time finishing her porridge. There was no reason to let Malokai know how unsettled she was by him, no reason to rush to suit his mood. He acted as though nothing anyone said or did had any emotional effect, and she wouldn't let him see that their interaction had disturbed her in the least.

When they got to Louella's, the diminutive healer was nowhere to be seen. "Louella?" Adrienne called.

"I'll be out in a minute!" Louella's voice sounded distant, and Adrienne thought she must be in the back storage room. "I'm mixing up a salve for Master Tyrn. His joints ache."

"Take your time," Adrienne said, crossing her arms and leaning up against the counter that housed some of Louella's herbs and healing supplies.

Louella emerged from the back room a few minutes later. "Hello." She greeted Malokai with her warm smile. "You must be Malokai."

Malokai looked startled by Louella's appearance, and his hand traveled halfway to the weapon strapped to his back before he controlled the telling motion. Adrienne watched him closely, wondering why the delicate looking Louella would elicit such a reaction from the warrior. "This is Louella," Adrienne said, studying Malokai's reaction. "She is a Talented healer."

Although Malokai looked calm enough now, Adrienne paid attention to the hand that had earlier reached for his weapon. It was back down by his side, but there was no relaxation in it.

"You're not sick, are you?" Louella asked, looking Malokai up and down with the eyes of an experienced healer. "Some of the healers can tell if someone is sick as part of their Talent, but I still have to ask." She shrugged, having accepted that having to ask after someone's health was not a terrible limitation in light of the things her Talent did allow.

"I'm fine," he said curtly. Adrienne didn't like the intensity of the looks he was directing at Louella. There were not many in this part of Samaro with such light coloring, but surely a man from the Modabi Mountains, which bordered Almet, would be familiar with such features. Adrienne knew that light skin and hair were normal in Almet, and Malokai himself had blue eyes.

"Good," Louella said, oblivious to the tension in the room. "When I first met Adrienne, we had a bit of a demonstration of my Talent," Louella said. "Since you both seem well and unharmed, someone would have to change that before I could demonstrate, if a demonstration is what you're after."

Adrienne remembered cutting herself so that Louella could study the particles in her blood, but decided that if Malokai wanted to see Louella's skills firsthand then he would have to be the one broken or bleeding. There was only so much Adrienne was willing to do to catch Malokai's attention.

"What kinds of things can you do?" Malokai asked Louella. Adrienne had hoped that meeting with Louella would make him interested in the process of becoming Talented, and it seemed it had. Whatever had provoked his initial response to the healer seemed to have been replaced by curiosity, for the moment at least.

"Well, so far as we can tell, the Talents people develop are in line with their profession," Louella told him. "My particular strengths when it comes to my Talent are healing cuts and sores and mending broken bones." She smiled, mischief glinting in her sky blue eyes. "Sewing and setting were my strong points before I developed a Talent."

Malokai studied Louella, his eyes as hard and cutting as ice. "What do you mean when you say you can heal cuts?"

"With my Talent I can heal a cut, like one from a knife, almost instantly," Louella explained. "The skin will heal over as if it had never been broken. More serious injuries can take longer, and it takes more time for the patient to recuperate, but I can heal wounds that would have been fatal had they not been treated by a Talented healer."

"The guards were attacked several weeks ago," Adrienne said, putting it into a perspective that a soldier—a warrior—would understand more readily. "Three of the men died. Two more probably would have, were it not for Louella and the other healers." She remembered the gruesome wounds that in any other city would have made it so that all that she could do was to try and make the men comfortable as they died.

"Adrienne was badly hurt as well," Louella added, glancing over at her friend.

"It wouldn't have been fatal," Adrienne objected, not wanting her own experience with healing to be central to the conversation. There was no reason for Malokai to know that she would have lost the fight—and her life—had she not had a Talent of her own.

"What about illness?" Malokai asked.

Louella wrinkled her nose. "My Talent in that area never really developed. My poultices and herbs seem to work the slightest bit better, but other healers have experienced great improvement in dealing with illnesses after discovering a Talent, to the point that they can cure the illness right then. For me, my Talent lies in healing physical injuries."

"Maureen's ability is more inclined toward illnesses," Adrienne added.

"Maureen?" Malokai did not recognize the strange name, and Adrienne tried to put herself in his place. He had not been in

179

Kessering for very long, and new information was being given to him very rapidly. It was a wonder he had kept up with their conversation so far.

"Another Talented healer," Louella said amiably. "There probably isn't a regular healer in Kessering anymore. No point, when the rest of us can heal better and faster. Those that weren't trained as Talented have all moved away." Louella rose to her feet. "Why don't we all go into the back room and have some tea? Perhaps send for Pieter?"

"That would be good," Adrienne said before Malokai could speak and possibly decline the invitation. She straightened up from where she had been leaning against the counter and grabbed Malokai's arm to steer him to the back room. Despite growing up around soldiers and being one herself, Adrienne was still impressed by the iron-hard muscles cording his arms.

Adrienne ignored the unfamiliar tug in her gut and focused on why she was here. She had heard Malokai say more since meeting Louella than at any time since the commission had questioned him, and she was curious to see what else he might have to say now that he was talking.

"Could you get the fire going?" Louella asked, pointing to the hearth that had only a few sullen red embers remaining.

Malokai moved toward the hearth, but Adrienne stopped him. "I've got it." In seconds the embers were flaring to life and Adrienne was adding logs from the woodbox to an already lively fire.

"How did you...?" Malokai asked, blue eyes growing wide.

"My Talent manifested in fire," Adrienne said. "It can be useful even for such mundane chores." She thought of the flames running up the blade of her sword to devour her enemy. The memory was stronger than any death she'd caused since her first, and she knew *that* was what her Talent had been meant for. She'd promised Ben she would keep looking for new ways to use it, but she had already found its purpose.

She could see that she had finally captured all of Malokai's attention. The normally stoic warrior could not fully hide the look of shock on his ebon face. "Didn't Ben tell you about my Talent?" she asked.

Malokai slowly shook his head. "I only knew that you had one. You, the healers, some blacksmiths, and a few others. He did not say what any of you could do. I know Master Ruthford can memorize, and another scholar can locate books..."

"Did you think all of our abilities were like that?" Adrienne asked.

Malokai's broad shoulders rose and fell in a shrug. "Master Ruthford only said he was hoping for a more active result with me."

Adrienne looked at the ceiling as if there were answers carved into the roughhewn logs. "Ben should have told you what we could do." Adrienne wouldn't have been too eager to discover a Talent herself if she had thought her future ability was limited to one like Ben's.

But she had learned about the Talents from Tam before she had ever read about them, and the commission had told her even more. She wondered for a moment why they had been more forthcoming with her than with Malokai, and came to the conclusion that they had trusted her more than they trusted him. She looked again at the dark, dangerous looking M'bai warrior and could see why the commission had made that choice, though she did not agree with it.

Adrienne knew what it was like to be eaten up with curiosity about what was being done in the small city and dissatisfied with the commission's decisions, and felt a new sense of kinship with Malokai. She realized he must be feeling now what she had felt when she first arrived in the city.

In a move of sympathy Adrienne explained what she could about her own Talent to Malokai, and passed the job of explaining Pieter's Talent to Louella.

"I don't think anyone really knew what to expect of blacksmiths," Louella said. "Not that they knew what to expect of the first healers, either, of course."

"So what happened?"

"Everything Pieter creates while using his Talent is better. It works better, lasts longer, stays sharper."

"Like a weapon?"

"He made my sword," Adrienne said, unsheathing the first couple inches so that he could see the blue-tinged blade."

"The color..."

"Part of his Talent," Louella explained. "He doesn't try to make things blue, but that just seems to be part of it."

Malokai nodded, as if that made perfect sense, and Adrienne realized that in a strange way it did. As much sense as any of what they were telling the M'bai warrior. They told him more, and he sat and listened attentively, asking questions occasionally.

Malokai might not be a soldier, but she knew from experience that he was an exemplary fighter. The commission might have doubts about him as a potential Talented, but to Adrienne that quiet intensity, that focus, was as important as the active skill of fighting when it came to making war. And to developing a Talent.

181

Pieter arrived while Louella was telling Malokai more about the Talents manifested by others in Kessering, and it wasn't until after the four of them had eaten lunch that Adrienne said she needed to see how the guards were doing without her there.

"Hopefully they kept up their training," Adrienne said as she rose from the table. The guards were getting better at obeying her even when she wasn't around to enforce their behavior, especially since the day Malokai had arrived and some of them had missed the impromptu three-on-one sparring session, but she didn't trust them for too long without her. Charles still refused to fully accept her command, and there were other guards who tended to follow him when the opportunity arose. They preferred sloth over the rewards of hard work.

She wanted to get rid of Charles, but could think of no way to do it that the commission would accept. Explaining to them why she removed an experienced guard from the watch would not be easy, and could wind up hurting her long term goals for the guards.

"How long are you going to keep them training all day every day?" Louella asked. "It's no wonder that they tire of it."

Adrienne knew that Louella didn't mean any offense, but the healer could not understand the time it took to become truly proficient in the art of fighting. "They don't train every day," Adrienne said. "Six of them are now on duty at all times, which means every five days they get a day to do little more than walk the streets or watch the gate."

"That still isn't a day off," Louella pointed out.

Adrienne ground her teeth. "Maybe if I had more than thirty guards I would be able to give them more time off." Adrienne's voice had come out more sharply than she had intended, mostly because she knew that Louella had a point—a good one. But Adrienne knew her own point was just as valid. Eventually, she would cut back on the training time, but not yet. The guards were too new, too undisciplined to be given time off. Too vulnerable, if there was another attack. If she eased off on their training early and one of them was killed because of it...

"I would like to see these guards," Malokai said in his musical voice, cutting through the tension between the two friends.

Adrienne had been hoping to get Malokai involved with the guard's training since his first day in Kessering, and she allowed herself a small smile. "Then follow me."

When they got to the training grounds, all of the guards who were supposed to be training were present, and all practicing as they had been instructed. Satisfaction turned to confusion when she realized that one of those men training was Edward, not Flynn.

"Guardsman Witter, aren't you on duty today?" she asked Edward. He was not the kind of man to skip out on guard duty, but she couldn't figure out why he would be at practice instead of where he should be.

"Yes, Lieutenant," Edward answered, sheathing his sword with practiced moves and snapping to attention. "However, due to your absence, I thought it prudent to oversee the training myself. Flynn agreed to take my place today."

Adrienne nodded. It was a smart decision on Edward's part; the other guards were more likely to listen to him than to young Flynn or anyone else besides Charles. Adrienne had been considering making Edward Captain of the Guard, and she knew that she would have to do so soon. He was a natural-born leader, and one of the most talented of the group. "Good work," she told him before turning to the group at large.

"Everyone, this is Malokai Kyzeka. He will be observing today." She hoped that he would also be participating, but she kept that hope to herself.

Everyone paired up for sparring, using only bare hands and knives at this point, and Adrienne pitted herself against Charles. Out of all of the guards, new and old, he had shown the least improvement in the last three months. She hoped that some more one-on-one training would be beneficial for him.

Or convince him to quit.

After twenty minutes Adrienne was frustrated to the point of screaming. Charles kept making the same mistakes, and no matter how many times she corrected him, he kept falling into the same pattern. She cursed ripely. "Malokai," she said, knowing he had been watching the pair of them the whole time. "Would you help me demonstrate this?" It came out sounding more like an order than a request, but Malokai just gave a small smile and stepped forward.

All activity stopped when Malokai stepped up to face her, but Adrienne did not tell the men to get back to work—more than just Charles could learn something by watching her and Malokai spar today.

"I'll be Charles," she said, explaining that they would run the same pattern as before. Malokai nodded and, without further words, slowly enacted the sequence Adrienne and Charles had run through again and again. It ended the same way it had before: with Malokai's knife pressed against Adrienne's stomach.

"Now I'm dead," Adrienne said. "Or at the very least out of the fight and in serious danger unless a healer gets to me soon."

There were murmurs amongst the men. Charles snorted. "Why would I be fighting without a sword?" he asked.

Adrienne had wanted them to fight only with knives because different weapons presented different weaknesses, but this had been Charles' argument all along. He had stated repeatedly that he would not go into a situation like this armed with only a knife. "Are you always wearing your sword?" she asked. "You never have it away from your person, even on the other side of the room?"

Since his sword was along the fence on the north side of the training area, the answer to that was obvious. "You told us not to use swords," Charles said, casting the blame back on Adrienne.

"And if we were attacked now, armed only with knives?" She didn't give the guard another chance to answer. "Same moves," she told Malokai. "Faster."

The speed with which she moved now was probably faster than Charles could manage, but Malokai's moves were equally fast, and the result was the same. Speed and agility were not the problem, or the solution.

"Fighting is about adapting," Adrienne told the men. "If you can't adapt and change your moves based on your opponent, you're going to end up dead."

She and Malokai repeated the moves again, but where Malokai performed the same move as before, Adrienne turned sideways and took half a step back at the last second. The knife went past her, and Adrienne was able to grab Malokai's arm and unexpectedly flip him over onto his back.

An experienced fighter, Malokai moved with the flip and rolled onto his feet, but he made no move to attack her. The exercise was over; Adrienne had proven her point.

"That time, I avoided getting stabbed," Adrienne pointed out somewhat wryly. "Being able to flip him was another advantage. Some men might have stayed down," she added, eyeing Malokai speculatively out of the corner of her eye, "but even if they don't, it buys time."

All of the assembled guards but Charles seemed pleased with the demonstration and impressed with Adrienne's abilities. Charles looked characteristically angry. "You expect me to flip you?" Charles asked. "You're a woman. You might get hurt."

"Then fight me instead," Malokai suggested, stepping forward. "Your lieutenant already has."

Another laugh nearly escaped Adrienne as Charles's eyes grew wide. He had backed himself into a corner with his last excuse, and could not get out of sparring with the large M'bai warrior without revealing his cowardice. "You're going to want to keep your center of gravity low for the flip," Adrienne advised Charles, hiding her smile with effort. Despite her dislike of the man on a personal level, she was in charge of his training, and that was more important than watching him get hopelessly flattened by the M'bai warrior.

Malokai went easy on Charles, letting him evade the knife as Adrienne had, but nothing short of Malokai jumping over Charles could help the guard complete the flip. There were a few laughs amongst the watching men, no doubt as they remembered the ease with which their short, much lighter instructor had flipped the large warrior. The guards had probably expected the flip to be the easiest part for Charles.

Adrienne knew there was value in knowing how to flip an opponent, but it wasn't a necessary skill for the guards, and was frankly more trouble than it was worth to teach them. "Luckily, Charles did not need to flip Malokai. Just grabbing the other man's knife-hand can be hugely advantageous." Adrienne caught and read the glint in Malokai's eyes. "Of course, it is important to be sure that your opponent has only one knife, and is not equally skilled with both hands."

Malokai pulled another knife from where it had been secreted behind his back. He rolled it end over end in his left hand—not the hand that he had been using before—with all the skill of a performer. Then he drew back and threw the knife so that it stuck in the fence post some twenty feet away.

Since knife-throwing was a skill Adrienne admired but did not possess to any great degree herself, she deigned to retrieve the knife while the guards clamored to ask Malokai how he had done that. By the time she returned—she had taken her time examining the expertly balanced blade—Adrienne thought she detected a hint of desperation in Malokai's typically unreadable expression.

"I think that is enough training for today," Adrienne said, mindful of what Louella had said earlier. "Report tomorrow at ten o'clock. Edward, see that the men on duty today learn of the new time."

"I will, Lieutenant."

The men seemed pleased that they were being released early, and that they would have a shorter training period the next day. Adrienne figured it was good for their morale, if nothing else.

"Some of them call you 'Lieutenant,'" Malokai said when they were on their way back to the inn.

"I'm a lieutenant in the army," Adrienne said. "It's a sign of respect from the men."

"Not everyone calls you that."

"Not my friends," Adrienne agreed. She couldn't imagine Louella or Pieter addressing her so, not in any serious way. Not only were they her friends, but neither of them truly understood the title or the achievement it had been to earn it.

"Master Rynn and the other commissioners? Do they refer to you as such?"

"'Lieutenant' is a sign of respect, and the commission doesn't respect any soldier," Adrienne said. Ben had called her lieutenant before the commission, on the occasions that he had found it necessary to speak up in support of her, but she knew he did not think of her that way. It was all a show.

"Do you respect them?"

Adrienne opened her mouth to say yes, that of course she respected the commission, but the answer did not come as quickly as she had expected. She hesitated. "I try to," she finally said. "I recognize their authority. I respect what they were assigned to do here."

She knew that none of that was the same as respecting the commissioners themselves. She just could not find it in herself to respect people with such misguided fears and hatreds. The fact that they let their prejudices get in the way of their goals was an obstacle Adrienne found almost impossible to overcome. "Do you respect them?" she asked Malokai.

Malokai shrugged his broad shoulders as he made his way through the crowd. It was easy for him to maneuver through the milling people in the streets; most people hurried to get out of his way. He didn't look at Adrienne as he gave his answer.

"I do not know them. I do not know the ways of cities, of commissions." He shrugged again, his eyes looking further into the distance than the shops and inns before him.

"Why are you here?" Adrienne asked.

"Duty brought me here."

"Duty," Adrienne said, wondering what duty Malokai could have toward the commission. "It traps you every time." Was it duty that had brought her here? Surely it was duty that made her stay.

CHAPTER ELEVEN

Adrienne's eyes flew open at the sound of a fist banging against the door she had locked before crawling into bed a few hours earlier. The banging was accompanied by the distant sound of screams, and Adrienne leapt from her bed and grabbed her sword. She was halfway to the door before she remembered she was naked.

She had just slipped on her robe when her door burst open and Malokai came barreling in. "Fire. In the stables."

Adrienne swore and took off in the direction of the back staircase. She could smell the smoke, and mingled with the screams from the inn's patrons were the screams of panicked horses. She could hear Strider's trumpeting cry of fear and rage, and knew that she had to get to him before he hurt himself, or anyone fool enough to try and lead him out.

Malokai grabbed her arm to stop her from charging into the stables, but she yanked free and threw open the door with a force that sent it bouncing back off the wall. Horses were kicking at the doors to the box stalls in an attempt to get free, and as Adrienne went by she opened stall after stall, fighting to see through the thick smoke as she made her way to Strider.

She could see the whites of Strider's eyes as they rolled in fear, and froth was forming on his mouth as the smells and flickering lights of the fire terrorized him.

Fire created a primal fear in horses that could overcome even the best trained animal, and Strider was no exception.

Adrienne knew better than anyone the dangers of the stallion's hooves, but the destrier was more than an expensive tool to Adrienne. He was the only thing she had from Kyrog, and a gift from Captain Garrett. If he was too overcome by fear to leave his stall now that the door was open, she would have to lead him out herself.

Adrienne tore a strip of fabric from her robe and slipped into the stall. She had no choice but to get close to the rearing stallion, risking his shod hooves to bind the strip of cloth over his eyes. His hooves caught her a couple times, painful glancing blows along her ribs and legs, but he never made full contact, and Adrienne finally managed to cover the warhorse's eyes.

Blinded, Strider stopped his violent plunging and stood quivering in the stall as the air grew thicker and thicker with smoke. Adrienne did not take the time to find a lead rope, but grabbed on to the chin of Strider's halter and led him out of the stall, past bits of straw that were catching fire in the aisle, to the safety of the street outside.

Away from the screaming horses and roaring fire, Adrienne could hear again. She scanned the crowd and saw Malokai calming a trembling gray mare with sweat dampening her coat. "Are they all out?" she asked.

Malokai nodded, then let go of the mare and stepped toward her. Adrienne frowned in confusion until he reached out and pulled the edges of her robe together, concealing her nakedness. "You might want to tie it tighter," he said, his teeth gleaming white in the flickering light from the flames.

Adrienne ducked her head in embarrassment as she knotted the belt tightly. She hadn't noticed the tie coming loose in her struggle with Strider.

Once she was covered again, Adrienne began to scan the crowd of people gathered around the burning stable. After the third perusal she realized what it was she was looking for. Thom was not amongst those gathered to witness the fire.

Adrienne did not realize she had said the boy's name aloud until Malokai was once more at her side, grabbing her by the arm. "I didn't see him," he said.

"The hayloft!"

They rushed through the stable doors together. People outside were throwing buckets of water on the flames, but the hayloft was consumed. If Thom was still up there...

Malokai pushed Adrienne toward the tack room and headed toward the ladder to the hayloft himself. Adrienne bellied down to get under the smoke and searched the small room, then went back into the main aisle. She saw Malokai coming back down the ladder with Thom's limp form slung over his shoulder and wondered how anyone could have survived up there.

"Get out!" Adrienne could not hear Malokai, but she saw his mouth form the words through the smoke and hesitated only a moment before doing as he said. Once outside, she hurried through the crowd, looking for someone who could help.

She saw Maureen standing off to the side and ran toward her.

Adrienne grabbed Maureen's arm and began dragging the healer in the direction of the burning stables, ignoring her protests and struggles to get loose. Adrienne was coughing out smoke, and her throat was too sore to attempt an explanation. No explanation was necessary once they got within sight of Malokai and the unconscious boy. Maureen rushed forward, kneeling next to Thom, her attention focused on him to the exclusion of all else.

Adrienne knelt beside her and gave in to the explosive coughing that had been threatening as her lungs tried to expel the smoke they had inhaled. Malokai was in much the same condition, and Adrienne could only imagine how thick the smoke had been in the hayloft. Just the thought brought on another round of coughing.

Through tearing eyes, Adrienne saw Maureen lift her hands from Thom's chest. Fear gripped her until she saw the boy's chest rising and falling by itself. Her head went light with relief and she sagged, forced to brace her hands against the ground to keep from landing on her face. "He's okay," she repeated over and over, her voice a harsh whisper as she tried to make herself believe them. "He's okay."

She looked up and saw Malokai watching her. "You saved him," she croaked.

"You thought to look for him." Malokai's voice sounded as though he had been swallowing razors, and Adrienne winced in sympathy. Her own throat felt as though it was on fire. It was at that moment that Adrienne realized that Malokai was shirtless, and that there were angry red burns on his chest and shoulders, and probably more on his back that she couldn't see.

Malokai seemed unaware of the burns.

"He'll be fine," Maureen said, coming over to the sorry pair. There was a moment of hesitation before the healer placed her hand on Adrienne's shoulder and closed her eyes. Adrienne felt quiet shivers coursing through her before Maureen broke contact.

Adrienne's lungs no longer spasmed, and her throat felt smooth and unharmed by the smoke. The painful marks left by Strider's hooves had begun to fade as well.

Maureen then turned to use her Talent on Malokai, and Adrienne noticed some of the tension fade from his face as the pain left his body.

"Thank you," Malokai told the woman he knew only by sight, his voice back to its usual musical quality. Malokai was as alienated from the other Talented as Adrienne was, but Adrienne realized for the first time that despite their differences, Maureen was not a bad person. She would not have had to heal Adrienne and Malokai, they had been in no real danger, but the healer had done so without being asked.

Adrienne was humbled.

"Keep an eye on the boy," Maureen told Adrienne.

Adrienne nodded. Maureen began to turn away, and Adrienne stopped her by putting a light hand on her arm. "Thank you, Maureen. You saved that boy's life tonight."

"So did you. Both of you." Maureen smiled, and there was respect in her eyes. "My Talent is with sickness," she said. "I did what I can, but have Louella check on you. And on the boy." She looked back at the burning stable. "How did it go up, do you suppose?"

Adrienne shook her head and Maureen walked back into the crowd.

"Go to Thom," Malokai told Adrienne once Maureen had gone. "I'll look over the horses."

"I need you to teach me Oneness," Malokai said.

Adrienne raised an eyebrow. She had been just about to climb into bed when Malokai had knocked on her door, and she was not impressed that that was all he had to say. "I was planning to sleep tonight," she said, readjusting the belt on her robe. She wore nothing underneath but the thin sleep shirt she had invested in after the incident with the stables, and she wished Malokai had come only a few minutes earlier, when she was still fully dressed. It was hard to look imposing wearing a robe.

"Teach me, and I will let you sleep."

Adrienne sighed and opened the door wide enough to allow Malokai entrance. She waved a hand and the candles scattered around the room lit so that more than the dying fire provided light. "Have a seat and tell me why you need to learn Oneness tonight and not tomorrow when I'm awake."

Malokai sat in the single chair in the room, pulling it away from the table to sit facing the bed where Adrienne took her own seat. The room was small enough that their knees almost touched, and Adrienne wished that she could adjust her robe over her legs without looking nervous. She was used to wearing her *swa'il* when in the company of men, not flimsy cloth.

"I finished the book. Ben said we would begin working on Oneness in a week or two, once we had discussed the book thoroughly." The disgust in his melodic voice was interesting, as was the fact that he had said "Ben" rather than "Master Ruthford." Malokai had never before referred to Ben informally, and Adrienne doubted it was friendship that had prompted the change.

"That sounds about right," Adrienne agreed, raising a hand to smother a yawn. She was tired; she'd spent the day training guards and practicing with her Talent. "Ben—all of the scholars—like to discuss and understand every bit of information before moving on to the next step in training."

Malokai growled. "I do understand the information," he said impatiently. Although they had talked regularly over the past week, especially since the night the stables had caught fire, Adrienne was surprised by the amount of emotion Malokai was showing. "We discussed the book for three hours tonight, and I didn't need any clarifications. I don't need another two weeks of talking."

Adrienne understood Malokai's frustration. She preferred action over long discussion herself and remembered keenly her own frustration when the commission had wanted to hold her back, but she had to carefully weigh her choices. This decision could mean bringing the wrath of the commission down on them both.

The wisest decision would be to not help Malokai with Oneness. She knew Ben and the rest of the commission would be against her telling Malokai anything; they would tell her to wait and to mind her own affairs. The soldier in her felt compelled to obey their unspoken commands, but there was another part, equally strong, that railed against wasting time. The commission wouldn't even know if Malokai could develop a Talent until he tried to achieve Oneness. It could take weeks—months—for him to do so once he started trying. She looked at Malokai, and thought that a two week head start wouldn't hurt.

"Oneness is about…Ben says clearing your mind, but I'm not sure that's the best way to explain it," she said. "I would say that you focus your mind and feel the connection we have with everything around us." She leaned toward Malokai, resting her elbows on her knees, forgetting for the moment that she was dressed in just a robe and a thin shift. "We are not separate from our surroundings, from the world. We are One with the elements, with each other, with everything around us. You have to feel that." She smiled ruefully and sat back. "The first step is to completely clear your mind."

Malokai nodded.

"From what Ben told me, and what Louella said, most people sit and meditate, but I found it helped me to move," Adrienne said. Malokai continued to sit there, seemingly unaware of anything else, before suddenly looking up.

"What is next?"

"You clear your mind, and in that state, you hopefully achieve Oneness, where you can feel that connection to everything. Asmov referred to a connection to the universe in his journal, and it really does feel like that."

"What's after Oneness?" Malokai asked.

"I don't know if I can explain it until you reach that level," Adrienne said. "I don't think it would make sense." And that, she knew, would be stepping way outside of anything the commission would allow. Stepping over those bounds would be beyond anything even she could rationalize.

Malokai closed his eyes for a moment, taking deep, even breaths. When he opened his eyes, the blue orbs were intense and locked on hers.

"I can feel your heartbeat," Malokai said in a voice that sounded oddly detached. "It sped up just now, when I spoke. I can feel the grain of the wooden table, the draft from the window." He turned as though he could see out the dark panes into the night outside. "Two men are arguing. Fighting in the street. I believe one of your guards is on his way to break it up."

A shiver raced down Adrienne's spine, and she slipped into Oneness as well. She could feel Malokai, his existence, but she had to concentrate to really feel his heartbeat: it was slow and steady, not the quick, almost nervous rhythm of her own. There were three people on the street below, but she could not feel anything more about them than their presence. She could not tell who they were or what they were doing. "You can feel all of that?"

Malokai looked momentarily puzzled by her question. "Can't you?"

Adrienne didn't know where to start. That he had achieved Oneness so quickly and with such apparent ease was almost unbelievable. The level to which he could apparently sense things was nothing short of astonishing. "No," Adrienne answered weakly. "I can't feel everything, not as strongly as what you describe."

The strongest things in the room to Adrienne were her sword and the flames of the hearth and candles. Those things seemed almost to reach out to her, standing out in the sea of sensations she experienced whenever she was conscious of her Oneness. Louella had said it was like that for her with injuries. For Pieter, he could most clearly feel his tools and the metal he was shaping.

"You can only feel some things?" Malokai asked, looking as puzzled as Adrienne felt.

Adrienne nodded. "Yes and no," she said. "I can feel everything, but some things I have an affinity for. Fire I can feel most strongly," she explained. "My Talent lies there, and fire feels...different to me than everything else. Pieter forged my sword using his own Talent, and what I feel when I focus on the sword is similar to what I feel for fire." Pieter's other tools also stood out clearly, but they did not call to her like the one made for her did. It did give her an idea, though. "What does my sword feel like to you?"

Malokai glanced at the sword that was leaning against the wall next to the bed, within easy reach had Adrienne been lying down. "Hazy," he said after a minute. "Not clear like everything else."

It was the opposite of what Adrienne had been expecting. "What about the fire?" she asked, wondering if, because he too was a fighter, he would have a Talent similar to hers. It was true of Louella and the other healers, after all.

He gazed into the hearth and winced. "The fire is clear, but if I try to...reach for it...it's hot."

That Malokai would try to reach for it, the only way Adrienne could describe what she did when using her Talent, was interesting. The fact that Malokai thought the fire was hot was just confusing to her. Adrienne was aware of the fire's heat when she used it, but never uncomfortably so. As far as she knew, Louella and Pieter had never been able to reach for fire at all, or at least had never felt compelled to try.

"Painfully hot?" Adrienne asked, wanting to understand.

Malokai tilted his head. "Had I kept trying, yes, I think it would have been painful." He shook his head. "What does it mean?"

Adrienne didn't know. Maybe Ben would have some idea, but telling him she had taught Malokai Oneness was not something she looked forward to doing. "I'm not sure," she told him. "How did you learn Oneness so quickly?"

"The Modabi Mountains are a dangerous place to be unaware of your surroundings. The skill of connecting to everything around you is essential for a warrior. Now that I have Oneness, how do I develop a Talent?" he asked.

Adrienne held up her hands to ward him off. "I can't help you anymore," she told him. "Ben is going to be upset enough about what I have already done. I can't add to that. I won't."

"Ben doesn't have to know," Malokai said. "When he wants me to try Oneness, I will, and I'll do it quickly, but he doesn't need to know it's not the first time I've done it. I've been using this Oneness since I was eight. Had Ben explained the concept to me, I would have discovered Oneness just as quickly with him as I did tonight with you."

"You can't keep this a secret from Ben," Adrienne protested, though she wondered what kind of eight year old would need such a skill. The mountains must be dangerous indeed to require such a connection to keep safe. "He's in charge of your training." Despite her earlier self-justifications, such a level of deceit was too much. Adrienne would tell Ben herself if Malokai refused.

"He shouldn't be in charge of our training in the first place," Malokai told her. "He lacks any real leadership traits; he shouldn't be in charge of more than chronicling what happens here."

"The commission put him in charge," Adrienne said. "Whether you like Ben or not, whether you think he should be in charge or not, he is. And you have to tell him."

Malokai's vivid blue eyes stared at her out of that dark face as if he was searching for something more. "They don't deserve your loyalty."

Adrienne refused to look away from those eyes, although she wanted to. Instead, she kept her voice firm, her back straight. "I am a soldier. My loyalty is with my commanding officers."

"Then I will discover my Talent without your help," Malokai said. "And I won't tell Ben what happened tonight. Whether you tell him is your decision."

Since Malokai had discovered Oneness so suddenly, the relationship Adrienne had been developing with him had become strained. Malokai continued to help her train the guards most days, often using his *urahu*, the strange spearlike weapon he had brought with him from the Modabi Mountains. Adrienne enjoyed pitting herself against a skilled opponent with an unfamiliar weapon, which he used sometimes like a quarterstaff, sometimes like a spear, and always with incredible effectiveness.

Her only regret was that what had passed between them nearly four weeks before, when she had refused to help him past the point of learning Oneness, had halted their growing friendship. They rarely spent time with each other when not training the guards, and when they were together their interactions were stiff and formal.

Ben had finally allowed Malokai to move on to attaining Oneness, and when Malokai had done so immediately, the scholar began trying to help him discover his Talent. So far there had been no progress on that front.

Although Adrienne had not really talked to Malokai since the night she had taught him Oneness without the commission's permission, she knew he was growing frustrated. She could sometimes feel the frustration radiating from him like heat from a hearth, and she thought that might be the only reason he still practiced with her and the guards. Physical exertion was a way to release some of the pent up frustration, perhaps the best way for people like Adrienne and Malokai.

And as far as Adrienne knew, Malokai did not have another outlet for his frustration. She still had her books, and the paper written in Almetian that she was bent on deciphering. The more she learned about the Dark Mage and the armies that had grown up around him, the more she thought that the mage and his armies, more than slavery, was the real cause of the rift between Samaro and Almet.

There was something there, some missing piece, that had led to King Zuka, who Adrienne had learned had been the son of King Ignatio, freeing the slaves after his father's death. It had not been, as Adrienne had been taught, a sense of justice that had caused King Zuka to free the slaves. There had been fear there, and an underlying benefit to freeing the slaves despite the fact that it had initially taken an economic toll on the country.

If only she could read the Almetian script, she felt she might have the answers.

Adrienne sat at the small table in her room, studying the copy she had made of the original text found in the book. The paper it had been written on was brittle and fragile, and Adrienne did not want to risk damaging it. The characters written on her copy were easy to see, but no easier to read despite their clarity. She studied the words, looking for more patterns in the text that might reveal some meaning. She could not read Almetian, but she hoped that if she studied it long enough she might find some similarities between the two languages.

When her study was interrupted by Malokai knocking on her door, she was surprised enough that it took her several seconds to invite him in. "I wasn't expecting you."

Malokai ran a hand over his tightly curled black hair, the first nervous gesture she could remember seeing from the imposing warrior. "I was wondering if you would accompany me to Louella's," he said, his words a bit rushed.

Adrienne was immediately concerned. "Are you sick?" she asked worriedly. Malokai didn't look ill, but she didn't doubt that he was one of those men who would look and act well until he passed out cold. Ricco was like that, and had once collapsed at her feet from a fever she had not even known he had. Luckily, he had recovered without the aid of a Talented healer, but the memory had never quite left her.

"No. I'm fine. I just want to talk to her. To you and Pieter as well."

"Okay," Adrienne said, feeling more relieved than was perhaps warranted in a city where Talented healers made sickness little more than an inconvenience. "We can go now," she said in an attempt to cover up the extent of her concern. "Pieter's home is on the way."

The streets were growing dark with the coming night, and Malokai was silent as they made their way through the city. Adrienne tried to figure out why the M'bai warrior would need to speak with all three of them tonight, and failed to come up with anything plausible.

Pieter asked no questions about why they had come to his home, or why they were now all going to Louella's. He had patience, something Adrienne all too often lacked, and was willing to let people tell him things in their own time. Given his size and strength, Adrienne thought it was probably good that Pieter was a patient man and not one given to rashness or violence.

Louella was obviously surprised to see the three of them when she opened the door, but she quickly put away the stockings she had been darning and invited them all in for tea. "What brings you by tonight?" she asked as she set the kettle over the fire to heat. "I have biscuits if you'd like something to go with the tea."

Louella prattled on as she got the biscuits and set them out along with plates and cups for the brewing tea, and Adrienne realized she was talking to ease any tension amongst the group. "Malokai asked us to come," Adrienne told the other woman.

"I figured as much," Louella replied calmly, making sure everything was placed on the table just so before sitting down herself. "I'm only wondering why."

"I need help discovering my Talent," Malokai told her, told everyone. He looked even grimmer than usual, with his dark face stony and his blue eyes serious.

Louella smiled in amusement, and Pieter shook his head, low laughter rumbling in his barrel chest. "We can't help you," Adrienne said, the corner of her mouth quirking up.

"Ben said I was to try and discover if I had an ability," Malokai told her. "You won't be disobeying him if you help me."

There was an edge to his voice, and Adrienne knew the words were aimed at her in particular. And she knew that she deserved them. "This isn't about Ben or the commission," she assured him. "We can't help you because our Talents are all different. We wouldn't know where to begin."

"It's true," Louella said when Malokai looked to her for confirmation. "I never could have taught Adrienne to do the things she can with fire. She discovered that Talent quite by accident when she was angry."

"What about you?" Malokai asked. "You weren't the first healer to develop a Talent. Surely you had help from the others."

"I did have help, to some degree," Louella agreed. "I had more help than Pieter and Adrienne, at any rate. Maureen Cassin helped me." Louella sat primly on her chair with her legs crossed and her hands folded in her lap like a lady about to give instructions on proper etiquette. "However, my Talent and Maureen's are not exactly the same, and so she could not show me what to do or how to do it. She did advise that I go about my healing while in a state of Oneness. Eventually, my Talent manifested itself while I was sewing up a particularly nasty cut. I was in a state of Oneness and suddenly I knew what to do to stop the bleeding and knit the flesh back together without the aid of needle and thread."

"So I'm supposed to maintain Oneness until I figure out what I can do?" Malokai asked.

"Not necessarily," Pieter said. "When I discovered my Talent, I was working on a particularly difficult tool. I was on the last stage of shaping it, a crucial stage where one mistake could ruin all of my previous efforts, so I took a deep breath to calm myself and something came over me. Oneness, I suppose, though I had not consciously reached for it."

Adrienne had never heard this story, and was as interested in it as Malokai seemed to be. "What happened?"

"I suddenly understood the metal in a new way. I could feel every strength, every weakness. The slightest difference in width or thickness was blazingly apparent to me in that state. And I knew just where and how to hit it to get the shaping exact."

"Did the metal turn blue?" Adrienne asked, her hand wandering to the sword at her hip. The other objects Pieter had forged using his Talent had been blue as well, though not all as brilliantly blue as her sword.

"In certain light," Pieter said. "The extreme color of your sword is because I used my Talent throughout the entire process, from heating to shaping to treating. Nonetheless, at the time I forged that tool it was my best work."

"So you weren't even trying to use an ability," Malokai said. "Not even trying for Oneness."

"Being in a state of Oneness while working at the forge had always seemed like a bad idea before that day," Pieter said without apology. "I still don't go completely into a state of Oneness to use my Talent. I don't find it necessary or useful to do so. I have used my Talent enough that I don't need to go that far to understand the metal."

Louella leaned over and placed her hand over Malokai's. "You can see now why we can't help you," she said. "All of our experiences are too different."

"There has to be some way," Malokai said, moving his hand and shoving himself away from the table. He paced the small room. The kettle over the fire began to boil and he stopped to retrieve it. He poured the scalding water into Louella's delicate teapot before replacing the kettle and resuming his pacing. His long legged strides carried him quickly from one end of the small room to the other, and Adrienne was reminded of the lion she had once seen in a menagerie. It had been contained in a small cage, and had looked just as restless. Though many of the spectators had thought the sight magnificent, Adrienne had felt sorry for the caged beast.

"Maybe Adrienne can be of some help," Pieter suggested. "The two of you have the most in common."

Malokai shook his head. "I thought about that," he explained. "I can't do anything with fire."

"Have you considered…" Louella looked apologetic for what she was about to say. "Have you considered that you might not have a Talent?"

"Of course he will," Adrienne said. "He can already achieve Oneness."

"Being unable to achieve Oneness means you will never develop a Talent," Louella said gently, her blue eyes compassionate in a face the color of fresh cream, "but being able to achieve Oneness is not a guarantee that you will be able to develop one."

"What?" Adrienne asked.

"There have been people in Kessering who have achieved Oneness but never become Talented," Louella answered. "Oneness is difficult, but can be learned with time and patience." She looked sympathetically at Malokai. "Evidence suggests that Talents can only be discovered, not taught. That they are inborn somehow."

"Why was I never informed of this?" Adrienne asked.

Louella shrugged her thin shoulders. "It would not have helped your training to know, and once you became Talented the information was no longer important."

Malokai was silent, but Adrienne refused to believe what Louella was suggesting. "I'm sure Malokai will discover a Talent," Adrienne said. "He must. The rate of his progress—"

"Doesn't mean anything," Pieter said bluntly. "To be honest, I'm surprised Malokai was brought to Kessering at all. He doesn't have a specialized profession, and that seems to be the one common link between everyone who has been able to develop a Talent."

Adrienne came halfway out of her chair in frustrated anger. "He's an excellent fighter. One of the best I've ever encountered." She was angry that Malokai's skill would be belittled. Worse, she was upset by the idea that she could once again go back to being the only Talented—or potentially Talented—fighter in Kessering.

"But he's not a soldier, not as his sole profession," Pieter said more gently. "Fighting isn't all he does."

Adrienne waved her hands angrily. "None of us here are only our jobs—" Her hand shot out and knocked into the porcelain teacup, sending it over the edge of the table.

She and Pieter, the closest two, reached for it automatically, though it was too late to catch it. When the cup froze a bare two inches from the ground, they looked from it to each other and stared.

"I didn't—" "Did you—" they both asked at once, eyes wide with amazement.

Louella turned and saw Malokai, his hand outstretched, attention completely focused on the teacup. Slowly, the teacup rose, shaking slightly as it made its ascent.

CHAPTER TWELVE

Adrienne and her friends were waiting nervously in the otherwise empty corridor outside of the commission's meeting room. Today, the commission would deliver its decision regarding what had happened two days ago at Louella's house. The day that Malokai had so unexpectedly discovered his Talent.

Malokai's extraordinary ability to move things with his mind had sent the commission into a flurry of activity—if intense meetings counted as activity. It was proof to them that Adrienne's Talent was not a fluke, that it was possible to create an army of Talented soldiers.

The commission was not as afraid of Malokai's Talent as they were of Adrienne's, but she knew that not all of the commissioners were happy with the state of events. She suspected that many of them had probably seen her ability to develop a Talent as an aberration and had not expected Malokai or anyone like him to be able to develop an ability.

And despite the fact that the commissioner's saw Adrienne's Talent with fire as being more dangerous, many of them still viewed the tall M'bai man as an inherent threat. To them, Malokai was a savage that could not be trusted with such power.

Adrienne thought that view was even more ignorant than the view the commission held of soldiers. At least the view about soldiers was a sweeping view that they had adapted before any of them had met any soldiers, but they knew Malokai now and still did not trust him.

"What do you think they're saying?" Louella asked. Like the others, she had wanted to be present for at least some of the discussion. Unlike the others, she had been surprised that they were not included.

"Ben is probably telling the commission that everything is working as planned," Pieter said. "The training is going well, the Talents the commission was looking for are finally being developed, and we should continue training more soldiers and warriors."

"And Lady Chessing is probably saying that even one more soldier in Kessering will threaten the entire city," Adrienne said.

Malokai said nothing.

"I heard some of them want to stop the training," Louella said. "They don't want more Talented."

"They're afraid," Pieter said, resting one of his big, dark hands on Louella's light one.

"And jealous," Adrienne added.

"What will they do with us if they end the program?" Malokai asked.

Louella looked up at the warrior in surprise. "What do you mean?"

"If they decide that they don't want more Talented. What will they do with the ones that they have?" He looked at Adrienne, and she knew that they were both thinking the same thing. Would the commission decide that their duty was done and send them home?

Although Ben had not said much, Adrienne knew that he was worried that the commission would end the training program. As the only Talented commissioner, ending the program would affect him in a much more personal way than it would the others on the commission. But he had not told Adrienne what would happen to her if the training was ended.

Adrienne stared blankly at the wall, transfixed by the fading pattern on the tapestry. She lost track of time, and the tapestry began to to blur in front of her eyes, the colors bleeding together until all pattern was lost.

"They have to say yes," Louella said. Adrienne jumped as the silence was broken, turning away from the tapestry to look at her friend. "The commission has to decide to train more people to become Talented," Louella explained, her face earnest. "They had such success with you and Malokai."

"With us as well," Pieter interjected.

"Yes, of course." Louella shot the blacksmith an exasperated look. "I only meant that they wouldn't stop now that there are finally Talented who could fight Almet. Right? Isn't this why the king formed the commission in the first place?"

Malokai shrugged, and Adrienne didn't know what to say. Over half a year in Kessering, living under the commission's rule, had taught her that the commission was not always logical, nor did their actions always seem to be in the best interest of Kessering or Samaro. Too often the decisions the commission made did not even seem to line up with their objectives, at least not the objectives given to them by the king. Adrienne wondered if perhaps the commission had its own agenda, separate from the one laid out for them by King Burin. Either that or King Burin was more of a fool than she had supposed and had picked the worst possible group to help him end the conflict with Almet. If the commission decided to stop using soldiers and warriors or ended the training program altogether, Samaro would have no way to end the conflict with the larger country to the north.

But Louella trusted the commission, as did most of the others in the city, and Adrienne did not want to damage that trust before she heard the verdict. Perhaps the commission would make the decision to continue the training program with more soldiers instead of less. If that was the case, all of her worry would have been over nothing. "I'm sure they'll do the right thing," Adrienne said, though her words were far from the truth.

"Of course they will," Louella said. "They—"

The door opened, and Louella popped up from her seat like a cork from a bottle. Adrienne and Pieter rose more slowly, and Malokai straightened from where he had been leaning against the wall with a false sense of casualness. They had all wanted to be here, together, to hear what the commission had decided, and Ben had finally agreed to allow it.

However, they soon saw that the door had not been opened in invitation. Instead, Ben came out of the room and closed the door firmly behind him.

"Elder Rynn has given me permission to inform the four of you of our decision," he said formally.

"Ben, I thought we were going to hear directly from the commission," Adrienne said, her voice sharp after two hours of anticipation. Her muscles were tense, as if she had been waiting too long for a battle to begin, not for a meeting.

"I am a commissioner, Adrienne," Ben reminded her coolly. "There was no need to have everyone stay behind when I can deliver our decision myself."

Adrienne's stomach twisted. She didn't have to hear Ben's words to know what the commission had decided. She could see the decision written on his unusually drawn face.

"The commission has determined that there is no immediate need for more people with abilities to be trained," Ben said. "It is now clear to us that some people are capable of developing abilities that can be used against an enemy. If the need for such abilities arises in the future, others will be trained, but until they are necessary the commission sees no reason to uncover abilities in more people." Ben nodded decisively, as though he were in full agreement with the commission's decision, but Adrienne knew Ben was disappointed as well.

She bit her tongue to keep from saying how stupid and ill thought out the commission's decision was. Anyone with even the most basic understanding of strategy knew that one didn't wait to train soldiers until they were needed, but kept them in reserve in case they eventually were. She wondered how Ben had felt when the rest of the commission had made the asinine decision, and if any of them saw the inevitable drawback of needing more Talented but not having them.

Ben knew better than any of the other commissioners how hard and precarious it was to develop a Talent. Not only was he Talented himself, but he had trained many of the Talented in the city. He knew that it was not a short process, and that it did not always work.

"But I thought the situation in Almet..." Louella trailed off, confused.

"The struggle with Almet has not escalated to the point where special abilities are necessary," Ben said. "Things are momentarily stable on that front."

Adrienne knew that by stable Ben meant that the normal amount of killing and looting was occurring. Civilians were being harmed and soldiers were dying in an ongoing struggle to keep Samaroans safe from being killed or enslaved by Almetian forces.

"So they are just going to wait?" Pieter asked. Louella let out a relieved sigh, and Pieter shot her a look. "You can't be happy about this?"

"If they can find a solution to open war," Louella hedged.

"They can't." Pieter looked fierce, and Adrienne remembered her old sword, which still hung proudly in Pieter's shop. The blacksmith understood better than Louella what this decision meant on a larger scale, and that sometimes bloodshed was necessary to maintain freedom.

"We don't *know* that," Louella said. "Do you really want to risk your life before everything else has been tried. Do you really want people to *die* if they don't have to?"

"Of course not," Pieter said. "But we've tried other ways." He looked at Ben in accusation. "Talented soldiers were supposed to *be* the other way. The Talented were the way to win the war."

"Until real war breaks out, abilities such as Adrienne and Malokai have developed won't be necessary," Ben pointed out.

Adrienne wondered if anyone on the commission had ever heard of making the first strike, or thought about how many would likely die in a war before enough people could develop useful Talents to make a difference. Compared to Almet, Samaro was too small to not take every advantage they could get.

She tried to believe that the commission was right, but their decision went against everything she had ever been taught. She wished to be back in Kyrog, where the orders made sense and, even if they didn't, she trusted the person who had issued them. She could not bring herself to trust the people here. "Wouldn't it be better to have more people with powers in reserve, ready to be called up when needed?" Adrienne finally asked, unable to help herself.

"We have decided that it is better to hold off on any further training," Ben said with finality.

"We can't stay here," Malokai said abruptly. He had been lying on the other side of the camp, looking up at the sky that was slowly turning a darker shade of blue as the sun fell toward the horizon. Now he sat up and looked at her out of those intense blue eyes.

Adrienne looked around the sparsely wooded area where she and Malokai had set up camp the night before. They had left Kessering after the commission's decision, needing space from the confines of the city. It would take only a few hours to walk back to Kessering from where they camped, but here they were momentarily away from the sights and sounds of the city, and the control of the commission.

Neither Adrienne nor Malokai had told Ben about their unexpected trip, though Pieter and Louella knew. Ben would likely be angry that they had left without first asking permission, but Adrienne no longer cared what Ben thought. The commission had decided against training any new Talented; they did not need to manage every part of Adrienne's life.

"Well, no, of course we can't stay," she said, hoping that Malokai did not mean they had to go back to the city right at that moment. It was peaceful out here, away from the bustle and chaos of civilian life. "We'll have to go back eventually. It's just nice to get away for a while." Not that there was much for her to get away from, now that her own training was at an end. She had promoted Edward to captain before hearing the commission's decision, and he was now solely in charge of the city guard. Except for Louella and Pieter, there was little in the city of importance to Adrienne. Her studies about the Dark Mage had come to a halt: no matter how hard she tried, she could not decipher the Almetian script. There was probably a book in the library that would help with such a task, but she could not ask the librarian or one of the scholars without giving away what she was trying to do.

"I meant we can't stay in Kessering," Malokai said, drawing her from those bleak thoughts and focusing her attention more fully on him and what he was saying.

"What?" Adrienne hadn't expected that.

"You heard the commission," Malokai told her. "They aren't going to train anyone else like us."

"They will," Adrienne told him. "Ben said they would, when it becomes necessary." They had all talked about it. Adrienne, Malokai, Louella, and Pieter had spent hours discussing the decision the commission had made, trying to understand it and what it would mean for them and for the future of the Talented. Adrienne and Malokai had continued to discuss the situation even after they had left Kessering, and she was sure Louella and Pieter had done the same.

She wondered about the other Talented in the city. With Adrienne and Malokai gone for the time being, it was likely that Louella and Pieter had spoken with the others. Did they find all of this wrong, too, or were they relieved? Grateful, even, that no more soldiers would be coming to their city for training? Adrienne had never gotten to know them, had hardly met any of them except for Maureen, and could not guess at their thoughts or feelings regarding the commission's decision.

"Who decides when it is necessary?" Malokai demanded. "The commission? How many need to die, in what numbers, before they decide it is 'necessary' to train more Talented like us?"

"I don't know." It was something Adrienne tried not to think about. She reached up and worried the cord of her necklace between her fingers. "Maybe the king—"

Malokai's harsh laughter cut her off. "You're counting on King Burin to make this right?" he asked. "You have no more respect for the king than I."

"He formed the commission," Adrienne said. "He must want—"

"He wants to keep his throne, and his head," Malokai said. "Even in the mountains we know this. He'll have to weigh whether or not people will be more upset by Talented with abilities far beyond their own or what is happening on the Almetian border. It could take the king longer to make a decision than it takes the commission. And if he decides that we Talented put his position in danger, he will never allow more of us to be trained, no matter what happens with Almet."

"Then what do we do?" Adrienne asked. "Talk to the commission?"

"No. We have to leave Kessering," Malokai repeated.

Adrienne rolled to her feet and began pacing, feeling suddenly nervous. The grass, brittle as they approached the end of the dry season, crunched under her feet as she turned to face Malokai. "We can't."

"Yes, we can," Malokai said, standing as well. He did not pace, but watched her movements like a cat watching a mouse.

"Even if we could," Adrienne argued, "what would that accomplish? We would be taking away the only offensive abilities they have." She doubted the commission would even bother to replace them if they left. She and Malokai leaving would probably result in making the commission even more hesitant to train soldiers in the future.

The two of them would no doubt be seen as a threat if they left, dangerous renegades who had slipped the chain of the commission's control. The commission might well consider it too risky to train more soldiers if they worried that those soldiers, upon developing a Talent, might leave Kessering and the control of the commission.

"We could train more Talented ourselves," Malokai told her, grabbing one of her arms to stop her pacing and spin her around to face him.

"We can't," Adrienne said, meeting those hard blue eyes with her own. Despite the fact that she felt herself teetering on the edge of breaking the chain of command by disobeying the commission, she would not allow that to happen. She would not allow this situation to change who she was. "The commission would never allow it."

"Forget the commission," Malokai growled, taking her by the arms and shaking her roughly. "The only thing the commission is going to do is get a lot of people killed."

"But we can't just go against them," Adrienne said. "We can't leave Kessering to go out and train others. The commission is in charge."

"In Kessering," Malokai agreed, "but not outside the city walls."

"The commission is in charge of us, Malokai. They're in charge of people with abilities. They're in charge of the Talented."

"Why?" Malokai asked. "What makes them our leaders?"

"King Burin," Adrienne said. "He chose the commissioners, he placed them in charge of finding a way to end the conflict with Almet. And the commission *made* us, Malokai. We are Talented because of *them.*"

"We are Talented because of *us*," Malokai told her. "All they did was show us how. They have no experience with war, no Talents that help them fulfill this mission. The commission is working against the cause, not for it. The only useful thing they've done is train us, and that's over now. They taught us to hunt and gave us spears, but now they forbid us to use them. They are not following the mission, they are following their own desires."

"I can't go against my leaders," Adrienne said. She struggled to cling to the person she was, the person who had been shaped by the chain of command she had followed all of her life. She was a part of that chain and couldn't separate herself from it, no matter how logical Malokai's arguments. Breaking that chain would break her as well.

Before Kessering, being a soldier had made her what she was, and she had owed everything to the army. Now she was Talented, and though the chains rankled, she owed the commission for that.

"To what lengths would you go to follow your leaders' orders?" Malokai asked. "If you knew the mission would fail and you would die, would you still follow their orders?"

"Yes," Adrienne said without hesitation. It was impossible to truly be a soldier without accepting the chance of injury and death. Adrienne had made peace with it long ago.

"What if your commander told you to murder a family?" Malokai asked. "Not people opposing you, not anyone armed or posing a threat, just an innocent family. A mother, a child." The intensity of his eyes was frightening, but she focused on the question he'd asked, not the emotion behind it.

"Why?" Adrienne asked.

"Does it matter? Your commander told you to do it."

Adrienne struggled with the question. "No army commander would ask that," Adrienne finally said.

"You know that's not true. You're not that naïve."

Adrienne tried to meet his eyes but couldn't. "No good commander would ask that," she amended, knowing even that answer was weak. "And that's not what the commission is asking of us."

"Through their inaction, the commission is facilitating the slaughter of families." The rigidity with which he held himself told her that his words were more personal than she could guess.

Adrienne started to say something, but Malokai wouldn't allow it.

"This struggle with Almet doesn't affect only soldiers," he said. "We could help stop it. Talented fighters could help stop it."

"I can't break the chain of command," Adrienne said in little more than a whisper, her eyes begging him to understand. "I am a soldier."

"Soldiers are meant to protect," Malokai said. "You told me as much. If that isn't what your commander has you doing, if he is instead forcing you to stand back and let innocents die to no purpose, then it seems that the chain is already broken."

Adrienne thought of Captain Garrett, who had told her to go to Kessering. He had believed that her mission was righteous, and that it would help the effort that they were all working toward.

She thought of the commission, who had trained her but wouldn't use her when she could be making a difference and saving lives.

She thought of King Burin, who only cared about himself and those that could help further his own needs.

Adrienne thought of families dying by Almetian blades while she sat uselessly in Kessering. The vice that had been constricting her chest fell away, and her mind was clear for the first time in what felt like ages.

She could think again.

"We have to leave," Adrienne agreed.

Adrienne and Malokai returned to Kessering the next day. They stopped at Louella's shop before bringing their things back to the inn, and found Pieter there as well, as though he had known they would be returning today.

"You're back," Louella said. She looked at them more closely, taking in their travel gear, and her face changed subtly. "But you're not staying."

Adrienne nearly smiled. Trust Louella to figure out their plans without them saying a word. "We can't."

Louella nodded and told them to sit down as she went about fixing an early lunch. "Ben has been asking after you. I told him that you and Malokai went camping, and that I didn't know when you would be coming back." She deposited plates piled high with bread, thinly sliced ham, and boiled yams in front of Malokai and Adrienne. "Will you tell him before you leave?"

Adrienne shook her head. "It's best if he doesn't know. I don't think the commission will be pleased that we're going, and he might try to stop us."

Louella nodded. "Then you had best let Pieter and I make most of the preparations," she said. "We'll buy whatever supplies you need, since no one will suspect us of leaving. You'll just need to get your things from the inn when it is time to go."

Adrienne surprised Louella by standing up and hugging the slender woman. "Thank you," she said.

Louella returned the hug, patting Adrienne on the back. "Sit back down and eat. You'll need to make me a list of everything you need. I've never traveled."

Adrienne and Malokai worked on a list of supplies while they ate, and soon Louella and Pieter went out to purchase what they could find. Adrienne was surprised by the sadness she felt at the prospect of leaving her friends, but knew that there was nothing else to be done. She and Malokai had thought of asking Louella and Pieter to leave with them, but at the last moment had decided against it. It was unlikely the pair would want to leave their homes, and Adrienne and Malokai were still unsure of where to go.

Adrienne wanted to return to Kyrog. She had told Malokai that they would not need to stay at the soldiering camp long, but Kyrog was close, only three weeks from Kessering, and if they really meant to train more Talented, then the elite camp was an ideal place to find soldiers for the task. She didn't tell him that she badly wanted to see her friends, and was afraid that if they spent months traveling to the Modabi Mountains too much time might pass in a camp like Kyrog. Soldiers did not stay in one camp forever.

Malokai had been just as adamant about returning to the mountains. There were other warriors there, as well as people skilled in other professions who might have the potential to become Talented in other areas, such as healing or smithing.

"The Modabi Mountains are months away," Adrienne pointed out once they were alone in Louella's house, starting up the argument they had been having since the night before. "Especially since you don't have a horse." And Malokai was adamant about not getting one. According to him, the M'bai did not ride. "We could go to Kyrog first. It's not in the direction of the mountains, I know, but then the months spent getting to your home could also be spent training new Talented."

Malokai shook his head, his dark faced creased with a frown. "More than two people moving across the countryside will call attention. Do you want the commission to know where we are going?"

She hesitated. "We don't know what they will do. What can they do, without soldiers?"

"This commission was formed by the king," Malokai said. "The king has his own army."

"It could take months for them to reach us," Adrienne said. "If they decide to pursue us at all."

"Are we to fight them if they do? Are we to fight anyone that the commission sends after us, soldiers or not?"

Adrienne didn't like the idea of fighting anyone sent by the commission. Leaving might anger the commission, but raising arms against them...It would be better not to let the commission find them. "They're going to guess that we went either to Kyrog or the Modabi Mountains," Adrienne pointed out. "Why would we go anywhere else?"

"They'll probably check Kyrog first," Malokai said. "It's closer. Even if they head to the mountains first, we will get there ahead of them."

"On foot?" Adrienne asked skeptically. Even the nags Tam and Ilso had ridden were faster than two people on foot.

"No one the commission sends is going to be willing to travel from sunup to sundown," Malokai said. "But you and I are."

Adrienne nodded. She would push if she had to, run if necessary, to stay ahead of anyone pursuing them. But she still wanted to go to Kyrog first. "I still think—"

She fell silent as Louella and Pieter returned. They each were loaded up with supplies, mostly food in fresh or dry forms. Pieter had recovered some tools from his shop, and Louella held what appeared to be a cloak.

"What's this?" Adrienne asked when Louella handed her the greenish cloth that was indeed a long green cloak. The material felt smooth as silk and shimmered slightly with every movement.

"A gift for you, from the Talented weaver."

Adrienne looked the cloak over more closely, achieving Oneness and examining it again. The fabric had clearly been made using a Talent, but other than the shimmer of the fabric and the surprising texture, Adrienne did not see how it was different from other cloaks.

It was a strange gift, and not only because it was from someone she had never met. In this part of Samaro, cloaks were unnecessary for the most part. Unless it was raining, a cloak would only add to the heat of the day. "I see," Adrienne said.

The color was nice, the silky feel rather decadent and decidedly unsuitable for travel. All the cloak would do was take up valuable room in her saddle bag.

"Aren't you going to try it on?" Louella asked.

The healer seemed so excited by the gift that Adrienne had no choice but to slip the cloak over her shoulders. It fell about her perfectly, and was lighter and cooler than she had expected, as if she was not wearing a cloak at all. Perhaps it would not be such a nuisance, though she still could not imagine wearing it while traversing the plains.

"It looks good," Louella said. "And you don't look excited at all." She laughed, as if she found something amusing in Adrienne's reaction.

"It's a nice cloak," Adrienne said, in case Louella was friends with the Talented weaver, though the healer had never introduced the woman to Adrienne in all of the months they had been friends. "I'm just not sure how useful it will be."

"You might want a cloak once we get to the mountains," Malokai said. "It gets colder there." But Malokai did not look impressed by the gift either.

"I suppose that you don't know what it does." Louella shook her head. "You never did get to know the other Talented. Barbara, the weaver, said that this cloak will blend into the background. It will help you to hide, should hiding become necessary."

Adrienne lifted an eyebrow skeptically.

"She said to wrap the cloak around yourself—cover yourself with it completely—and achieve Oneness. The cloak will hide you." Louella smiled. "It's also water proof and should keep you warm on a cold night, if hiding is not what you need."

Adrienne was not sure that she believed Barbara's tales, but the one thing she had learned in Kessering was that when it came to Talents, anything was possible. She nodded and folded the cloak into a small bundle before setting it on top of the other supplies.

"And Malokai," Pieter said. "I've made something for you." He handed over a knife in a plain leather sheath.

Malokai unsheathed the knife to reveal a blade of magnificent blue. Adrienne let out a whistle of appreciation. The slightly curved blade was easily six inches long, and she knew without testing that it would be wickedly sharp.

"I figure a warrior can always use another knife," he said. "I would have tried making a new blade for your *urahu*, but I wouldn't know where to start."

Malokai smiled and accepted the knife. "It's a great gift," he said. "Thank you."

"Thank you both for this," Adrienne said, pulling out her purse and taking out the coins needed to pay Louella and Pieter back for what they had purchased. "I'm sorry that we have to leave so soon."

Pieter nodded and offered Malokai and Adrienne firm handshakes and well wishes. Louella's smile was tremulous, and her eyes bright with tears. "I'm going to miss you so," Louella said as she pulled Adrienne in for a hug. "You're not mad that we aren't joining you, are you?"

"Of course not," Adrienne assured her.

"Because this is the only home I remember," Louella said. "I'm not ready to leave yet."

"Louella," Adrienne rested her hand on the blonde's shoulder and held it there until Louella met her eyes. "Don't feel bad about staying here. It's best that you stay with the other Talented here in Kessering. Both you and Pieter."

Louella smiled despite the tears that glistened in her eyes. "Can you at least say where you're going?"

Adrienne shook her head apologetically. "I don't want you to have to lie to Ben."

Louella nodded. "Be safe." She turned to Malokai and pulled him into a tight hug. Her head went only to his chest, and he tensed for a moment before relaxing into the embrace.

The initial tension Malokai had shown when he first met the petite blonde, which Adrienne had finally concluded must be due to Louella's obvious Almetian heritage, had faded as Malokai had gotten to know the healer, and Adrienne thought that he might now miss Louella as much as Louella would miss him. "Both of you be safe. Come back if you can."

Louella's eyes said that she knew very well they would not be back. Unlike her and Pieter, Adrienne and Malokai were not welcome in Kessering, not really. And the commission would probably not be friendly to them if they were to return.

"If you need anything, send for us," Pieter said. "There are hard times ahead."

Adrienne smiled and nodded curtly before she and Malokai took their goods and left before more words could be said.

Adrienne was grateful she had made it away without shedding any tears, though her eyes stung from the effort of holding them back. She hadn't cried when she had left Kyrog, and she would not cry now that she was leaving Kessering.

Thom watched her solemnly when they entered the newly rebuilt stable and Adrienne began saddling Strider. Between her saddlebags and Malokai's belongings, it was clear no one would be riding the horse.

And it was clear to the young stable boy that this would not be a short trip. "You're leaving, aren't you?" Thom asked, his eyes filled with dejection and a small dose of anger.

"Yes," Adrienne said. She would not return the welcome this boy—her first friend in Kessering—had given her with a lie.

"You can't leave. I'm not a good fighter yet," the boy said.

Adrienne smiled. "You were good enough to beat up the kid that was harassing you," Adrienne reminded him. She had lectured him afterwards about not resorting to violence, but she knew that the older, bigger boy had learned a lesson when Thom had beaten him in a fight. She didn't regret teaching Thom anything.

"I don't see why you have to leave," Thom said, wiping his arm across his face to get rid of the traitorous tears, so humiliating for a boy of his age.

"It's time," Adrienne said softly, her heart aching for the boy, and for herself.

"The least you could do is leave me your horse," Thom said, causing Adrienne to laugh.

"You wish." She walked over and ruffled the boy's hair, feeling most of the ache in her chest fade. "Thank you for taking care of Strider," she said, pulling a silver penny from her purse. It would be the last he would get from her, but he had earned everything she had given him and more. "If you could do just one more thing, and not tell anyone we left unless they ask."

"I won't tell them even then," Thom promised.

"You can tell them then," Adrienne said. "I don't want you to lie. Just wait until they ask."

Thom looked uncertain, as if he wanted to prove his loyalty by keeping her secret forever, but finally he surrendered to the will portrayed through her dark brown eyes. "Fine," he said with a heavy sigh.

"Thank you." Adrienne ruffled his hair again. "Ready to go?" she asked Malokai.

The M'bai warrior nodded, and they left the stable with the laden warhorse. Adrienne had her sword at her hip, and Malokai had his *urahu* strapped to his back. Both of them possessed Talents that most people could barely dream of.

And they were headed for the Modabi Mountains.